PRAISE FOR CB SAMET

"CB Samet has a way of bringing you into the hair-raising suspense, keeping you at the edge of your seat."

— VORACIOUS READERS REVIEWER

"This is an intense read that really sucks you from the get go! I loved this suspenseful and action packed story! Great characters! .... This is a definite page turner!"

— BOOKSPROUT REVIEWER

"Absolutely fantastic story"

— BOOKBUB READER

MCMILLAN FILE

THE RIDER FILES BOOK 3

CB SAMET

AVANTSTAR PUBLISHING

For Cheyenne and Stardust
for bringing happiness to people I love

1

In the darkened room, large figures towered over Mica. Blood oozed from a cut on her side. She tugged weakly on the rope around her wrists.

Who ties people with real, braided rope anymore?

Plastic cable ties or duct tape, sure—but this stuff was old-fashioned, thick rope, and as scratchy as a burlap sack.

Mica's side throbbed with pain, and her thoughts felt as foggy as her vision. She blinked repeatedly, which did nothing to improve her eyesight. She felt like she was peering through her grandma Myrtle's glasses—and the poor lighting of the warehouse didn't help. Who knew what empty buckets or shards of scrap metal were strewn about the place. Health hazards.

She twisted her wrists, a task which occupied Mica's thoughts while the men decided how best to torture her.

Tall figures loomed over her, leaching the unpleasant smell of cigarettes and body odor. Their scent mixed with the mustiness of the warehouse and the coppery smell of blood. Her blood.

Fortunately—or unfortunately—Mica had bled often enough so the familiar scent of her own blood didn't make her nauseous any more. That was probably a good thing because she figured she probably wasn't done bleeding yet.

Mica counted her assailants. Four men. None of them was the one she wanted to see. She'd have to wait a little longer.

"Let's see if *this* makes her talk." The man closest to her held something in his meaty hand—a box or cylinder. He poured white powder into his palm.

Crap.

This is going to hurt.

DAVID RIDER FINISHED SUTURING a four-inch laceration, the result of a brawl at a techno-disco. He snapped off his vinyl gloves and propelled them with precision aim into the trash bin opposite the patient's bed.

With his job done there, he headed off toward bed 4-B to check on an upper gastrointestinal bleed he'd been treating. That patient needed to be admitted to a floor upstairs, but there was no room at the inn.

Through a narrow window he passed a luminous moon shone from a starlit sky, but for David and the rest of the emergency room staff, a full moon on a Saturday night was a bad omen; one that usually preceded a busy night.

On a full moon, the urbanites would become restless and look for trouble. When they invariably found it, they got hurt. When they got hurt, they came to East Regional Medical Center.

As David passed the window, he caught a glimpse of himself. His hair was disheveled and probably had been since treating that cardiac arrest patient a few hours earlier. His skin looked pale from too many hours spent devoid of sunshine, working beneath the fluorescent, artificial lights of the emergency room.

"Dr. Rider," Maple, one of the ER nurses, called to him, "there's an EMS call."

David walked over to the radio on the counter to listen to the ambulance report.

"En route Code Three to your facility with an approximately thirty-year-old female found in an abandoned building. One laceration to her abdomen, mid-axillary. Patient is unresponsive, blood pressure one hundred over seventy-four, respirations twelve and shallow, bilateral breath sounds clear and equal, pulse sixty-two. Unable to obtain a history. Suspect narcotic overdose. Pupils dilated, ECG is normal sinus."

Overdose. Another one.

The paramedic continued, "We have an IV established with Lactated Ringers. Bleeding is controlled. Patient is on non-rebreather mask, receiving high-flow oxygen. Requesting permission to administer two milligrams naloxone IV. ETA is five minutes." The paramedic's voice sounded strained, evidence he was hard at work.

David picked up the radio mic, but hesitated to speak. Naloxone was fairly innocuous to administer, but a bolus dose could send a chronic drug user into withdraw or wake them into a raging fury. If this patient was calm, but stable, he worried the medic's dose—if not titrated perfectly—could land them with a belligerent patient in his ER, which would likely overwhelm an already stretched staff.

"Negative. Do not give naloxone. Just transport," he ordered.

The paramedic replied with agitation, "I copy you do *not* want naloxone to be administered to a probable overdose?"

"That's correct," David said. "We'll see you in five."

He replaced the receiver and typed in a patient's chart.

Maple shot him an incredulous look, which he promptly ignored.

Maple had short, full, bright red hair that might have made her *feel* younger, but actually enhanced the fine wrinkles in her face. It made her look every bit of her late forties, highlighting the thick, make-up covered lines earned after years of working late, stressful hours in emergency medicine.

Maple was still attractive and fit, and had made her interest in him known, but she was much older than David and a little too jaded for his interest. He also had a strict 'no dating in the workplace' rule.

Several minutes later, David watched two paramedics enter his emergency room with a female patient on their stretcher. She had an endotracheal tube protruding from her mouth, and her breathing was being assisted. They rushed her into one of the trauma rooms.

He frowned at the endotracheal tube, before looking disapprovingly at the paramedic, whose name tag read 'Raymond.'

"I don't recall you saying the patient was intubated," David commented calmly, as he slipped on a pair of gloves.

"No, we intubated about one minute ago, when her respirations dropped to six per minute," Raymond said pointedly, "as a result of her overdose," he added, moving the patient over to the hospital bed.

David slid next to the tall, thick paramedic. Maple and another nurse arrived at the bedside and helped with the move. Raymond gave a patient report to the nurses, as a respiratory therapist breathed for the patient by squeezing the thick plastic bag attached to the endotracheal tube.

David performed a quick primary assessment and ordered Maple to give naloxone to reverse the overdose.

Raymond gathered his paperwork and turned to Maple. David noticed her weak smile while Raymond rolled his eyes in response. Maple started to nod but stopped short when she noticed David looking over the patient at her, as he auscultated the patient's breath sounds with his stethoscope. Maple pursed her lips at him in response and left to fetch the naloxone.

David continued inspecting the patient. She had a minor laceration with no obvious damage to major organs or blood vessels. A quick ultrasound evaluation revealed no life-threatening injuries to her major organs. He looked at the bruises on her arms and the ligature marks on her wrists. Had she been assaulted? He inspected her hands, noting scraped knuckles. Whatever happened, she'd put up a fight. Other than a few old bruises and healed scars, no other signs of trauma marked her body. Importantly, he didn't find any signs of head injury.

"Hold on a minute before you give her that," he said to Maple as she approached with the opioid reversal agent.

When the naloxone worked successfully, the patient's breathing would become sufficient on its own, and the endotracheal tube could be removed. Once they reversed the effects of the drugs, the patient might wake up and become unmanageable.

David quickly assembled his suture material. He could stitch her side while the effects of the heroin still had her semi-comatose.

With his tray of equipment set up and his face shield in place, David cleaned the skin. After donning sterile gloves, he set to work suturing her injury.

Maple watched him treat the woman's laceration. "You may be an arrogant ass sometimes, but you're damn good at suturing."

He gave Maple a nonplussed look.

"Just saying, though—it wouldn't have killed you to let Raymond give her naloxone."

David pulled his attention back to his sutures and talked calmly as he worked, "If Raymond had given her too much, we could be dealing with a belligerent patient right now. As the situation stands, she's sleeping peacefully while I patch her up. If he'd *told* me her respiratory status was unstable and she needed a tube, then sure, I'd have approved the dose."

David had completed residency a few years ago and was well aware that even eleven years of intense education wouldn't automatically grant him the respect of the ER staff—many of whom had been in the trenches for decades. He'd have to earn their respect through his actions; arguing would be fruitless. David knew, though, that as long as he continued to keep the patients' interests a priority, he'd eventually win the ER team's respect.

"What do you think about her?" Maple asked, referring to the patient.

She looked to be mid to late twenties and in good physical condition. She had fair skin and short blond hair that curled just below her ears. Her underlying beauty was masked by pale, clammy skin and dilated pupils. Both were the result of the narcotic.

Sleeping beauty. Too young to look so deathly pale.

"I think our Jane Doe is in the wrong profession," David replied.

"Aren't we all," commented Robin, another nurse, as she walked past carrying a urinal.

"She doesn't have track marks," Maple pointed out, indicating that the patient wasn't likely to be a habitual heroin user.

David nodded in agreement. The woman's overall hygiene appeared too immaculate for drug abuse—with perfect teeth, manicured but unpainted nails, professionally dyed hair, excellent muscle tone, and moisturized skin. He finished the sutures and bandaged the patient's wound.

The emergency room staff made a game of guessing a patient's personal history, blood-alcohol level, and other 'to be discovered' information.

"Could be a prostitute," Maple shrugged, "with her first heroin experimentation."

Even as she said it, David cringed at the thought.

The game was usually stereotypical and callous, but more often than not, accurate.

They knew nothing about the patient, so she became Jane Doe; the first, no doubt, in a line of Jane Does who would come in that night. And one of many more that had come through the emergency room doors since the hospital's opening.

David left the patient and did his rounds. Activity in the ER was picking up pace, and as the evening progressed, the emergency room quickly filled. Later, after a trickle of intravenous naloxone, Jane Doe's breathing tube was removed, and she was moved into the hallway to make room for other trauma patients. There she could sleep off the remaining drugs in her system as she waited to be admitted to the hospital.

MAXINE RIDER SPUN her legs round and round on the exercise bike. Sweat dripped from her forehead. She felt like a damn hamster.

From the reflection in the window overlooking downtown Atlanta, Maxine saw Claire enter the workout room. She wore blue jeans and an Atlanta Braves t-shirt. Because the company's computer tech didn't watch sports, Maxine wondered if Claire had gotten the shirt as a gift.

"You've been working out a lot since Antigua," Claire noted.

Maxine slowed her legs for the cool-down portion of her work-out, while recalling her recent trip to Antigua. One of her best employees, former-Ranger Ryan Walsh, had married his soul mate on the island. No man deserved the happiness Ryan found when he'd wooed the pretty critical care physician. Maxine wished Ryan and Jenna a lifetime of happiness—provided he *not* quit Rider Security and Investigation, which he hadn't.

But the wedding in Antigua had also been the day Maxine's arch nemesis, Lucius Wallenius Titan, of rival security company Titan Enterprises, had threatened her son. It had ruined the trip, and led to agonizing months of worry afterward. As yet, though, Lucius hadn't made good on his threats.

Claire stood beside Maxine as she pedaled. The young woman tucked the strand of blue hair behind her ear. "You wouldn't be trying to impress a certain handsome Russian warlord, would you?"

Maxine scowled. Antigua had also been when Vladimir Pronin, leader of the Russian mafia, had danced with her. He'd flown all the way from Moscow to Jenna's wedding and while he was there, had the audacity to ask Maxine to dance. She couldn't remember the last time she'd danced. It probably coincided with the last time she'd worn a dress.

Vladimir was an enigma. Other than a few mutual enemies, they had nothing in common. Yet he flirted and flashed discon-certing smiles at her.

"I'm trying to rid myself of the stress of worrying about David." Maxine eased off the bike, already feeling the ache in her hip bones.

Getting old is a bitch.

The combination of age and hard, physical living during her youth as a Marine had culminated in an abundance of arthritis.

Claire waved a hand at her. "David is fine. He has the new top-of-the-line security system at his apartment. The parking garage is card access only. *And* he has your number if he needs anything."

Maxine dragged a towel across her face before slinging it over her shoulder. "My number is only a benefit if he releases his disdain of me long enough to call it if he's in trouble."

Maxine's relationship with her son had been strained for decades. When she'd been overseas in the Marines for months at a time, he and his father had grown to resent her. Her lack of 'emotional range', as Claire called it, didn't help the situation either. When David had left for college, their barely-speaking relationship fizzled into one of silence.

Maxine literally had to track him like a covert agent—through his college graduation, white coat ceremony, medical school, residency, and now his job as an emergency room physician. Tragically, she couldn't figure out how to insert herself back into David's life. After the threat from Lucius Titan, the last thing she wanted to do was call David to explain how *her* company had put *him* into someone's crosshairs. *She*'d put him in danger; and that would just give David another reason to resent her.

Instead, Maxine had one of her operatives stage a break in at an unoccupied apartment on the same floor as David's. When the burglary prompted David to upgrade his security systems, Maxine secretly made sure he got the best money could buy.

"He may be safe at home," Maxine agreed, "but that leaves a lot of uncovered ground."

"You're tracking his phone and his car," Claire offered hopefully.

Maxine walked to the water cooler and filled a paper cup. She let the cool liquid tumble down her throat. "Those devices aren't going to tell me if he's injured." She didn't have the manpower to put protection on David around-the-clock. Her team was already spread thin, and Maxine was actively recruiting to bolster her numbers. Finding the right combination of skill, savvy, and moral aptitude in ex-military personal, who'd be expected to work hard for modest pay, presented a challenge.

"Maybe Vladimir can help," Claire suggested.

Maxine felt her eye twitch. "I only used his help when I had no other options. I would never..." she stopped as Claire's mouth quirked. Evidently, Claire was now congratulating herself for riling Maxine.

Claire chuckled.

Maxine threw her sweaty towel at her.

Clara shrieked and dodged it. "Gross!"

As Maxine walked out of the exercise room, she called out over her shoulder, "Back to work. Find me more employees."

"Fine! But I'm going to tell them what a grumpy boss you are."

Maxine stalked down the hallway from the gym into her office, where she prepared to pack up for the day.

Claire's words riled her.

Grumpy? She wasn't *grumpy*. Except perhaps compared to Claire—who was infuriatingly bubbly and always overflowing with optimism. Claire only needed the blue wings to match her blue hair and she'd become the Good Cheer Fairy.

Perhaps someone with as much idealism and buoyancy as Claire would naturally see Maxine's calm, collected demeanor as grumpy.

But it still riled her.

The mobile phone on Maxine's desktop dinged. She unlocked it and looked at the text. Vladimir Pronin had sent her a message asking her how she was. A light sensation skittered up and down her spine.

Maxine swore.

What game was he playing? Taking an interest in her?

Maxine didn't have time to entertain romantic relationships and *certainly* didn't want the short lifespan likely incurred in a relationship with a man whose billion-dollar industry revolved around everything she stood against.

DAVID HAD a break between patients and approached the plain-clothed police officer who was waiting to speak with him.

"Dr. Rider? I'm Detective Bose."

David shook the outstretched hand. The detective's grip felt firm. He had a friendly smile despite the three a.m. hour. David, a foot taller than the cop, could see the fluorescent lights reflecting off his bald head.

"Pleasure." David wondered which one of his misfit patients from that night had earned the attention of Atlanta P.D. "How can I help?"

"I'm here to question Mica McMillan."

"Who?" Something struck David as familiar about that name.

"The woman in the hall over there. The petite blonde?"

"Oh. That's one of our Jane Does. Heroin overdose. She didn't have any ID on her." David stuck his hands in his white coat pockets. "You said her name is Mica?" His mind tried to catch the significance of that name, but it slipped his grasp.

"Mica McMillan," the detective repeated.

"Well, she's stable—just sleeping. You're welcome to question her, but we don't have anything more private than the hallway over there."

Detective Bose chuckled. "I think she earned her rest, but I'll hang around for her to wake up."

David's brow knitted. "Earned her rest?"

Bose grinned. "She just handed me the bust of the year."

"Bust?"

"She took down two drug dealers."

Maple appeared suddenly beside him. "Dr. Rider, bed four is dropping her oxygen saturation."

"Excuse me, detective." David cast a long look in Mica McMillan's direction before leaving to go see the crashing patient.

2

After David intubated the critical patient and spoke with the admitting physician in the ICU, he walked back to the break room to grab a soda. There was something magical in those effervescent bubbles capable of reviving him during the long shifts.

A thought—*the* thought—finally emerged from the depths of his high school memories and struck him. Mica Greyson McMillan. *That's* where he knew the name.

David recalled that Mica had been a tomboy, always sporting scraped knees and scuffed knuckles. She'd played softball, but had more bruises from picking fights than playing sports. She'd been a brunette in high school and worn superhero shirts while claiming to have her own Justice League. As a senior, he recalled thinking Mica was a strange little thing, someone with whom he'd had very little interaction.

Except for one night after school.

He'd just finished swim practice and exited the building with his gym bag slung over one shoulder. By the light in the parking lot, he saw a girl with clenched fists yelling at Andy, one of the juniors on the swim team. Andy stood a foot taller than Mica, with shoulders twice as broad as the little twig standing up to him.

David approached and could discern some of her angry words. She was accusing Andy of groping Caroline. Why did this girl care? Was she jealous?

Andy's posture shifted from dismissive to irritated, then to tense-shouldered, white-knuckled fury. Andy shouldn't need to blow out his chest and flex his muscles to intimidate a girl that size.

David had picked up his pace. He needed to intervene before Andy knocked Mica onto the pavement. One blow with his hammer of a fist and she would have a broken nose. Meanwhile, that tough girl wasn't backing down. What was the matter with her?

David remembered easing close enough to see her face by the yellow glow that spilled from the light above them. Mica McMillan. Mad Mica, people called her. She'd been wearing a Wonder Woman t-shirt and blue jeans.

Kids had cracked jokes about Mica behind her back, but truthfully, everyone had known she was scrappy in a fight. Football players turned up with black eyes, claiming to have gotten them in practice (including in the off season). Some would even say their old man took a swing at them before they would admit that a ninety-pound girl had been the culprit.

David remembered nearing the commotion that night. That was when Andy had shoved Mica. She twisted and caught his wrist, and then used Andy's own momentum to hurl him past her. Andy stumbled, but stayed on his feet. Whirling around in frustration, he lunged at her and took a swing.

Big mistake.

Mica was such a slight thing back then—her body a small and

fast target. After Andy's blow missed as she ducked, she came up from her crouch and launched an uppercut into Andy's abdomen. The punch had the full weight of the upward momentum of her body behind it.

David remembered how Andy had heaved out a surprised and pained grunt, before crashing to the pavement.

"Don't touch girls if they don't ask for it." Mica had sneered at Andy.

When David's footsteps crunched over the loose gravel on the parking lot surface, Mica spun around, fists raised.

"Easy there, Mica. I'm not your enemy."

Wild eyes became tame as she focused on him. Mica transformed from a fighter into a small girl. Her big, brown eyes looked up at him intensely.

"Are you okay?" David asked her. "Your knuckles are bleeding."

Mica stared down at her hands and shrugged.

He glanced around at the dark parking lot. "Is that your bike?"

She nodded and then stared at the ground, kicking at the gravel beneath her feet.

David wondered if she'd been waiting in the parking lot until Andy was alone to confront him. Had she planned this entire event? "Well, you can't bike home in the dark. I've got a truck. I'll give you and your bike a lift."

Mica glanced up at him. "Thanks."

He remembered blinking. The girl who'd been giving Andy a tongue-lashing seconds ago could now only muster a single word toward him. Weird. She clearly wasn't operating with a full deck.

Andy had crawled into his car and peeled out of the parking lot.

David loaded Mica's bike into his truck bed and opened the door for her. She climbed into the passenger seat and fastened her seatbelt. He walked around, buckled in, and started the engine.

"Where'd you learn to fight like that?"

"My dad."

David gripped the wheel tighter as he drove. After a moment, he asked, "Does he beat you?"

Mica turned to him and stared at David as if he had three eyes. She stared so long, he eventually reached up to rub his forehead to make sure he hadn't really grown a third eye he'd been unaware of.

"No," Mica finally told him. "He was a Marine."

As if that explains everything.

Did all Marine dads teach their little girls how to beat up boys twice their size? If that was the case, David would need to ask Margaret Collins what her father did for a living before he asked her to prom.

Other than directions to her house, the little sprite didn't say much to him. He dropped Mica and her bike off at her driveway. They never spoke of that night. In fact, they never spoke again—at all. Occasionally, back at school, he had noticed her watching him with those intense brown eyes and he had waved. Mica gave him a nod from her perch on the brick ledge in the school quad, as though she was sheriff in this town, acknowledging the passing by of someone she permitted to live in it.

David shook his head, returning to the present. He finished off his soda and returned to work in the ER.

He thought of the beautiful stranger he'd seen in his emergency room.

Mica.

He thought about her scraped knuckles and the laceration he'd sutured. He shook his head with a wry grin. Over ten years had passed since he'd last seen Mica, and she was still picking fights.

Vladimir Pronin looked into his niece's eyes as they danced.

Her striking beauty seemed to only grow with maturity. She was no longer the spoiled supermodel she'd once been. She was still a sought-after model, and always had her choice of jobs, but now she engaged in his side of the business.

"*Smotret'*, Natasha," Vladimir murmured as they danced. "Look around you. Four generations of our family are at this wedding."

Her eyes roamed the room as they stepped in rhythm to the Russian pop ballad "I Am You" by Murat Nasyrov.

One of Vladimir's cousins was getting married, and more than a hundred people were in attendance at the reception, all drinking, dancing, and socializing.

As Vladimir swayed with Natasha on the dance floor, he continued, "This is why we do what we do. If we don't look after our family, no one else will. Governments call us criminals because we kill and we traffic drugs. Yet those same governments kill and execute, and they take money from pharmaceutical companies for payoffs and political gain. They murder. They traffic drugs." He spoke slowly, explaining but not defending his business. "*Eto to zhe samoye.* Yet, *we* are the criminals, and *they* are justified. I tell you, we are better than they are. They think only to line their own pockets, while we think to protect our family."

"I support you, *Dyadya.*"

Vladimir smiled, knowing she spoke the truth. "I know, and I'm so proud of who you've become."

Natasha beamed, and her eyes glistened.

"I won't always be the patriarch of the organization." He paused, but she remained an active listener without interjecting, more evidence that her youthful haste had dissipated. "Sometime soon someone will need to replace me."

Her face looked stricken. "*Dyadya* ..."

"Natasha." He half spoke, half chuckled her name. "Look at your expression. You assume I speak of my replacement as a forced retirement—perhaps one where I have a new home in Novodevichy Cemetery!"

Her eyes grew wide. "Don't say such things."

"On a serious note, I'm referring to a *standard* retirement. One where I choose a successor, and I voluntarily step down. Sometimes I imagine living on a remote beach somewhere quiet. A tropical island."

"Not alone, I hope."

"Not alone."

"Maybe with Maxine Rider?" Natasha half-suggested, half-teased.

He smiled at the mention of the American woman's name. He also smiled at Natasha's line of questioning. A caring niece would ask about her uncle's companionship. A greedy, ambitious, self-centered person would have asked who he might name as his successor.

"And what is it you think you know of my relationship with Ms. Rider?"

Natasha's full, red lips curved in a grin. "I know your face beams at the mention of her name. I know you flew all the way to Antigua just to dance with her. Don't shake your head. You did. And she was flattered. I saw the way you two danced."

"You are young. There are some gaps even love cannot bridge."

"It can ... if you give it a steel frame and suspension beams."

He chuckled and kissed her forehead. "Perhaps, *moya plemyannitsa*. Perhaps."

MICA SLOWLY REGAINED consciousness but lay with her eyes closed. She ached miserably, as her head throbbed and her throat felt as though it had been scoured with sandpaper. The sounds around her seemed grossly amplified. Words like "chest tube," "GI," "syringe," and "patient" were spoken around her. She guessed the obvious; she was in a hospital but couldn't remember why. She strained against her aching head to remember what had happened.

She recalled sitting in a cold, metal chair in a dark, musky warehouse with her hands bound behind her. Cigarette smoke filled the air, and a small dim bulb had emitted a dirty yellow glow overhead.

She couldn't remember her assailants' faces, but she'd known who they were. Now, however, their identities eluded her. There had been three or four of them, and they'd been scared. She could smell their fear and the stench of their body odor as they puffed nervously on cigarettes. They had wanted something. Information. Yes, they wanted to know who she worked for—FBI, DEA, or undercover cop?

Then they'd dumped salt on the cut on her side, and Mica had screamed. She screamed disproportionately to the amount of pain inflicted in hopes of being heard and deterring her attackers from causing her any more pain.

As her memory returned, Mica opened her eyes to her current reality and squinted against the bright fluorescent lights lining the ceiling above her. Her eyes continued to burn and her head throbbed like someone was squeezing it in a vice.

Drugs.

They used drugs on me?!

What kind?

Mica tried to sit up, but a sharp pain coursed through her side, forcing her back down. Lying flat, she lifted her head, moving her hospital gown aside. She looked down to see a bandage on the side of her abdomen. Mica remembered getting cut. Yes, there'd been four men—one armed with a knife—and they had all rushed her at once.

A nurse loomed over her briefly, saying, "Sit still. We'll be with you in a minute." He quickly left.

Mica nodded and sighed at the irony. At the moment, she couldn't have moved even if she wanted to.

A short woman in a flowery scrub uniform, pushing a cart with a computer and printer on top, approached. She abruptly raised the head of the bed to a forty-five degree angle.

Mica winced at the pain in her side as the stitches tugged at her skin. Her head slowly cleared.

"Name," said the woman.

"Mica Greyson McMillan." Mica rolled her head around, stretching her sore neck muscles.

"Age?"

"Twenty-eight."

The woman looked at her briefly, as if to ascertain Mica's age for herself.

"Past medical problems?"

Mica wondered if the woman was capable of constructing a complete sentence.

"I had asthma as a child," she offered.

"Allergies?"

"None."

"Insurance?"

"Self-pay."

"Uh-huh," the woman looked up from her clipboard to give a disapproving glance. She continued with her questions.

Mica fought to control the spinning room.

· · ·

David typed furiously on the computer at the central cluster of desks within the ER, trying to complete a patient's progress note. Once he finished this documentation, he could go home and enjoy his few days off.

"Dr. Rider," Maple called to him, "Jane Doe number one's awake. Want me to get a history for you?"

He looked over at Mica. She sat up now, slowly rubbing her temples. Her skin was flushed instead of the pale, ashen color it had been when she'd arrived a few hours ago. Her curly, blond hair had dried to a rumpled fullness.

Maple stared at him staring at the patient, but he ignored her bemused look.

"I'll talk to her," David said. "If she's a first-time heroin user, she may be salvageable..." His voice trailed off. He logged off of the computer he was typing at and walked to Mica.

"What's up with *him*?" Robin asked, her curly brown hair bobbing up and down with the sway of her head.

"Oh, Reverend Rider is off to save another lost and destitute soul," Maple joked.

David walked away from their gossip.

Occasionally, the staff, nurses and doctors alike, would get motivated to preach to their patients about the consequences of their lifestyle choices. No one knew how much good the pep talks did. Science had proven that physicians pestering patients to quit smoking increased quit rates. David doubted the same applied to street drugs, but he put forth the effort anyway.

As he approached Mica, the admissions clerk took her cue and hauled her computer-on-wheels away from them. She handed David a sheet of demographic information as she left. He looked down at the sheet of paper to see the patient's name, Mica McMillan, and title, Miss. So, it *was* her.

He glanced around the ER, but didn't see Detective Bose.

"Miss McMillan, I'm Dr. Rider," he offered a hand.

She shook it distractedly, fidgeting with the bandage on her side.

"Do you?" She asked.

He looked at her, puzzled.

She smiled and clarified: "Do you? Ride, that is. Boats? Motorcycles? Helicopters?"

He was caught off guard—as much by her question as someone in his emergency room actually smiling.

"Oh, well, if driving my sports car counts," he said.

"But you don't have time very often, do you?" Her voice was thick with empathy.

David shook his head and averted his eyes momentarily. He paused for a moment, regrouping. The routine quickly re-initiated.

"How do you feel?" he asked, doctor to patient.

"Hungover." Mica slowly swung her legs over the edge of the hospital bed. She braced herself, with her arms extended and her hands holding the edge of the thin mattress. As she stared at the floor, she took several deep breaths.

David noticed her grimace, undoubtedly from the sutured laceration in her side.

"Heroin is pretty dangerous stuff. You're lucky all you have is a hangover." He spoke in his most patriarchal tone.

"So *that's* what they used." Mica frowned.

"You didn't know what drug you were taking?" He leaned closer.

"Receiving," Mica corrected him. She finally looked up, making eye contact and focusing her gaze on him.

David stared in confusion, both at her words and her beautiful, warm eyes.

Mica McMillan.

"It wasn't voluntary." She rubbed her temples.

"Oh." His train of thought fractured as his righteous script—mechanically delivered after frequent use—was no longer applicable. He had a sense that Mica told the truth. Her direct, unabashed answers gave weight to that truthfulness—as did the signs on her body from a fight.

"Are the ones who injected you the same ones who stabbed you?"

She rummaged through the plastic bag of her belongings and withdrew her coat. As she nodded, she checked the pockets of the coat.

"Jerks." The insult came out like a low growl.

She's been assaulted and acts like it's nothing more than a fender bender.

David felt completely enthralled. Mica had been attacked and drugged, but psychologically didn't seem affected. She had no anxiety, no disorientation, and no paranoia—nothing that usually accompanied traumatic events.

Had the dangers of the event not hit home yet? Was the heroin still sedating her? She was alert, but calm and evidently not interested in sharing the details of the evening's occurrences.

What series of poor lifestyle choices had Mica made to end up stabbed and drugged in his emergency room? She might be cavalier about it now, but if she didn't alter the course, she could end up in worse shape.

He thought about Detective Bose. He'd implied she was instrumental in apprehending drug dealers, but had never implied she was a cop. "Are you with law enforcement?"

Mica stiffened. "No." She held up a pair of sneakers. "Where are my clothes?"

"The ambulance crew had to cut them off to treat you."

She slipped on her shoes.

Noticing Mica was thinking of leaving, David added, "We're going to move you to one of the floor rooms for a couple days for observation."

"I'm sorry, but I have a lot of work to do. I can't stay." She said the words as casually as though she was declining an invitation for espresso.

Work?

3

ica stood and steadied herself, keeping one hand
on the bed for balance.

Heroin? Bunch of amateurs.

"Well," Dr. Rider stood also, "I don't advise this, and I'll have to
document this AMA—Against Medical Advice."

Mica could tell he was trying to sound stern, but the concern
in his voice overrode his efforts. His attempt at trying to be authoritative failed.

Charming.

So were his rumpled brown hair and lush green eyes, but Mica
didn't like authority figures on principle, and she wasn't interested
in his patronizing tone.

Not to mention we were in high school together.

How mortified would she feel if he remembered? Her high
school crush had seen her in the worst condition of her life
tonight. She thought she'd sensed some recognition, as though the
windmill in his mind was churning, trying to place where he knew

her from. It was only a matter of time before he remembered, if he hadn't already.

Mica pulled on her long, suede coat, wrapping it over her hospital gown.

At least I have my coat.

"Also," Dr. Rider continued quickly, "the police will want a statement. You were assaulted and drugged."

The coat reached her knees, concealing the wrinkled, faded gown. Whoever designed these hideous gowns was evidently aiming to avoid anyone wanting to steal them. Hopefully, she could pass as 'not homeless' long enough to get a taxi.

Mica tied off the coat at her waist, took a deep breath, and exhaled slowly to clear her mind. There was so much to do, but first she needed sleep.

She realized Dr. Rider was continuing to watch her—like he expected her to obey.

"The police only need a statement if a) I'm pressing charges, or b) a gun was involved. Because neither is the case, I'm free to go."

Dr. Rider flustered a reply, "You… You don't want to press charges?"

"You can't press charges if you don't know who assaulted you."

Or can't remember. Dammit.

Loss of her recent memories imbued Mica with immense frustration, because she prided herself on having a photographic memory.

She waved her hand dismissively. "Thank you for your help, Dr. Rider."

When she took a first, unsteady step, Dr. Rider placed a hand on her elbow. Long fingers gripped firmly, but gently. Heat radiated from his touch.

Must be a side-effect of the overdose.

"I'm okay." She took a deep breath.

"Wait, Mica. It's six am. You have no ID, no credit card. How do you plan on even getting home?"

Mica turned to look at David. The way he'd said her name made her realize he'd finally remembered her. He'd dropped the clinical tone and sounded genuinely concerned.

David continued, "My shift is over. I'll give you a ride home."

Mica gave the doctor a wry grin. "Seems like our last conversation went something like this."

His eyes sparkled. "I wasn't sure you remembered."

Mica would never forget the one person in high school who was nice to her. Other boys feared her or avoided her, but David Rider had treated her like a human being.

"Go Cyclones," Mica said, without the prerequisite enthusiasm one was supposed to muster when cheering the high school mascot. "I remember, but that doesn't mean we're not still strangers."

David gave her an adorable, lopsided grin. "I'm still a respectable guy. And you could still probably kick my butt."

Mica grunted but didn't disagree. There was no harm in accepting a ride home, and his offer was generous, especially because he was getting off work from a long night shift and was probably exhausted.

Still, he'd seen her after a rough fight, with who-knows-what still in her hair from the floor of that warehouse. All Mica wanted to do was run away from him.

She opened her mouth to conjure another decline when she saw Detective Bose of the Atlanta PD through the corner of her eye. He was drinking a cup of vending-machine coffee and chatting with a nurse. He must have been waiting to talk to her about the events in that warehouse. How did he even find her? Perhaps he'd gotten a description from the cops or paramedics on scene.

If he saw she was awake, he'd come loom over her, asking questions.

Sh... Sugar.

She didn't want to talk to the police yet. They'd have questions, and she didn't have answers. She needed to clear her head first.

"Okay. You win." Mica hooked her arm around David's and turned the both of them away from the detective. "I'll take that ride."

DAVID HAD Mica sign a 'leaving against medical advice' form. He exchanged his white coat for a leather jacket and then led her to the parking garage.

She gaped at his dark gray Aston Martin—stick-shift, fully-loaded—parked in the hospital garage. "This is a step up from your old pickup truck."

David unlocked the vehicle and opened her door. A cool October wind whistled through the garage, and he noticed Mica shiver as she sat down in the passenger seat.

"Yeah. It's a good thing you don't have a bike anymore, because I wouldn't have a place to put it." He climbed into the driver's seat.

She chuckled. As she looked around in obvious admiration at the plush, mocha-colored interior, she ran a hand along the soft fabric. "This must've cost a fortune."

Although she sounded jovial, David sensed an uneasiness in her expression.

He smiled. "Just my first born. Actually, I just bought it last May. I'm still paying for it."

"C'mon, Dr. Rider," Mica teased, "I thought doctors made enough money to pay for one of these every month."

After they buckled up, David pulled out of the parking garage.

"It's David. And not emergency room doctors working at charity hospitals. Sorry to disappoint you."

"I judge people on their actions, not their bank accounts. I assure you—you don't disappoint."

David glanced at Mica, wondering if she'd meant to sound flirtatious or if he'd read too much into her words.

As he pulled onto the street, she told him to take I-20 West.

"So ... emergency room physician? That must be a pretty challenging and rewarding field," she said.

"It has its moments."

Mica looked at him briefly. "Oh? That sounded like a 'but' is attached to it."

"*But* you get burned out when you see the same brutality every night. Beatings, shootings, stabbings, drug addicts, miscarriages. Big cities are like war zones."

Wow, very smooth, David. Complain about your job.

He caught himself at that strange thought. He didn't care about impressing her. Did he?

"Did you know what you were getting into?" she asked.

He nodded. "It's an adrenalin rush for a while—and still is, sometimes. You feel pretty good when you cheat death. But when the same people and the same problems keep calling, you wonder what you've accomplished. The gratitude in this field is somewhat scarce, too. You tire of patting your own back." His voice trailed off into sadness, tinged with a little too much borderline self-pity for his liking.

Why was he spewing his deep, dark feelings?

"Well," Mica said cheerfully, "you saved *my* life, and *I'm* grateful. I'll pat your back for that anytime."

When he chuckled, he noticed her cheeks flush.

"What about *your* career choice?"

. . .

MICA STARED out the window of David's luxury car.

What career?

"I think that's a conversation best held when I haven't been in a brawl and drugged with heroin."

His expression turned doleful. She preferred the smiling, chuckling version of David with his sparkling green eyes and dimples showing.

"Is this the first fight you've ever lost?" he asked.

Mica leaned the seat back and closed her eyes. "Who says I lost?"

"Wait. What?"

It was her turn to chuckle.

"Detective Bose said you fought two against one."

"Four against one." Opening her eyes, she turned to look at him. "You talked to Bose?"

"Not at any length. He said you helped with a drug bust." His statement ended with an inflection, making it sound partially like a question. David obviously wanted details.

She didn't have them. Not yet.

"It's all a little foggy. That's the drugs, right?"

He glanced at her, his eyes stormy with concern. "Could be. Do you recall any head trauma?"

"I'm not sure." She added: "Next exit is mine." Mica directed him through a series of turns to her home, which was well off the beaten path.

Home.

White shutters stood in contrast to the dark, red brick of the house. The morning sun spilled across her small wooden porch and illuminated the white walkway up to the front door.

David parked the car, but remained seated, examining her house and the woods that surrounded it. "You live alone?"

She arched an eyebrow at him.

He shook his head as his ears turned red. "I didn't mean it like *that*. If you have a concussion, you need someone to watch you for twenty-four hours."

"I'll be fine." She got out of the car. She didn't need a babysitter and definitely didn't need David's extravagant car sitting in her gravel driveway passing judgment on her one-story house.

David hopped out and stood by her side. "Mica, I know you're tough. This isn't about how strong you are. This is about protecting your health. If you don't want me to stay, at least call a friend or family member."

Mica thought about who she could call. Not her dad; he'd want all the details of the fight, so he could tell her how he'd have done things differently and with a better outcome. She couldn't call Eddy. He'd read too much into her asking him for a favor.

Her lack of options depressed her. Reaching her front porch, Mica jabbed the keypad to enter the code and unlock the front door.

"I'll be fine," she reiterated, the irritation crisp in her voice. She wasn't angry with David, but at her situation. Part of the problem of working alone was not having backup.

She was Superman with no Lois Lane, except that Superman didn't have to get kidnapped to lure out the bad guys. Oh! Her memory *was* returning. Still, "I'm Batman without Robin."

"Beg your pardon?" David followed her inside and closed the door behind him.

Mica scrubbed a hand across her face. "Nothing. Thank you for the ride."

Her last statement was meant to indicate the time for David's departure had arrived. Instead, he helped her out of her coat and laid it across the kitchen chair.

Ugh. She was suddenly reminded that she was still wearing

that hideous hospital gown. She undoubtedly looked as frightening as she felt.

David cocked his head to one side. "Okay, Batman. Let me be your Robin for the day."

Mica knew she could argue with him, but that would just mean spending more time in front of the handsome doctor while she looked like something that had just crawled out of the psych ward.

"Fine," she said. "I'm going to take a shower."

AJ SCHLAU SQUEEZED the stress ball, as Lucius Titan jogged on the treadmill in his office.

"Have you made headway with the Argentinians yet?" Lucius asked.

"No, boss. They're still upset about losing the plant and..." He stopped short when Lucius sent him a sharp look.

The failed attack on Vladimir Pronin in Moscow a year ago was a sore subject for Lucius. His plan to remove the head of the Russian mafia as a demonstration of power, thereby earning the favor of the Argentinian drug cartel, had back-fired when Vladimir escaped his death.

As one of Lucius' top men, AJ had learned about events. The attempted hit had taken months of planning and hundreds of thousands of dollars to execute. When it failed, they spent another six months assembling the pieces to understand what went wrong. Inexplicably, Maxine Rider and her rinky-dink security company were in Moscow with Pronin at the time of the hit.

Even in a far-fetched scenario in which Vladimir had wanted to hire her team, he'd known Maxine wouldn't accept. She considered herself above protecting criminals—a mindset which should have put her out of business by now. Yet not only did she foil Lucius's expensive attempted hit—during which Lucius safely maintained his alibi at a gala in London—she then had the audacity to retaliate on Vladimir's behalf by blowing up a major production facility outside Aldao.

AJ squeezed his ball tighter. "We also have another issue."

Lucius took a swig from his water bottle without slowing his pace.

AJ continued, "That sweet little PI we've been manipulating is onto me. She tried to lure me to a warehouse. Took down two of my men in the process."

"How does she know about you?"

"She doesn't yet, but she's getting close. She's digging too much."

Lucius's jaw ticked, making AJ's abused stress ball grow slicker with sweat from his palm.

"You have a solution?"

"Yeah, boss. I've been thinking we need to eliminate her before she assembles the pieces connecting me to you."

"And?"

"I'm still thinking on how best to do that. Something clean. Something tidy. No investigation needed."

"The amateur bank thieves she jailed are being released. Hire them to take her out. They'll leap at the opportunity for revenge. And any investigation will be open and shut."

AJ nodded slowly as he registered the genius of Lucius's plan.

Lucius slowed his treadmill to a walk. "You'll make it happen?"

"Yeah, boss. What do you want me to offer them?"

"Start at ten-grand a piece. Top it off at twenty-five if they negotiate." Lucius drank from his bottle of water and electrolytes.

"Okay, boss."

AJ could work with the price range—negotiate the price down

and then claim the bank thieves, known as the Sunset Sliders, had asked for more; so he could keep the difference. They'd eliminate his problem, and he'd get paid for being the middleman.

———⚬———

IN THE SHOWER, with the heat from the steaming water penetrating down to her bones, Mica began to recover her memories. She felt as if her mind had been as numb and chilled as the rest of her.

As she scrubbed every inch of her body except her brand-new stitches, events resurfaced. After the shower, she inspected the sutures. Tight work. Dr. Rider wove a respectable thread. The scar would be thin.

Unlike some of my other ones.

Mica now remembered her assailants, and she knew how to find the ones that got away. They'd have to wait a day, though, as she couldn't go anywhere until she had her truck back, and Mr. Overprotective—sorry, *Doctor* Overprotective—was unlikely to agree to drive her back into town to pick it up today. There was probably some physician's rule about not letting a patient drive if there was any suspicion of a head injury.

When Mica emerged from her bedroom, she followed the scent of bacon and eggs to her kitchen. Standing before her stove was an attractive man in khaki slacks and a black scrub top. She caught herself staring at his backside and the biceps protruding from his shirt. All of her sophomoric desires for David Rider resurfaced—except they didn't feel like the desires of a teenager any longer.

"Your color is better," he commented, as he turned around and scraped omelets onto a plate.

And he cooks?

Mica felt a blush spread from her neck to her face. She walked to the fridge to bury her head in the cool air. "A warm shower will do that."

She reached for the orange juice and poured two glasses. David carried the plates to the table as she carried the glasses.

"Those eggs look amazing."

"All ingredients from your fridge, so if you don't like something that's in your omelet, you have yourself and your long shower to blame." He winked at her.

Mica had taken a particularly long shower, partly as a stall tactic so she wouldn't have to face Dr. Rider, and partly because she'd lost herself in contemplative thought about how to catch the criminals on her list.

"I remembered last night." Mica grabbed forks and knives out of a drawer.

They sat down at the table.

"Oh. You want to talk about it?"

Why not? David had already surmised that Mica had a bizarre life, and she still needed to explain how she had *not* lost that fight —despite her visit to his ER.

"I'm investigating what I think is a covert, illegal operation," Mica explained. "In an effort to lure out one of the leaders, I made myself an easy target. I was jumped coming out of a park after a jog. I'd hoped the ringleader would make an appearance, but the heroin injection interfered with that. Charlie is the one who cut me, but Kyle gave me the heroin."

David, who'd been eating his omelet as she spoke, sat back in astonishment.

Mica shook her head. "The guy's never taken heroin before, and he thinks he's going to give me a dose to loosen me up for interrogation." She shuddered, remembering that awful euphoria spreading through her as the heroin latched on to the cells in her body. "I had to bide my time waiting for their boss to arrive, which meant enduring torture and a dose of narcotics. After Kyle took a phone call, it became clear they had the kill order and my target had no intentions of making my acquaintance. I liberated myself from my restraints and took them down." Due to the effects of the drugs she'd felt invincible while fighting, but the sensation was followed by a horrendous exhaustion.

"And now the guys who assaulted you are in Detective Bose's custody?"

"Two of them. The other two—Charlie Bush and Kenny Serrano—escaped the police," she explained.

"Why did they kidnap you?"

"I'd made tailing them and asking questions about their organization pretty obvious for the past week. They wanted to know who I was, who I worked for, and why I was following them. Basically, they wanted to determine if there'd be any repercussions for killing me."

"And what was the answer?"

Mica looked puzzled. "If there would be any repercussions for killing me?"

He laughed. "Hell, no!" He shook his head and said, "Who *are* you? And who *do* you work for?"

Mica drank her orange juice. "I'm self-employed," she explained. "I have a bachelor's degree in criminology, and I do investigative work, including tracking down criminals, missing criminals and bail-jumpers."

"So, you're a bounty hunter."

Mica's nose wrinkled at his use of the term. "I prefer 'fugitive recovery agent' but I do private investigative work, too."

"How in the world did you start that line of work?"

Mica settled back as she chewed and swallowed, debating how much to divulge about her dysfunctional life. She found herself oddly un-averse to sharing details with David, which was weird, because she normally held her secrets close.

"I was an FBI agent, green and naive. Three years ago, I took an undercover assignment to infiltrate bank thieves. My FBI work, which up until then had been desk work with outdated technology, suddenly became exciting; all because I was the right age and gender for the assignment. So, I infiltrated the 'Sunset Sliders', but they didn't trust me with the details. The job launched early, and I was on my own to stop it. During the heist, a security guard got trigger-happy and botched the whole thing. I took a bullet. The Sunset Sliders were arrested."

His eyes briefly flickered to her chest before darting back to her eyes.

Mica flushed, realizing David must have seen the bullet-wound scar when she was unconscious. She'd shown up drugged and battered in his ER, and now she was sharing her past failures with him. He must think she was a mess.

Mica stuck another bite of food in her mouth to keep herself from sharing more about her grisly past with David, lest she sink even lower in his esteem.

avid found himself fascinated with Mica as they talked over breakfast.

He wanted to know more—to understand more.

So, she'd been shot in the line of duty. Perhaps that explained why she was so calm in his ER after being assaulted. He'd noticed the small puckered scar on Mica's chest. He found himself sitting at the table with her and distractedly thinking about the soft, white skin beneath her collarbone.

David forced his attention back to the conversation. "You did your job and caught the criminals—so why leave the FBI?" Had he not known how physically tough Mica was, he'd have been tempted to think her exodus was related to getting shot, but Mica McMillan wasn't the type to quit something because of fear or pain.

Mica appeared reluctant to answer the question, but finally spoke, "I wasn't in control of the situation. For the first time in my life, I quit something. I walked away. I couldn't work for people without mutual trust."

David took a drink from his orange juice and tried to comprehend her life choices. "Then what?"

"Then," Mica sighed, "I cut off all of my mousy brown hair and dyed it blonde. I went to Colorado for six months, where I improved my Judo and Aikido, hiked in the mountains, and ate a diet of granola and fruit."

He laughed lightly. "And what did you conclude?"

"That I didn't want that life."

"A life in which you didn't have control?"

"Exactly."

David leaned forward. He could faintly smell an enticing, jasmine-scented body wash.

"Do you want the one you have now?" David asked softly.

"No."

It was not the answer he'd expected. Mica had such confidence and control. Surely the immense effort put forth could only come from an equally immense enthusiasm for her work.

He sat back again. "Then why do you do it?" As he asked, he recalled Mica's 'Batman without Robin' reference.

"Because I'm good at it," Mica said with a shrug. "And because this is how I make a difference."

Her honesty and openness mesmerized him. David felt like he could talk with her for hours, no days. Maybe even a lifetime.

For several long minutes, they ate their eggs and bacon in silence. David respectfully gave her the opportunity to say more if she wanted.

Then, suddenly, David heard the sound of a car pulling into Mica's driveway. She frowned and stood up. Walking over to the window beside the front door, Mica peered out.

She gave a laborious and irritated sigh. "Eddy."

"Trouble?"

"No, he's a friend," she grumbled. She opened the door and stepped out onto the front porch.

David joined her and watched a clean-shaven, impeccably groomed man in a navy suit emerge from a black sedan and approach the house.

Just a friend... Who arrives unannounced in the morning looking like a New York stockbroker?

When the unexpected guest smiled a set of gleaming white teeth, David decided he looked more like someone out of Abercrombie and Fitch.

"Don't give me that look, Mica. I tried your mobile first, and you didn't answer." Eddy stepped onto the porch and gave her a hug, even though she pointedly never uncrossed her arms.

David stifled an odd twinge of possessiveness toward Mica.

"Detective Bose told me what happened. I want to make sure you're okay." As the man said his last words, he turned to David.

Mica uncrossed her arms and introduced them. "Eddy, this is David Rider. He's a friend from high school."

Eddy smiled and extended a hand. He seemed unconcerned that Mica had an early morning guest.

"David, this is my friend Eddy Finch."

"Nice to meet you." David shook Eddy's hand. The man's grip felt firm, with no hint of aggression. David couldn't help but wonder why Mica hadn't called Eddy to stay with her for the next twenty-four hours.

None of my business.

"Sorry to interrupt. I didn't know you had company. You're okay? Detective Bose said you snuck out of the ER."

Mica shook her head. "I'm fine. We just finished breakfast."

David blinked at Mica. Did she have any idea what that statement implied?

Mica continued, "David is an emergency room physician and has prescribed a day's rest for me."

Eddy seemed to regard David more carefully. "This one *needs* a personal physician." He nodded in Mica's direction while still talking to David. "Don't get me wrong, she's good at what she does, but she forgets she isn't bulletproof."

The more he talked, the more Eddy's New England accent seemed out of place on the porch of this small house in Georgia.

"...or knife-proof," David added.

Mica shot him a look of heated irritation, which he found adorable.

Eddy frowned and looked down at Mica.

"I'm fine." She glared at the both of them.

"Well," Eddy began, taking retreating steps down the porch, "I see you're well and in good hands. When your day of rest is done, I've got news. Call me."

Mica took a step toward the edge of the porch. "I can hear what you have to tell me now."

"Rest first," Eddy called to her as he opened the driver's door of his car. "Doctor's orders." Even from the distance, David could hear Eddy snicker.

David straightened his almost-grin when Mica whirled to face him. He cleared his throat, walked back into the house, and began clearing the dishes. He waited to hear the complaint she appeared to be on the verge of unleashing...

Instead, she began quietly helping him.

"Thank you for breakfast," Mica said softly. "You don't need to stay ,though. You must be exhausted after your shift."

He lathered a sponge and scrubbed the dishes. "Do you have a landline?"

"What?"

"You don't have a mobile. You said it's in your truck. If you don't have a landline, then you don't have a way to call anyone if you're not feeling well. I'll stay. You have a comfortable-looking couch. I'll be close by, but out of your way. If you don't mind, I'd like a shower." He kept a bag with a change of clothes in his car for after his pool workout. David was skipping the pool today, but at least he had clean clothes.

"I don't mind at all. I'll show you where everything is."

MICA WORKED QUIETLY while this charismatic Good Samaritan slept on her couch. David had taken a shower, joked about smelling like jasmine and vanilla from having to use her soaps, and then fallen asleep within minutes of closing his eyes.

Mica stared at her office wall, as she often did, and pondered the connection between the criminal elements. Perhaps there *was* no connection—no conspiracy. Perhaps Jeremiah Hughes had really just died in a car accident and his sister had read too much into his anxious behavior in the days before his death. Mica had been trying to unravel the tangled yarn of the mystery for the past six months. Last night, she'd finally been close to the criminal malefactor who could perhaps shed light on what Jeremiah had been working on before his death.

Mica had allowed herself to be kidnapped and waited in the chair, restrained with rope, until he arrived. What she hadn't anticipated was them using heroin on her. After she'd felt the high of the liquid narcotic coursing through her veins, the men had received a phone call. Their stiff posture and submissive tones suggested their boss had called. They'd glanced at Mica with just a hint of remorse or pity, which had tipped her off that the boss wasn't coming and had ordered her death. Shortly after that, she'd freed herself from the rope she'd already worked loose, and left her assailants bloodied on the floor.

After *winning* the fight, she'd had no energy left to question them or chase after Charlie Bush or Kenneth Serrano. She'd crashed out on the warehouse floor and woken up in Dr. Rider's emergency room.

With a cup of warm cider in hand, Mica walked out of her office and looked at David on the couch again. She didn't have time for a relationship, especially given that they were polar opposites. Besides, she was reading too much into him helping her. David was a nice guy—that was all. He had helped her in high school because he possessed an innate courtesy toward other people. She didn't need to interpret any deeper meaning into his similar actions today.

He was just so easy to talk with. Mica had told him about her brief work for the FBI, though she'd simplified events for him. The truth was a much longer story, interwoven with deep feelings of inadequacy.

Watching David sleep made Mica crave her own bed. She set her cider down, closed her bedroom door, and crawled under the covers. Cool sheets and a soft pillow welcomed her.

David woke and sat up on Mica's couch. Checking his watch, he saw he'd had six hours of sleep. Through medical school and residency, he'd trained his body to sleep anywhere—cots, couches, and call rooms. He could fall asleep quickly and feel refreshed after a few hours here and there. In fact, given that, he hadn't expected to sleep quite so long at Mica's house.

Yet her isolated home possessed a calming quiet—none of the horns, sirens, truck engines, or helicopters of the big city.

He walked to her closed door. "Mica?"

When no response came, David eased it open. She slept soundly in her bed. The physician in him wanted to check on her pupil response and heart rate, but he wasn't about to walk into her *bedroom* and lean over her as she slept. Who knew how she might misinterpret that action?

David closed the door and walked away. Another door to a different room was open, and through it, he caught a glimpse of an office. When David leaned on the doorway and peered in, the organization and detail laid before his eyes surprised him. Head shots covered one wall. The pictures of various men each had notes beneath their pictures, and they were all linked to different men in a confusing web. In block letters on the side, Mica had written various statements:

CONSPIRACY?

WHO IS LEADER?

MISSING LINK?

David could tell she'd down-played her job as a bounty hunter —*err,* 'fugitive recovery agent'. Mica was a private investigator and something had her working overtime, unless the case was personal.

He looked over the names, but nothing linked her to these men. According to Mica's notes, they were all either criminals or ex-military, and some were both.

His stomach growled. Moving to the kitchen, he decided he'd make dinner. He didn't find much starting material, though: Hamburger buns but no hamburgers, bologna but no cheese, and just a few condiments. Well, he'd have to make do. Having grown up with a father who didn't cook, David had been self-taught from a young age.

He chopped olives and mixed them with Italian dressing, then set the mixture aside in a bowl. He buttered the buns and seared them on a pan before cooking the bologna.

"You're cooking again."

He looked over to see Mica watching him.

He smiled. "I was hoping you'd wake up while it's still warm."

She cocked her head to one side. "What is it?"

Gold curls framed her rosy cheeks, and her eyelids were still heavy from sleep, causing dark lashes to hang sensuously low.

"Muffulettas, except with bologna because you didn't have any genoa salami, capicola, or deli ham. And if you don't like it, it was this or omelets again."

"I've never had anyone cook anything for me, so this is a treat. Twice in one day!"

David turned to assemble the sandwiches. He drizzled the olive dressing sauce over the seared bologna and then put the bun on top. He struggled with a mix of emotions. How had no one ever made this gorgeous woman a meal? And why did he feel excited to be the one to perform this small gesture for her?

He turned and handed her a plate. They sat down to eat at the kitchen table.

"You slept okay?" she asked.

"I did."

"You?"

"Yeah."

"Do you feel okay? Headache? Blurry vision? Nausea?"

"I'm right as rain."

He chuckled.

"Wow," Mica said around a mouthful of food. "This is pretty good."

"Good." He ate his sandwich.

"Any chance we could pick up my truck tonight? I need to get it and my cell phone, which is in the glove compartment."

"And you need decent groceries."

"True."

He debated her health in his head as Mica waited. She seemed well enough, so she should be fine to pick up her truck. After that, they would go their separate ways. In a few hours, the twenty-four-hour mark since her assault would pass.

Then what? She could go back to solving her case, and he'd be back at work in a few days. Separate lives. Yes, that was a reasonable next course of action.

"Yes. We can go pick up your truck after dinner. I do need to examine those stitches in a few days, though."

Did he? A primary care physician could do that for her.

"Absolutely. I really appreciate it."

Fortunately, she didn't seem to see through his excuse to see her again.

"HELLO?" Maxine answered her mobile phone.

"Max, *moy milaya.*"

She jerked up in her chair, bumping her desk and knocking her coffee cup onto her papers and nearly her keyboard. She swore under her breath. "I just spilled coffee on everything. Hang on."

She heard Vladimir's familiar chuckle as she set down her phone and pushed the speakerphone button.

She mopped up the mess with tissues. "You can't call me," she scolded him. "*Why* are you calling me?" They'd had an understanding. Text only, and always routed through their chess game, never directly. He was calling from an unknown number, so at least he'd thought to use a burner phone.

Vladimir's baritone and Russian accent transmitted crisply

through the phone. "I've been worried about you. One minute we're dancing at Dr. Masters' wedding and the next, you're racing back to Atlanta."

Maxine dragged the pile of sopping tissues into the trashcan. "I told you: I was worried about David."

"*Da*. But you won't tell me *why* you are worried about your son."

She sighed. "This line is secure?"

"Of course."

"You know of Lucius Titan?"

"Titan Enterprises," he concurred. "He's private security, like you."

"Not like me." Her tone was sharp.

"That's true. He's more worried about profits than people."

"His morals leave something to be desired."

She could practically hear Vladimir shrug into the phone. What did the leader of the Russian mafia care about morals?

"Anyway," she continued irritably. "We don't get along. I know he's a scumbag, and he knows I've got one of his former employees. Until a few months ago, that was the extent of our loathing. At the wedding, though, he called to tell me he knew about the Hellfire."

Maxine let the silence set for a moment. When she had visited Vladimir in Moscow on behalf of one of her clients, Vladimir had been attacked and Maxine's team was caught in the crossfire. At the time, she and Vladimir deduced that an Argentinian drug lord had perpetrated the hit. Maxine had retaliated by blowing up one of their drug manufacturing plants.

She continued: "Lucius is pissed about it."

Vladimir took a hefty breath. "Meaning Titan is the one who orchestrated the attack on me?"

"I believe so. In fact, I assume he's the unknown competitor who tried to outbid you for the Argentinian drug market." She paused. "He threatened to go after David."

"Maxine," Vladimir snapped. "You should've told me this sooner. I had a right to know."

She paced her office, stretching her chronically aching knee. "Why? So you can start a war with Titan? A war where good people might become victims? Collateral damage?"

"You and I could figure something out."

"There is no *you and I*. I'm a private security contractor. You're the *mafia* for God's sake. I can't work with you."

Except she had worked with him—first in securing Aurora Meridian's safety and then in negotiating Jenna Masters' debt to him. Both of her clients needed creative and unorthodox solutions.

"But we make a good team."

Was he pouting?

They *had* made a good team. With a car on fire and bullets flying in Moscow, they'd worked together and got their employees to safety. After that, Maxine had the additional satisfaction of destroying an illegal drug plant.

With less gusto than her previous statement, she added, "We can't be a team, Vladimir. Our entire life objectives are different."

"I disagree."

She sat heavily in her office chair and stared at her phone.

Vladimir continued, "We both put family first. My family consists of my blood relatives, and everything I do is to secure their future. Your family is David and the Rider team. The infrastructure of your country enables you to function within the law—mostly. Russia is different."

Maxine pinched the bridge of her nose.

"Let's work together, Max. You tell me what you know about

Titan. I tell you what I know. Together, we keep David safe, and I keep *my* family safe."

"That's a bad idea." Her soft reply lacked conviction, and she knew it.

"I'll come to Atlanta, and we'll discuss the problem."

Vladimir disconnected the call.

Dammit!

Maxine lay her forehead down on her desk. The solution to being in over her head with a mammoth like Titan was *not* to enlist the help of a ruthless man like Vladimir Pronin.

Or was it?

If she pitted the two giants against each other, could her team step out of the rink and into safety?

Unlikely. Not with her shitty luck.

She and Rider SI would get trampled during their scuffle. And what was this nagging aversion to using Vladimir to better her situation? What did she care if the criminal overlord put his organization and his life at risk to fight a bottom feeder like Lucius Titan?

The thought of her—even inadvertently—causing harm to Vladimir invoked something akin to sadness inside her. Surely those feelings could *only* be because she didn't use people as a general principle. Her worry couldn't have *anything* to do with the way his eyes crinkled in delight when he smiled at her, or how much she enjoyed their long chess games, or their playful bantering.

Now, he planned to come to Atlanta.

When had things grown so complicated?

5

*A*fter dinner, Mica pulled on her boots and grabbed the spare key to her truck. David led her to his car, and once inside, she directed him to where she'd left her truck.

In under ten minutes, he parked next to her Ford pickup truck. "This is where you chose to go running at night?"

She grinned at the sight of the overgrown trail and rusty swings. "It's a nice park."

"It's a sketchy part of town. And I don't see *any* street lights."

"Exactly."

He shook his head. "Too bad you didn't get your guy."

"I'm persistent." Mica got out of David's car and unlocked her truck.

Fortunately, no one had broken into it or stolen the tires while it sat there; although with peeling paint on the hood and a crack in the windshield, her vehicle wasn't exactly an appealing vehicle to boost.

When Mica started the engine, though, it resolutely groaned to life and was soon purring like the oversized mountain lion it was. She pulled out her phone from the glove compartment and began charging it.

David stood by the open driver's door. "You look like a woman on a mission."

She turned to him. "Just a few errands. Thanks again for all your help today. And last night."

David scrutinized her expression. "Okay, Mica McMillan. Can I check in on you in a few days?"

Mica didn't think she needed any further medical attention, but at the same time she didn't want to draw out the conversation with more questions, so she simply answered, "Yes."

She half-feared that if David kept watching her—with those intensely green eyes of his—she would do something moronic, like ask him out on a date.

Instead, they exchanged numbers and discussed a day and time for her follow-up exam.

Finally, Mica watched as David got back in his car, before she drove out of the park and down the road.

As she powered the old truck through the streets of Atlanta, her phone recharged and displayed an array of text and voice messages. When she pulled over to fill up on gas, she scrolled through them.

After she finished fueling, Mica climbed back into her truck and returned a call from Detective Bose.

"Ms. McMillan. You're alive," he said blandly.

"You have Kyle Byrd in custody? I need to talk to him."

"I waited hours for you in the ER, and you snuck out on me. I need a statement about the events that transpired in that warehouse."

Mica grimaced. "Yeah, okay, but when I come to give a statement, can I talk to Kyle?"

"Can a civilian talk to a prisoner in custody for drug dealing? No."

"Five minutes."

"What are you after?"

Bigger fish.

"I need to know who he works for. His boss may have some involvement in the death of my client's brother. I almost had him."

She had a first name: AJ.

"You're relentless, you know that? The story I heard was that you were on your deathbed when the ambulance came for you. 'Course, I *also* heard you had Kyle and Will restrained and the others running for their lives before you collapsed."

"Yes, well, the scenario didn't go as planned. I didn't account for getting a heroin injection."

"Are you saying you planned your own kidnapping?"

Mica started the truck engine and switched to speakerphone. "These guys are hired bimbos. I need their boss—AJ somebody."

"If you saw this AJ character, I can have a sketch artist ready for when you stop by in a few minutes."

"He didn't come to the warehouse. I never saw him."

"So, I'll see you tonight at the precinct?"

"Okay. Give me about an hour. I'll be there."

When David had watched Mica drive out of the parking lot, he'd suspected she wasn't going straight home. She'd been a little too eager to say goodbye, as though her mind was already racing to her next destination. Her other giveaway was how she'd changed into blue jeans and combat boots before they left her house—an outfit that clearly meant business.

That was why he chose to follow her, keeping his distance in his less-than-inconspicuous Aston Martin. After refueling and a ten-minute drive, she'd turned the corner and parallel parked on the curb across from the Sundown Motel. It had a large, flashing neon sign with the L of "MOTEL" burned out. The building consisted of faded and graffiti-laden brick walls—even the windows had been painted black. Every other streetlight was broken or burned-out. A few men played dice on the sidewalk a block down the road.

Knowing he'd been spotted, David parked behind her.

As he climbed from the Aston Martin, Mica got out of her truck and watched him with her arms crossed. Her eyes narrow, she hissed, "What are you doing, David?"

"I could ask you the same thing. You're supposed to be headed home for rest."

"I rested earlier today. Right now, I need to pick up Charlie Bush."

"The one who got away?"

"*One* of the ones who got away."

"I'll come with you."

Mica shook her head. "Absolutely not. I work alone, and it's not safe."

He shrugged, smiling, "I told you: I'm your Robin for the day." David looked at his watch. "Besides, you technically require two more hours of medical surveillance before your twenty-four-hours is up."

David watched Mica try to suppress a grin...

...and fail.

Strong though she may be in the face of danger, Mica seemed weak to his charm. That was a relief, especially considering he hadn't used that 'charm' in so long he was worried it would be rusty, or dusty, or crusty. Maybe all three.

Seeing opportunity in her poorly concealed smile, David added, "I won't get in the way. I'll strictly be an observer. Besides, you know what I do for a living. Let me learn about what you do."

Mica stepped up close to him and lowered her voice. "You do exactly what I say *when* I say it. Charlie is a buffoon, but I don't want you getting hurt."

As they approached the "MOTE," Mica glanced at David intermittently. She was obviously still uneasy about allowing him to accompany her. David's apprehension escalated. He stole a look back at his car in the dim light of the setting sun, hoping this wouldn't be the last time he ever saw it.

He recalled everything the car dealer had told him: The car had an advanced security system that would send an alert to his phone if anyone touched the car. It was supposed to be jimmy-proof. Besides, the most stolen car on the market was the Honda Accord. Who'd want an Aston Martin?

He swallowed. At least he was fully insured.

"This won't take long," Mica reassured him.

Her voice comforted David—at least until they entered the motel. As he followed her inside, he instantly forgot about his car and hoped instead he'd walk away from whatever was about to happen.

Mica casually approached the motel counter. A man of about fifty years sat smoking a cigarette and reading what looked to be a vampire romance novel. His coarse, gray hair was pulled back into a ponytail, and bifocals rested on the end of his nose. He wore blue jeans and a faded Aerosmith t-shirt from the 1980s.

"Hello," Mica said cheerfully.

The man slowly looked up at Mica. He paused then took off his glasses to look again at her more closely.

David smiled to himself. Several times today, he'd also looked twice to make sure Mica was definitely still there. When Mica entered a room, something akin to a pleasant breeze swept through the door with her. Some would sense the breeze would glide right past them, leaving them to wonder if it—and Mica—had just been an illusion.

Once the man at the counter seemed certain there was, indeed, a beautiful woman in blue jeans standing in the lobby of his run-down motel, he raised his eyebrows as if to ask her what she wanted.

"Can I get a room number for Charlie Bush?" she asked.

The man's face hardened. "You a cop?"

"Nope."

He seemed inclined to believe her, but shook his head, leaned back in his chair and slipped on his glasses. Mica reached into her pocket and pulled out a pair of hundred-dollar bills and set them on the counter.

David could feel his jaw sinking to the floor.

The man peered at the money over the top of his glasses and without moving said, "Room three-twenty."

Mica winked at David, and for an instant he lost himself in her eyes. All he could see was her, and he forgot how he'd willingly entered a bad part of town and stood in the lobby of a sleazy motel just to be with her.

The moment passed quickly as they came to the stairs. Paint was flaking off of the steps, walls, and handrails. The stairs creaked with each step as they climbed them, and David's eyes strained against the dim lights. The rails didn't appear as though they'd bear even the slightest weight.

"What does he look like?" David whispered.

"White guy with a broken nose."

"You broke his nose?"

Mica replied matter-of-factly, "The jerk *cut* me. Do you have any idea how hard it is to get abducted, looking like you're *trying* to escape?"

"Uh, no."

They reached the third floor and strode cautiously down the corridor. Mica walked fearlessly ahead, while David tried to slow his rapid breathing and speeding heart, swallowing his fear at the potential danger they were willingly walking toward.

Moans and groans of pleasure emitted from the rooms.

"Business is good," David remarked quietly, trying to mask his nervousness with humor.

Mica looked at him with a wry grin.

As they arrived at room 320, Mica reached into her coat pocket and withdrew a lock pick kit. She bent down, eyes level with the keyhole, and fiddled with the lock. A deep groan came from within the room.

"Isn't that illegal?" David kept his voice at a whisper, as he bent down beside her.

Mica glanced at David and gave him a quick up-and-down, but didn't seem bothered by his sudden nearness. Instead, she shook her head and explained: "I'm just entering, not *breaking* and entering."

David's brow furrowed in confusion, until he realized she was being facetious.

Mica returned to work, quickly picking the lock with silent ease. As she opened the door, he heard gasps come from inside the room. David followed her inside but stopped in the doorway. Beyond the door, a man in his late-thirties stood in the far corner. He jerked his pants up around his waist while a woman in a sheer robe quickly scooped up her belongings from around the room. She evidently didn't want to be part of whatever was going to happen next. David could empathize.

"Hello, Charlie." A jagged coldness cut at the edges of Mica's voice.

The man—Charlie, apparently—trembled nervously at the

sight of Mica's familiar face. "They said you wasn't dead." He fumbled with his zipper.

He had a large, hairy chest with a small gut hanging over the waist of his pants. His glasses magnified a lazy left eye, which seemed to stare in the direction of the window. Brown, shaggy hair clung to the side of his face from the sweat that still poured down his cheeks. A white bandage was draped over his nose.

The woman, presumably a prostitute, pushed past David and hurried down the hallway.

"They'd said you came back to life," Charlie grunted, squeezing into a dark-green turtleneck that had been lying on the end of the bed.

Mica shook her head and took a step forward. "Don't believe everything you hear." She motioned with her index finger for Charlie to turn around.

Charlie spun around, placing his arms against the wall, and spreading his feet apart. He'd apparently been arrested enough times to know the appropriate position.

David watched in awe as Mica calmly pulled Charlie's arms behind his back and fastened a plastic tie around his wrists. He was a grown man twice her size, yet he whimpered in fear at the sight of Mica McMillan.

Astonishing.

She wasn't even pointing a gun at him. Where *was* her gun? David realized he should have probably thought to ask her that earlier.

Instead, he followed Mica as she escorted Charlie down the rickety stairs.

"Where's your gun?" David asked as they descended the stairs.

"I don't carry one."

"What?" David said loudly, then dropping his voice back down to a whisper. "You go after criminals and you don't even carry a gun? You didn't tell me you were suicidal!"

"I have a pocket knife," Mica countered encouragingly.

"That doesn't make me feel any better."

"There'll always be someone with a bigger weapon. When you pull out a gun, people become nervous. Nervous people do stupid things."

"Yeah, like exactly what you tell them to do because you have a gun."

Mica continued, "If a person thinks they're in control because they're armed and you're not, they'll remain more relaxed. Relaxed people aren't trigger-happy. That gives you more reaction time when an advantage presents itself."

David shook his head. "They've got the gun. Where's the advantage?" He didn't give her time to answer. "I can't believe you're unarmed!"

"I wouldn't exactly say that," Mica countered.

"Oh, right. The pocket knife." David shook his head, following closely behind Mica as they descended the stairs.

Charlie led the way, continuing to whimper quietly.

"The human body can be a weapon," Mica explained, as they walked. "Boxers, for example, would be charged more heavily for a homicide if they killed someone bare-handed because their fists are considered weapons."

"Yes," David agreed, "but a boxer's *arm* weighs as much as you do."

Mica shot him a you're-too-cute look.

David shut his mouth. Voicing his concerns clearly wasn't earning him any macho points.

They reached the bottom of the stairs, and the Aerosmith fan at the counter never even lifted his eyes from his book as they led Charlie from the motel.

David felt a moment of relief as they walked away from the roach-mote. Relief instantly turned to terror, though, when he suddenly saw five strangers standing between them and his car. There were two black men, two Caucasian men, and one Latino man. They didn't appear armed—at least not with weapons-in-hand—but the threat they posed was unmistakable.

They were waiting for the owners of the vehicle parked on the curb. Did they want money? The car? David didn't care; they could have it all.

He wondered how Mica had managed to stay alive when trouble seemed to gravitate toward her no matter where she went. Flushing with anger, he scolded himself for blindly following her here, accompanying a woman he knew nothing about. Nothing except her magnetism to danger.

The hairs on the back of his neck stood straight. What would Maxine do in this situation? His mother, a former Marine, ate danger for breakfast; the same way she ate her eggs—with a dash of Tabasco sauce.

Then, suddenly, David realized Mica had walked right into the middle of these men—totally undaunted. He quickly shuffled to her side, just in time to hear her ask, "Can we help you gentlemen?"

They all laughed, nodding their heads. The circle around David and Mica grew tighter.

Nothing 'gentle' about these men.

One of the black men stepped forward. He had short hair and a mustache. He wore blue jeans with a white shirt and black vest. Large gold rings protruded from his fingers on each hand.

Rings? Or brass knuckles? Hard to tell in the lighting, although David imagined either would leave the same bloodied, battered appearance to flesh.

"Yeah." The black stranger looked from David back to Mica

and then down at Charlie who was trembling, nearly in tears. "Yeah, you can help us. We want your mothafuckin' car and all your mothafuckin' money." They all laughed again.

David tried to swallow, but his throat felt as dry as sandpaper. He started to nod. The exchange seemed reasonable to him. He and Mica got to live, and the gangbangers got his car and money. He only had about thirty dollars in cash on him. Was that enough to buy his life?

"The car's got a GPS system. You won't get very far in it. I suggest you settle for the money instead." Then Mica asked, "A fair fight?"

The man looked at her in disbelief. "You sayin' you wanna *fight* for the money? Geeze, how much money you got, lady?"

"Enough to fight over, not enough for anybody to get shot over," Mica stated. "I'm proposing one-on-one, old-fashioned, hand-to-hand. Me against whichever one of you wants the challenge. A last-one-standing-keeps-the-money fight."

Although he kept his composure, David couldn't believe what he'd just heard. Perhaps he'd misunderstood Mica over his own pounding heart. Surely these men would pull out a gun at any moment and shoot all three of them.

In fact, Charlie's reluctance to make eye contact with the thugs led David to believe the man with amblyopia thought the same.

The leader of the five thugs smirked. "Yeah, okay." He stepped back. "Leo? Kill the bitch."

The tallest black man stepped forward. He took off his hoodie and tossed it to one of his colleagues. From his fitted sweat pants to the bulging biceps that stretched through his short-sleeved shirt, the man called Leo looked to be a muscular one-hundred-eighty pounds. His condensed breath, floating out of his mouth and over his dark eyes like smoke, gave him a demonic appearance.

A few drops of cold rain fell from the sky.

Mica passed Charlie to David and curtly ordered, "Trunk."

Then, mechanically, she pulled out a pair of black gloves from her back pocket and pulled them on.

David complied with Mica's orders, unlocking the trunk of his Aston Martin and opening it for Charlie who eagerly climbed inside. He lay face down, curled into a ball to fit into the small space, his hands still secured behind his back.

David felt disturbed to suddenly discover that a human could fit in the trunk of his car. He knew the dimensions cited by the car dealer were over six cubic feet; but *still*, seeing a man curled up in that space unnerved him.

Yet Charlie might ultimately be the only one of them to survive this ordeal.

David closed the trunk and rejoined the group, which had formed a circle around Mica and Leo.

David started to step forward into the ring, but the leader of the gang blocked him with his meaty arm. David stood there, in the middle of the city road, in the light of a streetlamp, about to watch a woman be brutally beaten, and he could do nothing to stop it.

Maxine would know what to do. She had her security business and a small army of loyal men ready to do her bidding.

Mom would have been prepared for something like this.

David's brain worked like a medical computer, figuring out all the potential dangers. One blow to the ribs would collapse Mica's lung. One blow to the back would send her in kidney failure.

One blow to the head would surely kill her.

6

Raymond closed his eyes and drummed his fingers on the steering wheel of the ambulance. Small drops of rain began to cover the windshield. They commingled until they were finally heavy enough to stream down the glass.

From his view behind the windshield, the city morphed into a shadowy Monet painting. His favorite song played on the radio: "What It's Like." The tune by Everlast was dark and melancholy, but it was his song.

Because, maybe, if more people walked a mile in others' shoes then they might know what it's like.

Or so the song says.

Raymond stared at the tall, letters: 'Regional Medical Center' that loomed on top of the hospital. The blue, fluorescent light beckoned to the wicked streets below: *Bring me your weary, your lonely, your ill, your weak, your injured, your intoxicated, your waywardly, your wasted.* Those blue letters promised more than they could deliver—a cure for everyone's ailments. A hospital, a hotel, a refuge, a comfort, and a cure. As though a single massive building could provide for people what they were unable or unwilling to provide for themselves.

What was the hospital really? It was a place of pain, psychosis, nosocomial infection, and prolonged misery. A place where idealistic physicians turned cynical and where nurses turned callous.

Perhaps not always.

Perhaps not forever.

Somehow—amid the piercing screams of the psychotic, the crimson flow of blood on the stained yellow floors, the sickening smell of alcohol as it seeped from the pores of the inebriated, the putrid smell of urine, bile, and vomit that soaked sheets, the constant screech of the intercom, and the sickening sweet stench of perfume and air fresheners—moments of powerful compassion brought hope, and lives were truly saved.

Tonight, Raymond had been called into work and had found himself stuck with a rookie partner, which probably explained why he felt more jaded than usual. As a shift captain, he often had to work when others called in sick, or with family emergencies. The overtime wasn't worth it but wasn't as though he had family waiting on him at home.

This wasn't his usual truck or zone, but Raymond felt comfortable with the area, and the closest hospital was still Regional. The rookie he'd been partnered with only had forty-eight hours on the truck since he'd earned his paramedic license. Raymond studied the new paramedic. One jittery knee bounced up and down, nearly colliding with the dash. The rookie was nervous—wanting, waiting, and panting for the first trauma call of the night.

Easy little terrier.

For Raymond, the streets produced too much trauma—stabbings, shootings, motor vehicle crashes, lacerations, eviscerations, head trauma, fractured bones, spinal cord injuries, burns, blunt trauma, dislocations, shearing forces, puncture wounds, pneumothorax, hemothorax, pneumohemothorax.

What a mess!

Raymond would never be labeled a "trauma junkie." What could he do for them? Wrap them up and ship them to the ER. They needed a surgeon, not a ditch doctor. He preferred cardiac calls, because at least the ambulance carried numerous drugs to treat patients with heart disease.

A high-pitched tone suddenly emitted from the radio: "Unit twenty-one. Signal twenty-four. Two-five-four-eight Third Street."

Raymond put the ambulance in Drive and flipped on the emergency lights and sirens.

"Unit twenty-one en route!" his partner shouted into the radio.

Raymond cringed. He wanted to give his partner a sedative.

Signal twenty-four was an obstetrics or gynecological call.

Maybe it's not a delivery.

The dispatcher's voice came back over the radio. "Unit twenty-one. You are responding to a twenty-eight-year-old female, eight months pregnant. Caller reports the woman is complaining of abdominal pains."

Yeah, those are called contractions.

He shook his head.

Birthin' a baby with a rookie.

From the corner of his eye, Raymond could see his partner anxiously squirm.

As he approached the address, he turned off the siren. In these neighborhoods, better to draw as little attention as possible; although legally, if the lights were on, the siren was supposed to be.

.   .   .

DAVID WATCHED in horror as Leo assumed a boxing stance, rising on his toes, shifting his weight back and forth with fists balled and tucked close to his body.

Mica, meanwhile, moved steadily with her arms up in some kind of martial arts pose. She kept a calculated distance from her opponent but was still in arm's reach of his huge fists.

Fists? More like jackhammers, thought David.

Weapons.

As Leo swung, David winced. When he opened his eyes a split second later, though, Mica still stood. She'd dodged his swing.

The boxer came at her repeatedly, his arms swinging. Each time, Mica gracefully and quickly avoided the blow, although sometimes only by inches.

After several swings, David wondered if she was toying with Leo, or just waiting for an open shot. Looking at the faces around the circle, he saw amusement, disbelief, and growing irritation. They'd underestimated her—as had David.

One of the white men of the group, short and wiry, with a bald head and loose, blue polyester clothing, stood in one spot while bobbing his head and jerking his arms, as if mimicking the actions he saw before him.

The Latino man stood with his arms crossed, bunching up his heavy leather jacket. Lastly, the third black man wore a permanent smirk as he stood with his hands on his hips.

On Leo's next swing, Mica ducked and then kicked upward into her opponent's side. He let out a grunt and stepped back to regroup. Sweat poured down his face and Leo panted heavily. Mica seemed to be letting him tire himself out.

After several more missed blows, the gang lost their patience. At that instant, Mica kicked again. This time she aimed lower and struck the man called Leo in the side of his knee. He fell to the ground with a short, piercing cry.

David winced. Mica had no doubt torn several ligaments and tendons with that kick, and Leo would be limping for quite a while.

The gang members seemed to realize they'd lost this wager—if they'd ever had any intention of honoring it in the first place. The three men suddenly closed in on Mica, and David could hardly believe what happened next.

With graceful kicks and rapid punches, they all fell to the ground like flies.

Throughout the skirmish, Mica remained untouched. The Latino thug got back up and lunged at her with a knife, but Mica caught his wrist and twisted it behind him. She snatched the knife right out of the thug's hand and hurled it in David's direction.

The leader of the gang, standing beside David, had reached into his jacket pocket seconds earlier, but that was before Mica's knife embedded itself into the man's forearm.

He screamed, dropping the gun he was pulling out from inside his jacket. David's jaw was hanging open, and he snapped it shut as he reached to pick up the gun.

RAYMOND TURNED the corner and let his foot off of the gas when he saw a street fight ahead of him. A woman was holding a man's wrist, forcing him to bend over awkwardly, while two other men slowly clambered to their feet, apparently having already been beaten to the ground.

Ten feet away from the brawlers, two other men stood next to a parked car. One of them was clutching his arm, mouth gaping wide. The other was stooping to snatch something up off the ground.

The scene was freeze-framed in the headlights. Then the

flashing lights of the ambulance spun dizzily against the build-ings, and the men scattered.

As they ran, Raymond recognized the woman who remained.

No way!

It wasn't possible. The heroin overdose patient from the night before stood in the street.

Events seemed to move in slow motion as Raymond drove closer. Seconds had passed, and all but one of the men had dispersed, frightened by the oncoming lights. The woman seemed calm and collected as she walked over to the remaining man who stood next to the car.

Dr. Rider?

The entire scene seemed surreal. It *couldn't* be, but it *was*.

As Raymond drove past them, he could see Dr. Rider's face clearly as they briefly made eye contact.

And, as if to confirm it, that was the doctor's car he was standing beside!

The 'James Bond' car they'd joked about at work, claiming Dr. Rider needed it to compensate for his manhood; even as Raymond had secretly envied the car.

Raymond turned to the right two blocks down and pulled off to the side of the street, pulling the ambulance up against the curb. His mind quickly shifted back to the call; he could ponder that street fight later.

A signal twenty-four. If they took the stretcher up now, they could bring the pregnant woman down immediately and reach the hospital before she delivered.

MOMENTS EARLIER, David had watched the ambulance drive-by in a slow blaze of blinding light.

As the mammoth vehicle had passed, David had peered in

through the window and recognized Raymond staring back at him. He imagined he looked as strange and out-of-place as he felt, standing there holding a gun.

David turned his astonished look toward Mica.

She patted his shoulder, stood on her toes, and kissed him on the cheek. "Time to go, David." She was breathless with flushed cheeks.

With the gun aimed down, David pressed the magazine release with his right thumb. He removed the magazine with his left hand, pulled the slide back and checked the chamber. Confirming the weapon was empty, he handed her the disassembled Strum Ruger 9mm and got into his car.

As he started the engine, Mica climbed into the driver side. She stared at him with a mix of astonishment and heated desire.

David winked at her. "You're not the only one full of surprises. You don't grow up in the home of a military parent and not know your way around firearms."

"Color me impressed," Mica said.

"What about your truck?"

"I'll come back for it. Let's stick together."

David shifted into gear, feeling a wave of relief as he pulled away from the curb. How close had he come to death? Mica had saved him.

Mica looked at him carefully and asked tentatively, "Are you okay?"

Kick, punch, bam! She'd taken them all to the ground. The moves and the knife-throwing had been phenomenal to see. Watching her fight was like watching a choreographed dance.

"I felt like I was watching a Jackie Chan movie! I didn't even help you."

"Jackie's a little faster, I think." Mica smiled. She slipped the pieces of the dismantled gun into his glove compartment.

"Besides, you *did* help. You didn't join the fight. If you'd jumped in, the fighting would have escalated faster. Instead, I had time to take down the strongest of them before having to fight the rest."

"You *knew* they wouldn't let us go."

"Of course they wouldn't. But I needed a strategy that didn't have me fighting all of them at once."

David turned the corner and saw the ambulance that had passed them. The flashing monstrosity was parked on the side of the road two blocks down. He slowed the Aston Martin and watched intently through the window. A medic was frantically grabbing boxes and bags of medical supplies from the back of the ambulance. With his arms full, he rushed into the entrance of a four-story apartment building. Raymond must have been inside already.

"Do you want to stop?" Mica asked.

He knew Raymond wasn't particularly fond of him, but perhaps this represented his chance to rectify that. Raymond's partner, laden down with supplies, looked panicked, and the least David could do was to offer some help.

"Yeah," he said slowly. "Yeah, that sounds like a good idea." He parked the Aston Martin behind the ambulance.

David hopped out and headed for the apartment building. He hesitated. "I just remembered you put someone in my trunk. I'm a doctor. I can't drive around with someone in my trunk!"

"Go ahead," Mica called. "I'll check on Fearless Wonder and make sure he isn't puking in your trunk."

He tossed her the keys. "*That's* not what I'm worried about."

"I know. I'll make sure he's not in distress. As soon as we're done here, I'll take him to the police station."

David nodded and turned to face the four-story building. He entered and paused for a moment in the lobby, allowing his eyes to adjust to the bright lights. He climbed the staircase directly in front of him, careful not to step on any of the rotten-looking planks or grab the handrail that hung loosely from the wall.

When David reached the second floor, he could hear a woman screaming. He hoped he wasn't walking into another violent situation. Following the screams to the fourth floor, he had to push his way through a crowd in the hallway. He came to the doorway, where a gaggle of people were gathered outside. A shrill scream resonated from behind it.

David recognized the intermittent screams; he'd delivered his share of babies. He pushed past the crowd, knocked twice, turned the knob, and walked inside.

He immediately saw a Hispanic woman lying on the floor with her legs spread and a sheet draped over her. Her eyes were wide with fear, and they rolled back with pain.

With mask and gown donned, Raymond faced the woman and arranged supplies on the floor around him. The other paramedic stood at the head of the woman, holding a bag of IV fluids that flowed into the woman's left arm. He rocked nervously from one foot to the other.

At his feet sat a blue bag filled with supplies—blood pressure cuffs, bandages, and other equipment. A large, orange box containing vials of medication lay next to the woman. A cardiac monitor was connected to the woman's chest with fine wires. From a distance, it seemed to display a normal heart rhythm.

The ambulance stretcher had been pushed out of the way, up against a table next to the wall.

A man stood pacing in the kitchen, mumbling in Spanish.

Raymond turned to see who had joined them in the room and didn't conceal his surprise when he recognized David.

"Can I help?" David asked.

Raymond's gaze flickered over to his nervous, bumbling partner. He seemed to consider David's request. Raymond's partner appeared virtually incapacitated by fear and adrenaline. Raymond's surprised expression turned to anger briefly when David offered to help. This was soon followed by resignation as Raymond nodded and tossed David an isolation kit.

"How close are the contractions?" David donned the gown, mask, and gloves.

"Close enough," Raymond said. He lifted the sheet, revealing a soaked pad beneath the woman. At that moment, the top of the infant's head was already crowning.

"Para one, gravida three," Raymond said as he knelt down. This was her third pregnancy, and she'd miscarried the previous one. "Her blood pressure's up a little. Has a history of asthma, no known allergies. She doesn't speak a word of English."

David nodded. "Do you speak Spanish?"

"Not enough to translate anything, Doc."

David adjusted his gloves and readied himself. "*Puje!*"

David had called for her to push. Sadly, that was pretty much the extent of his foreign language capabilities.

AFTER MICA HAD CONFIRMED that Charlie was still breathing in the trunk of the Aston Martin—and promised to get him out soon— she followed in David's footsteps into the apartment complex. As she took the stairs, she wiped moisture off her face from the drizzle outside.

She found the apartment where the commotion originated and entered the room to the overwhelming smell of pungent urine and coppery blood. The larger of the two paramedics knelt on the floor of the apartment, holding a baby's head as the infant protruded from a woman lying on the floor. He suctioned the baby's nose and mouth with a small blue bulb.

Dr. Rider held a blanket, kneeling nearby and ready to receive the infant when it was free from the captivity of the woman's birth canal.

"*Puje!*" the medic yelled.

A sound like the cry of a banshee filled the room, as the woman screamed her way through another push.

The second paramedic, thin and timid, stood at the woman's head and jumped at the sound of her wailing.

Mica went to the woman's head and knelt down beside her.

"You don't speak Spanish, by any chance?" David asked.

"*Mi nombre es* Mica," Mica answered, by speaking to the woman. "*Cual es tu nombre?*"

"Anita," the woman said meekly.

"It's a boy!" Raymond cried.

"*Tienes un niño,*" Mica told the woman.

She smiled and began to cry. Mica took her hand in hers.

Mica watched David as he cradled the child, who was covered in thick, white mucous. Beneath the coating, the baby's body appeared blue and limp-looking.

Not normal.

The paramedic placed two clips a few inches apart on the umbilical cord and briefly felt the cord in the middle. After cutting the cord, he hollered for the woman to push again.

Mica observed David move a few feet away with the infant. He knelt on the floor, reaching for instruments spread out next to the blue bag. He grabbed a curved metal device. As he extended it, a tiny light shone from the end. The other paramedic slid a canister with long tubing across to David. A sucking noise rose from the tubing. David inserted the metal device and appeared to be suctioning deep inside the infant's mouth. His motions were swift and fluid yet gentle. The tubing vanished down the infant's throat as it suctioned.

In the kitchen, the baby's father voiced concern for the baby's health. His anxious chattering and questioning wasn't helping his wife through her delivery.

"*No estas preoccupado*," Mica said. "*El hombre es un doctor*."

"*Un doctor!*" the man said excitedly.

"*Hay una problema?*" Anita asked wearily. "*Donde esta mi niño?*"

David left a breathing tube in the infant's throat after suctioning twice. He un-hooked the suction and connected a tiny, oval-shaped plastic bag to the tube. He squeezed the bag in delicate motions, breathing for the infant. Mica gaped in awe as the infant turned from blue to pink. Squirming, the baby choked on the tube. David pulled the tube out and the infant released a scream.

"*Mi niño!*" the woman cried in delight, straining to see the child.

Mica saw the paramedic, who'd just delivered the infant, catch the woman's placenta in a plastic bag. It was huge, Mica thought. It looked like a giant roast—round and a dark redish-brown. And the *smell!*

Ugh.

She suddenly felt nauseated, and the room seemed too small with too many bodies packed inside of it.

"Hey," the larger, calmer paramedic called to her. "I need you to rub right here, firmly." He was pointing at the woman's lower abdomen, just above her pelvis bone.

"Is she going to be alright?" Mica followed his instructions.

"So far, so good." The paramedic scooped equipment and supplies together, while the other paramedic took a blood pressure reading from the woman.

"I'm Raymond." He introduced himself as he laid a clean, dry dressing on the middle of the stretcher. He pulled off his gown and gloves.

"Mica." She continued to massage the woman's abdomen.

David swaddled the infant, and he carried him Anita so she could hold her newborn child.

"*Cual es el nombre de tu niño?*" Mica asked.

"Cristóbal Hernandez Segovia," Anita said proudly. The man in the kitchen rushed over to see the child. His eyes filled with tears, causing a chain reaction throughout the room.

David's eyes were the first to moisten with tears, followed by Raymond, and then Mica. Finally, the other paramedic had to bury his own head in his sleeve for a moment to compose himself. The moment felt both strange and miraculous as they all looked at each other, grinning from ear to ear.

RAYMOND SHOOK his head in disbelief. If there was ever a call he would want a physician to mysteriously appear at, this was it. In addition to David's fortuitous presence was a calm, linguistically-talented woman.

"Unit twenty-one status?" The dispatcher's voice came over the radio.

Raymond pulled his radio from his belt and keyed the mic. "Twenty-one's 10-4 on the scene with two patients. We'll be en route to Regional in about ten. No need for further status checks."

"Dispatch clear."

The radio would have picked up the child crying in the background.

The new mother had stopped bleeding and held her baby. After trading their gowns and masks for a set of clean gloves, Raymond and Dr. Rider loaded Anita onto the stretcher. Because the mother couldn't safely hold the baby while being carried down the stairs on the stretcher, and the father was still hysterical, Mica wrapped her arms around the swaddled baby and carried him down to the ambulance. Raymond's partner followed behind, carrying all the equipment back to the ambulance.

It had been quite the effort to climb the four flights of stairs up to the apartment in the first place, so Raymond knew coming back down with a patient on the stretcher would be tough.

They maneuvered carefully down the creaking, rickety stairs, and somehow managed to arrive at the back of the ambulance. Dr. Rider proved to have quite the upper body strength, and, once again, Raymond found himself reluctantly grateful that he'd arrived seemingly out of nowhere.

"I have to stay with the patients," Dr. Rider was saying to Mica, as they paused outside the ambulance.

Raymond narrowed his eyes as he watched the doctor excuse himself. What was the story there? Had they been on a date? In *this* part of town?

"No problem," Mica said warmly. She handed the baby to the physician and walked back toward his car. "I'm going to take Charlie in, then I'll come to the hospital and pick you up."

Charlie? Raymond wondered.

"Okay," Dr. Rider nodded, watching her go.

The way the blond woman looked at Dr. Rider—that slight smile, with her head tilted to the side and her eyes locked with his —was pure attraction. It made this situation even more confusing. If *this* had been Dr. Rider's idea of a date, rumbling in the streets of downtown Atlanta and jumping calls with ambulances, Raymond would have to impart a little romantic advice to him.

Shaking his head free of such distractions, Raymond turned his attention back to his patient—*patients*.

Raymond slung the doctor a spare stethoscope before cranking the heat up in the back of the ambulance. The interior would grow toasty, but his discomfort was secondary to keeping the newborn warm.

As Dr. Rider held tubing a few inches from the infant's face, blowing oxygen toward him, he listened to baby Cristobol's heart sounds.

Raymond's rookie partner closed the back doors of the ambulance and took his place in the driver's seat up front. As they pulled away from the curb, he turned on the lights and sirens.

7

"*A* citizen's arrest?"

Mica looked up from her paperwork to see Detective Bose standing over her with his hands on his hips.

"Charlie Bush was at the warehouse. He was one of the men who assaulted me."

"*We* could have apprehended him. I thought you were coming here to give your statement, not drop off more perps."

"Don't worry, I'll do that too." Mica rolled her shoulders, shrugging off her fatigue. She'd *had* to be the one to apprehend Charlie so she could ask him about his boss, AJ.

As fearful as Charlie was of Mica, he was clearly more afraid of AJ. He'd clammed up during the car ride to the station and turned pale at the mention of his boss' name. Charlie had been cooperative—congenial, in fact—right up until Mica had asked about AJ.

Charlie wasn't motivated to talk about the one person Mica needed information about despite the fact that she'd delivered him unharmed to the police.

"What's this AJ person to you anyway?" Detective Bose asked. "Can't be a bounty if you don't even have a full name."

Mica felt a lump in her stomach. She was reluctant to divulge her conspiracy theory with other members of law enforcement and potentially lose what little credibility she had left. But she also needed Detective Bose's cooperation.

"A client hired me to look into the death of her brother. AJ's name came up during my investigation, so I suspect he may have answers."

Or, he may be the murderer.

"You're talking about PI work. Are you licensed for that?"

Mica's jaw tensed. "Yes, I am, and it would be helpful if I could speak with Kyle Byrd."

Bose crossed his arms. "I want to help you, Mica. Really, I do. Your father and I were in the Marines together. But you can't interfere with our investigation while you're experimenting with PI work."

"Can you at least ask him for AJ's last name and text me if you get it?"

"I can do that."

"Thanks."

"The Feds still shadowing you?" Bose asked.

"Just one," Mica admitted. She finished the last form she'd been completing and leaned back in her chair.

"Does your father know about him?"

"We're just friends." They hadn't always been 'just friends,' but she and Eddy maintained 'friend' status now, and that wasn't about to change.

MICA PARKED David's sports car in the "Physicians Only" parking section. She walked through the doors to the Emergency room marked "Patient Entrance." The lobby was surprisingly sparsely occupied with barely anybody there except the janitors sweeping and mopping the floors. They gave off a pristine shine that she knew would soon be coated with vomit, saliva, blood, and dirt from the next onslaught of patients.

Mica turned the key ring over in her hands before stuffing the keys in her pocket. She would pass David's keys back to him... And then what? Say goodbye once and for all? She could catch a cab or hail a ride back to her truck.

Mica knew David had been scared ... but scared *off*? Why was she even wondering that? As if she was planning a relationship with him?

Mica shook her head. There were *plenty* of reasons why a relationship with her wouldn't work out. She was strong, mentally and physically, which intimidated a lot of men. She also sometimes worked in dangerous areas... Well, *most* of the time.

But Mica wouldn't sugarcoat her work for any man. This was her life: violent, disordered, irregular, and subject to constant change. She loved the hunt and the danger. She had no deep-rooted psychological desire, no childhood trauma that drove her into battle. She could walk away from four armed men with her prey in handcuffs and everybody still alive, and she felt good about it. This was her talent—not music or dance or surgery or palm reading, but finding and apprehending criminals.

Mica knew she could tackle the streets, one bad guy at a time, and with each one she captured, the world was minus one more villain; provided the prosecuting attorney could beat the crook's hired lawyers.

That was the final hurdle, so much so that Mica had even briefly thought about law school once. Very briefly. She'd been deterred by the thought of having to put a great deal of time and effort into a case that would ultimately be decided by a judge and jury. The lack of control didn't appeal to her.

Mica could only imagine the frustration if the accused was acquitted on some technicality, or found not guilty by a sobbing, sympathetic jury. Or, worse, if the accused *was* found guilty, but was actually innocent.

No, she'd just deliver offenders into the system and then hope that system worked.

In the same vein, Mica had also thought about going back into actual law enforcement. The FBI had been her dream until she'd discovered it consisted of ninety percent desk work with outdated technology. Being shot had merely been the final call-to-action to leave the bureau.

Mica walked toward the double doors that led into the emergency room. A large security guard in a brown and black uniform stepped up in front of her and held out his right hand.

She stopped.

"I'm sorry ma'am. Patients and staff only."

She explained politely, "I'm a friend of Dr. Rider."

"I'm sorry, but you'll have to have a pass."

Mica frowned before digging in her pants' pocket.

The guard took a defensive step backward and moved his hand to the handle of the revolver at his waist. He cocked his head to one side and raised his eyebrows in warning.

Mica pulled out a set of keys. "Will Dr. Rider's keys do?" She held them up for the guard to see.

The black, plastic lock button connected to a gold key chain with the classic Staff of Hermes design, imprinted with the initials D.F.R. The guard took the keys and examined them closely, *too* closely. Mica wondered if he needed glasses. Eventually, the guard stuck his bottom lip out.

With a bob of his head, he led her through the doors and toward a counter where David, Raymond, and several other people in scrubs or white coats were standing. David was the only one who looked oddly out of place, still in his slacks and jacket.

"Dr. Rider," the guard called out as they approached.

Everyone turned to look.

"Mica!" David turned and walked toward them, smiling broadly. He seemed genuinely happy to see Mica and without a moment's reservation to suggest he held any regret about their adventure.

The guard held out his keys, and David took them.

"I figured if she was cleared to drive your car, she was cleared to come back here."

David nodded and offered the man his hand.

They shook hands. "Thank you. Thank you very much, Jerry."

Jerry nodded and retraced his steps to his post. Mica suspected the ER staff of a downtown emergency room knew each member of the security staff personally.

David smiled again at Mica. For a moment, she sensed he wanted to give her a hug or a peck on the cheek–or maybe just throw a casual arm around her shoulder in a gesture to show they'd bonded over battle, and blood, and babies.

Instead, he invited her to meet everyone. He led Mica to the counter and introduced her to Raymond—who she'd met earlier that evening—plus two nurses, Tom and Robin, and Dr. Cruz, an internal medicine physician who explained how he moonlighted in the ER to pay for his children's college.

"Thanks again," Raymond began, "for helping with the call."

Mica shrugged. "It was sort of spur the moment."

"Where'd you learn Spanish?"

"Well, I minored in it in college, but never learned the language until I had to go to Mexico about two years ago."

Tom jumped into the conversation. "So, Dr. Rider tells us you're a private detective. Were you in Mexico, ya know?" He held his fists up in the air with bulging biceps, unable to grasp the words he sought. "Hunting bad guys?"

He made her work sound as though she'd been head hunting in Aztec ruins somewhere. Tom smoothed a hand through his dark, wavy hair as he flashed his blinding white and perfectly straight teeth at her.

Mica leaned against the counter. "I had to go to Cuernavaca to pick someone up."

Tom leaned forward with an expectant expression of wanting more details.

"I've heard Cuernavaca is beautiful," Robin said. Her voice resonated with an irritatingly high pitch.

Mica nodded. "It's the land of eternal spring."

"So, what was he wanted for?" Tom continued. "Murder one?"

"Murder one?" Mica asked blandly.

"Yeah," he nodded.

"No," Mica shook her head. "She was wanted for arson."

Tom nodded enthusiastically. "Cool."

"How long have you been in that line of work?" Dr. Cruz asked, his own curiosity evidently piqued.

"A few years..." Mica began.

"Where do you keep your gun?" Tom asked, using his question to let his eyes roam her body.

"Is Cuernavaca south of Mexico City?" Robin squeaked.

Mica replied. "I don't carry a gun. And, yes, it's south."

Tom shook his head. "How do you bring in criminals if you don't carry a gun?"

Cruz spoke next. "What kind of money do you make in that line of work?"

Raymond, of all people, stepped in to shield her from the

barrage of questions. Focusing on Tom's inquiry, he grinned. "Are you kidding? This woman is all the weapon she needs. We turned the corner downtown, and there she stood, kicking three different guys' asses..."

"Depends on the criminal and the crime and who hired me," Mica interrupted, answering Dr. Cruz's question.

"Three?" Tom said in disbelief, still listening to Raymond.

"Is it dangerous there? Like Tijuana?" Robin was still on the subject of Cuernavaca.

Raymond smirked at Tom. "She'd kick *yours*."

Mica faced Robin. "No more than any big city."

Dr. Cruz continued, "About how many criminals have you brought in so far?"

Tom looked down at his chest and muscles. "I don't think so."

Mica looked disparagingly at Tom. She could take him in under sixty seconds, but she didn't fight for show.

"Okay! Okay!" David shouted, taking Mica by the arm and interrupting the flurry of questions. "I'm rescuing my friend. This is my night off, and we're getting out of here before you get busy and expect me to stay."

Waving goodbye, they left the emergency department.

***

David pulled into Mica's driveway. They'd opted to leave her truck downtown and retrieve it in daylight. There seemed to be no appropriate way to end such an unbelievable evening. David had explained the infant delivery to Mica on the ride back, and he'd been happy to report that Cristobol was healthy and resting in the neonatal unit at Regional.

He knew he was talking just a little too fast, but all the excitement had him revved. He'd delivered numerous babies over the years, but none under those conditions and never immediately following a street fight.

He glanced over at Mica. "Sorry. I'm doing all the talking."

"It's alright," she reassured him. "At least I know you're not distraught about the danger I put you in."

"I certainly don't envy your lifestyle, but you seem well-trained for it." He put the car in neutral and turned off the engine.

"No more than you and yours," Mica commented, turning in the car to face him.

"Yes," he agreed, "but my life isn't at stake when I do my job."

Mica nodded. "Your *patients*' lives are at stake. Many would argue that's a bigger responsibility."

David thought for a moment. "Perhaps." He was unconvinced.

He exited the car and walked around to her side, but she'd already stepped out and was closing the door. He noticed her wince.

"Your stitches?" His brow furrowed in concern. Her agile movements during the fight could have damaged her wound.

"I'm fine."

"Mica," he said sternly. "Inside. Let me see them."

When they got inside and she disarmed the alarm system, David flicked on the kitchen light and ordered her to sit.

Reluctantly, Mica did so.

David knelt and lifted her shirt to just below her breast in order to examine her abdomen. He sighed with irritation. Around her bandaged laceration swelled a large, fresh bruise.

Mica strummed her fingers on the table, feigning annoyance.

"I thought you said you were fine?"

"I *am*," she replied.

David shook his head before poking and prodding at her side. He made her take deep breaths, stand, and stretch.

"You want a cartwheel next?"

"Well, the stitches are okay, but you should have x-rays anyway."

Mica gave him a pursed lip smile. "Nothing's broken."

As David stood, the proximity of their bodies induced a boyish nervousness in his stomach. He could smell her floral scent—soft, sweet, and enticing. Her wide eyes stared into his. She didn't make the slightest attempt to turn away from him. Instinctively, David reached out and rested his hands on her hips. He slid them up her sides while gently pulling her closer. She obliged, and their bodies almost touched.

Mica's phone suddenly rang.

She jumped, and as she pulled it out of her pocket, she stepped away from David. Although Mica instantly sent the call to voicemail, the moment of near-intimacy was broken.

David stuffed his hands in his pockets. "Good thing we got your phone back. You're in high demand."

She set her phone on her countertop and plugged it into the charger.

He tilted his head to one side. "I'll see you tomorrow to pick up your truck?"

"I can fetch it tomorrow. You don't need to keep chauffeuring me around, though I do appreciate it. Your twenty-four hours of post-assault monitoring is up, Robin."

David arched an eyebrow. "I'll pick you up, and we'll get your truck in daylight like we agreed. I'm off tomorrow. Maybe we can grab lunch while we're downtown." He backed away toward the door. "After that, I'm back on nights for a few days, so you'll be on your own, but you know where to find me."

She smiled. "Goodnight, David."

"'Night, Mica."

David left, closing the door behind him. She hadn't trusted herself to ease closer to say goodbye. Part of her wanted to find out where that moment of proximity to each other would have led, but Mica's rational mind chastised her for wanting to kiss David. But she had wanted it, badly. And more. Her fingers had wanted to slide under his shirt and feel David's swimmer's physique—those broad, muscular shoulders...

Get a grip, Mica.

She couldn't afford to let a high school crush resurface and interfere with her work. David might find her to be an entertaining distraction for a short while—like all the other men in her life had—but she wouldn't fall for his charm. If she did, she might not survive the landing.

DAVID ARRIVED home after dropping off Mica.

He kicked off his shoes, filled a glass of water, and turned the television to whichever college game was playing. He didn't watch the TV, though; instead, he paced his apartment as he sipped his drink.

David had fully intended to kiss Mica before her phone had interrupted them. That urge wasn't normal—not for him. David didn't kiss women he'd only just met. None of this was normal. He didn't drive women home from his ER, watch over them as they slept, or root for them in street fights. Yet, he felt like he *knew* Mica—at least part of her. He felt like he hadn't been doing these things for or with a stranger; but how well could he truly know someone he hadn't seen since high school?

David set down his glass of water on the counter and walked to his bedroom. He pulled a plastic bin out of his closet, popped open the top, and waved a hand through the dust which spewed from the surface. He imagined most people had fancy wooden chests filled with keepsakes. Instead, David owned a single black plastic bin in which all his memorabilia lay.

He dug through awards, photo books, and graduation caps until he found what he was looking for—his high school senior yearbook. Thumbing through the pages, he stopped at the sophomore class photos.

Yes, there she was.

Mica had been two years younger than him. His eyes fell on the photo of a gangly girl with short brown hair. Mica Greyson McMillan. She was a beautiful woman now, but still fighting in her own Justice League. He smiled.

David felt a mix of emotions he couldn't yet define. Needing a distraction, he grabbed a change of clothes and added them to his swim bag before heading to the pool.

8

Mica paced her bedroom with her closet door open. She was *never* indecisive about what to wear. Why was she today?

Maybe today's clothing struggle was because she would be having a nice lunch with a handsome man she'd once had a crush on, followed by her work. Just a lunch, though. This was *not* a date.

Did David consider it a date?

Mica looked at the one dress she owned—a black, sleeveless, knee-length outfit. Wearing *that* would be completely over-the-top and completely impractical. Her remaining choices were blue jeans or cotton stretch pants. She pulled on the jeans and a black sweater.

When Mica looked in the mirror, she frowned. Her hair looked smooth and buoyant, but the outfit seemed wrong. Well, it was appropriate for dealing with criminals, but it was a little bleak for a lunch date.

Growing up, she'd never made friends with the types of girls who might have shared grooming tips. And salon visits were certainly never a requirement in the FBI. In the world of private investigation, though, make-up and disguises—whether to blend in or stand out—were part of the trade.

Mica knew what to wear to blend in or stand out, whether the venue was a fancy club, local bar, or sleepy motel. But for this? A casual lunch with an attractive man she fantasized about kissing? Not part of her wardrobe repertoire.

She dusted on make-up, added a dash of blush and mascara, and topped it off with lip-gloss. She added a pair of silver earrings. Conservative, but passable. Interested, but not trying too hard.

DAVID ARRIVED to pick Mica up at her house. She looked rested after back-to-back nights of fighting. She stuffed her phone and cash in her back pocket as he waited by the door.

"Truck first, or lunch first?"

"Lunch," Mica replied as she pulled her front door shut and set a key code to lock it.

David noticed she was wearing make-up. Was that a sign that she was interested in him? Mica was beautiful without it, but the effort suggested she'd put thought and consideration into today's excursion.

He opened the passenger side door for Mica and ushered her in. When she didn't wince at the bending of her torso, he wondered if the cut she'd received didn't bother her anymore or if she knew he was watching her and was hiding her discomfort.

He slid into the driver's seat and powered the engine. "Once you have your truck back, do you have more fugitives to apprehend?"

"Kenny Serrano." Mica spoke the name harshly. As she glanced at David, she continued, "The four men who apprehended me were Charlie, Kenny, Will, and Kyle. Kyle and Will are in police custody, and they won't let me question them. Charlie, we picked up last night. He wouldn't talk to me. Kenny Serrano is next."

"And you want them to tell you who's leading them?"

"I need to know who's pulling the strings."

David drove them to the Big Easy, near Underwood Hills off I-75. He didn't speak in the car, struggling for what to say. He didn't want to sound overprotective. Mica had obviously been doing this long enough to know the dangers. He also didn't want to appear cowardly by harping on those dangers. A woman like her would have a low tolerance for cowardly or overprotective men.

After they parked and walked into the restaurant, they were escorted to a table.

"You've been uncharacteristically quiet for the last few minutes," Mica commented as they sat.

"You're just going to go after this guy?" David asked, unable to keep a measure of incredulity out of his voice. He laid his napkin out across his lap as the waiter came and told them about the lunch specials.

Mica smiled, as if touched by the concern in his voice. "Yes."

David laughed, shaking his head. "You have amazing confidence."

She's tough, like Mom.

Crap. He needed to tell her about Maxine and her propensity to investigate everyone. He puzzled for a moment. He didn't normally tell any of his dates about his mother. But, this was lunch. Not a date. Right?

The waiter brought glasses of water and took their order: two shrimp po-boys.

David took a sip of his water and tried to comprehend Mica's choices.

She, meanwhile, countered with, "You're an emergency room physician with all of those years of intense school and training behind you. I'm sure you have confidence in your ability to do your job."

"I suppose that's a fair comparison."

"Here's a question: All this time being a physician and you're not married with children yet?"

David wondered briefly if Mica, in her role as a private investigator, had investigated *him* in some form prior to this not-a-date, but he realized she didn't have to. Obviously, he wasn't dating anyone, because he'd spent an entire day and half the night in Mica's company, and he hadn't once received a call or text from anyone.

The waiter brought their sandwiches and sides of fries and coleslaw.

"I've had a few relationships," he admitted as they ate. "The women looking for a lasting relationship don't like the hours I work. Others drive the car once, go out to eat once, and when they hear how in debt I am from medical school, I never hear from them again. The trophy hunters go for the surgeons and specialty doctors. Emergency room medicine is not quite as glamorous as it's portrayed on television. When women learn what I really do, the title loses its appeal."

David took a bite of his shrimp po-boy and swallowed.

"You're appealing." Mica made the statement as though it was a simple fact. "Their loss if they're only focused on your finances."

As the conversation continued, David thought they might emotionally or existentially connect, but Mica checked her phone twice.

He guessed the mid-afternoon distraction was Mica's mind on her mission. Time seemed to pass so lightly while they sat and talked. He wanted more if it.

.   .   .

Mica had mentally planned her afternoon by the time lunch concluded.

"Important rendezvous?" David asked.

"Sorry." She hadn't meant to be rude by checking the time.

"Serrano?" he asked.

The doctor was attentive for sure.

"Yes. Reconnaissance first, though, because I don't know exactly where he is, like I did with Charlie."

"Can I come?"

"Um, *no*. Last time you joined me, I almost got you injured. Or worse."

"Just for the reconnaissance portion?"

Mica weighed the risks. There wasn't much danger or excitement at her next stop. Then she paused. Was she actually considering taking her date on her job? Was this even a date?

"Okay," she eventually capitulated, "but I'm sure you have better things to do on your day off."

David's grin widened and she tried not to stare at the way his smile accentuated his emerald eyes.

When the bill arrived, they both reached for it.

Their eyes met as their hands hovered above the slim piece of paper.

David spoke first. "I'd like to pay, but I've seen you in action so I know better than to insult you."

Mica curled her fingers and withdrew her hand. "I won't be insulted. Thank you for lunch."

So, it was *a date.*

After David paid, they left the restaurant.

"Can I drive?" she asked.

David tossed the keys over the car to her. Mica slid into the driver's seat; the supple leather and suctioned seat felt like a perfect fit.

Her dad had become an auto mechanic after his duty in the Marines was fulfilled, and Mica could expertly operate most any vehicle; however, she was interested to know how David had trusted her with his expensive and powerful car yesterday and again today without knowing her level of driving experience.

After they'd strapped in, Mica pulled onto the road, accelerating rapidly and smoothly.

She tried to grasp the extent of his interest in her. Would the novelty of what she did fade for him? Mica realized they *did* have some things in common: they both sought to cure the ills of society, albeit in very different approaches.

As she drove, Mica glanced across at David again, who half-smiled, before she faced the road again. David was tall and attractive. His short, disheveled hair gave him a friendly appearance. Although he hadn't shaved since before the night shift when she'd arrived in his ER, he was still handsome—with a firm jawline and defined nose. His blue blazer accentuated the green in his eyes.

An effervescent warmth spread through Mica when she saw him smiling at her appraisal. The sensation was pleasantly distracting. She turned her attention back to the road.

David watched Mica shift his car smoothly and drive it with more finesse then he ever had. She was 007 in female form. Although he didn't know their destination, he felt content to enjoy his day with this beautiful woman.

They took a series of lefts and rights as they drove downtown. He felt a tingling excitement at the adventurous afternoon. They were a million miles away from the buzzing fluorescent lights, irritable staff, suffering patients, and hysterical family members at the hospital. Instead, the street bustled with cars, and pedestrians, and the obnoxious noises of trucks and city transit—all of which he welcomed over the ringing phones, alarming monitors, and screeching intercom of the emergency room. High above them even shone a beautiful sun.

"Where are we going?" David asked, bemused that Mica had gone from being skeptical about even grabbing a bite to eat together to suddenly being willing to extend their time together.

"We're going to visit a special friend of the FBI. She's a mystic, palm reader, and homeopathic healer who believes in the power of the soul, healing hands, and aromatherapy." Mica's tone oozed with sarcasm.

They arrived at a quaint shop with a tacky neon sign in the window, advertising palm readings. The window was cluttered with chimes, posters of serene landscapes, and displays of tiny colored bottles, all claiming to contain various potions.

"And this relates to the FBI *how*?"

Mica parked David's car at the curb in front of the shop. Turning to him, she smiled and winked.

"She *also* believes in the power of money. She makes fake IDs. The FBI *knows* she makes IDs. She knows they know, but the bad guys don't know they know. So, she stays out of jail by letting the FBI know when certain bad guys buy fake IDs."

"Uh, huh." David raised his eyebrows. "Why doesn't she let them know about all the bad guys?"

"Too many busts being traced back to the same ID forger would throw up a red flag. Somebody might put her out of business," she said solemnly.

They got out of the car, and Mica gave the keys back to David who made sure to press the automatic LOCK button on his key fob.

"I take it you don't mean out of business in the laissez-faire, capitalist-economy sense," he said.

Mica shook her head. "No, more like Darwinian survival-of-the-fittest sense."

David blew out a puff of air as he opened the door for Mica. Seeing the products of a violent world from within the confines of a steel building and the plaster walls of a hospital was an entirely different experience to living them first-hand.

"Mica McMillan, what a pleasant surprise." A voice floated toward them like diffusing incense.

As they entered the shop, a woman approached wearing a long, fitted cotton gown splashed in warm pastel colors and dotted with rhinestones. The dress hugged her shapely figure. Her tanned face was accentuated with colorful shades of purple eye shadow and an abundance of blush.

She smiled warmly as she gave a small bow, her long, dark braided hair falling forward. Shifting her gaze to David, the woman bowed again, observing him from head to toe and then back to his head again. He felt mild discomfort as the stranger's eyes seemed to dance over his physique. The smell of lavender that surrounded her store assuaged his uneasiness.

The store had soft, gray carpeting and closely packed shelves that sold miracle cures, herbal remedies, massage lotions, and more. David knew some of the products could cure mild ailments. Did the woman know how to advise her buyers of usage and dosage? And none of it was FDA approved.

"David, this is Vanessa Vogel. She goes by Vivi," Mica introduced them.

He noted a twinkle in Mica's eyes, as though she enjoyed David's mild discomfort at Vivi's gushing sensuality.

Vivi's eyes crinkled in delight as she led them to a room in the rear of the store. They passed through an entranceway guarded by a hundred dangling, metallic-colored plastic beads. Pushing them aside, they left the realm of faith healing and entered an ordinary-looking office with plain white walls. A cluttered computer desk occupied one wall. Shelving stacked with equipment, cameras and film, plus a row of overflowing file cabinets, were crammed along the other two walls.

They sat down across from Vivi in uncomfortable metal chairs. The woman adjusted her computer screen.

"You have a name?" Her voice mimicked her personality—a polyester blend, pleasant in appearance but not something David wanted to be too near.

"Kenny Seranno," Mica replied.

Venessa's eyes flickered with recognition, and then she frowned slightly. "He can't be worth much."

She typed his name into her database.

"It's personal," Mica explained.

"Money is personal," Vivi remarked. She leaned back in her chair and crossed her legs.

David ignored Vivi as she shot him another long, lingering glance, trying to see if he was looking at her exposed calf. He was unimpressed with the woman, who seemed to think slow and proper speech added to her mystique. She was attractive enough, but he wasn't interested in charlatans. The bracelets on her wrist jingled as she adjusted a dangling earring.

Mica pursed her lips and squinted her eyes. "Do you know where Seranno is or not?"

Vivi slowly cocked her head to one side. "You're not the violent type. They don't offer much reward for corpses, do they?"

Mica stared her down.

Vivi shrugged. "Pool hall on Fourth Street, across from the deep-dish pizza place."

"Got it. And I have another name for you to look up."

Mica gave Vivi another name—this time one the fortune teller apparently didn't know off-hand. She searched for it on her computer, but found nothing.

Tapping a long fingernail against her lips, Vivi mused, "Give me the afternoon. I'll text you tonight."

"Thanks. I owe you."

"Oh, yes. You do."

Mica stood to leave, and David followed suit.

As they left, Mica thanked Vivi with a not-insubstantial amount of cash.

In return, Vivi gave David a eucalyptus candle, a business card, and a warm invitation to return *any* time.

TEN MINUTES LATER, David pulled his car up to Mica's truck so they could part ways.

Mica hopped out of his car and reached for her truck door. She was clearly a woman on a mission. David didn't want to interfere with her work, but he wanted to make arrangements to see Mica again.

"Don't follow me."

He raised his hands in surrender. "Robin is sitting on the sidelines for this one."

Mica slid behind the wheel of her truck.

"Can I call you sometime? Tomorrow?" David asked.

"I suspect my next target will take me out of town, but I do want to hear from you again," she said warmly.

"Target?" David asked. He remembered she'd also gotten information on someone other than Serrano from Vivi.

Mica nodded. "Buzz Lynch. He knew my client's deceased brother, who I'm trying to help."

"Easy target? Or will he be reminiscent of the last few nights?"

"He's a black belt in Karate."

David nodded and frowned. "What color is your belt?"

Mica started to smile, as if his question was a joke, but then straightened her mouth after processing the concern in his voice. "Sparkling silver. Oh, nope. That's my tiara. I'm always getting those two mixed up."

David's mouth quirked, but he didn't laugh.

She added, "I don't do Karate."

"But you're better than he is, right?"

"We'll find out."

Mica leaned forward and touched a hand to David's jaw. "Don't worry about me, Dr. Rider." She smiled and winked.

He melted into her reassuring smile, but worried nonetheless. He wanted to end their day on this note—a beautiful smile and the feel of her hand against his skin.

"I'll be in touch, Mica McMillan." He winked back.

Her smile widened, making her face radiant. After watching Mica start up her truck, David drove away.

⁂

AJ Schlau grimaced at the stench of decay and rotting flesh. He hated this dilapidated apartment complex. The whole place needed to be condemned and shut down. *Burned* down.

He stepped over someone reeking of cheap bourbon passed out in the hallway.

"It's this way," Manny said.

AJ followed the lanky distributor and pimp. The degenerate reminded AJ of one reason this building *couldn't* be burned down —the massive amounts of heroin sold in places like this.

Manny unlocked the door and swung it open. All AJ could

think was: Thank the unholy devil it wasn't summer, or this corpse would stink even worse than it already did now.

"*Shit.* How long has he been dead?"

Manny shrugged. "Biddy called me an hour ago."

Biddy? Was that really the whore's name?

Biddy came out of the bedroom in hysterics, screeching in a high-pitched Ukrainian accent. "Manny, thanks for coming. What am I going to do?" She clung to Manny as streaks of dried mascara and frayed hair made her look like something out of a horror movie. Any minute she'd start gnawing on Manny's flesh.

"What happened?" AJ snapped in a tone that suggested she better pull herself together.

Biddy swallowed, and AJ saw a glimpse of fear and recognition in her eyes. He wondered if she was one of the girls he'd bought and sold over the years.

She looked apprehensively at the half-dressed corpse's prone body on the floor. "He got too rough. I shoved him and he fell. He hit his head on the little square table and didn't get back up."

AJ watched her hands shaking. "And you huddled in this apartment and waited to call Manny until you needed a fix?"

When they trafficked women for sexual exploitation, they gave them regulated doses of heroin. Once the women were addicted, they were more than willing to work for drugs. Unfortunately, heroin addicts weren't known for their logical decision-making—like calling for help *before* a corpse started to liquefy.

"I could use a dose. Just to calm me down." She glanced eagerly back and forth from AJ to Manny.

Now that Biddy had accidentally killed someone, she was a liability. He couldn't have her talking to the police. Even if the death was ruled an accident, she could still run her mouth to the police about Manny, or even himself.

AJ placed a hand on her cheek. "We'll take care of this. And we'll get you your fix."

Biddy gave him a grateful smile.

As AJ walked out of the apartment, Manny followed. He pulled the door shut. AJ retrieved a handkerchief from his pocket and wiped the moist tear and mascara from his palm. He sniffed in disgust.

Turning slightly to Manny, AJ said, "Give her an overdose. Leave two bodies to be found. Make sure your prints aren't left behind."

Manny nodded and went back inside the room.

9

David drove back to his apartment, feeling uncharacteristically energetic. Usually, after working four twelve-hour shifts, he preferred to spend most of the next day sleeping, until he finally had to drag himself to the grocery store to restock his refrigerator.

Today, he'd woken, paced the floor, and then started chores, biding his time before seeing Mica for lunch. After lunch with Mica—and another few fascinating hours with her, including meeting an eccentric palm reader—he still brimmed with energy. David decided he'd grab his pool bag when he got home and go back out for a swim.

Then his phone chirped.

A reminder: Mom's Birthday.

He parked at his building and stared at the screen. David started to type a Happy Birthday text message as he did every year, but for some reason, the gesture felt wrong. For the first time in ten years, he felt the urge to call his mother.

They'd seldom talked since he left home. Maxine Rider was

hardly a doting, embracing mother. She was a battle-hardened Marine who'd been in Afghanistan for large chunks of his grade school years. While other mothers were carpooling kids to soccer practice, she was off somewhere killing insurgents. During the times she had returned home, David had always felt like part of her still resided overseas and was still out there fighting.

Her dedication to her country during her youth had made Maxine a hard woman. In addition, she'd blown her knee skydiving and suffered from an ungrateful husband; two events that made her even more cantankerous.

During one of her Afghanistan tours, David's father had cleared out Maxine's belongs into a storage shed and drawn up divorce papers as a homecoming present. She'd missed large segments of time of her son growing up, and the subsequent barrier David had erected had persisted to this day.

And yet Maxine apologized for nothing. She felt her family should have been grateful for her military career and not trying to drown her with guilt.

After the divorce of his parents, David was stuck between ugly and uglier. His sole adolescent mission became to leave home and never look back. He'd eventually succeeded and was estranged from both parents.

Maxine had tried to reconnect with him through the occasional phone call. After military retirement, she'd started her own private security firm. By that time, David finished college and was on to medical school. He'd felt disinclined to make time for her, because he still resented how his childhood had been neglected due to her absence.

But today, he contemplated calling her.

"Hello? David?"

Had he dialed her number? He must have.

"Happy birthday, Mom."

A long hesitation made him wonder if she was crying. Not Marine Max, though. A little pool of guilt sloshed in the pit of his stomach. Had he been too harsh? Was David only carrying on the anger his father had seeded in him?

"Thank you, David."

At the sound of Maxine's coarse voice, he recalled her stern face—battle-hardened and bulldoggish like the rest of her. He suddenly had an odd desire to hug her.

"How's the ER?"

"Work's fine."

I vacillate between elation at saving lives and burning out at the futility of half the diseases I treat.

David seemed stuck in a cycle of treating patients who were victims of other people or victims of themselves. He worked too many shifts, always being the single guy with no kids who could fill-in at a moment's notice or cover the holidays.

"How's private security?" Phone pressed to his ear, David exited his car and took the stairs to his apartment.

"The usual. Babysitting people who complain about life while driving cars that cost more than most people's houses."

David gave a dry chortle.

That would be me.

But she already knew that. Was she making a jab at him?

"I met a woman who reminded me of you."

"Oh, yeah. Beauty queen?"

"Her toughness reminded me of you." He unlocked his door, deactivated his alarm, and closed the door behind him.

"Ah. Kill a man with her bare hands?"

"Um. I don't think so. She was assaulted and took it like a Marine. Then she beat several men in a street fight." Retelling events had him in awe of Mica once again.

"Oh, yeah? Military?"

"Her dad was a former Marine. She worked for the FBI, but had a falling out with them."

"What's her name?"

"Mom, I just met her."

"Name?"

"Mom, you're *not* running a background check through your agency on my lunch date."

"Date?"

"Yes. No. I don't know."

It was only lunch, and he'd had to twist her arm. But Mica *had* worn make-up *and* let him pick up the check.

"Name?"

David sighed as he sat down on his couch. Bulldog with a bone. "Mica McMillan."

Why had he called his mom? Why had he told her? He'd had dates over the years and never once shared a name with his mom. David pushed aside the troubling thought that he wanted to know what Maxine might unearth.

A curdling feeling that he had somehow schemed this scenario struck him. He would have to be open with Mica about who his mom was.

"When do you see her again?" Maxine's interest sounded genuine.

"Probably in a few days." The thought occurred to David that his mother had never remarried, and he had no idea if she'd even dated after his dad evicted her.

He stood and stretched. "Well, I'm going to let you go. I've got some errands to run."

"Okay. I appreciate the birthday call."

"Bye, Mom."

Mica tried to concentrate on the road ahead, despite constant thoughts about David. If she'd lingered in his car, she would have kissed him. His green eyes had flecks of azure and gold, making them look like a tropical ocean sunset. When she'd looked into them, she'd felt their warmth. His full lips and firm jaw beckoned for her to kiss them, working her way from his neck, to his jaw line, to his lips.

Mica blinked rapidly. She needed to re-focus. Surely her attraction stemmed from her high school crush and wasn't representative of any true feelings. Besides, they likely weren't compatible, and she had no interest in being the doctor's fun little distraction until he tired of her. Yet, that judgment of him felt harsh. In any case, once he returned to his work routine, he wasn't likely to call ... and then the matter would be settled.

Mica's phone rang. She put it on speaker while driving. "Eddy?"

"You were supposed to call me. Important information, remember?"

"I remember you being cryptic."

"I was being *discreet*. I didn't know how much you wanted your new boyfriend to know."

Rather than engage in a discussion about how David was *not* her boyfriend, which was something that was none of Eddy's business anyway, Mica snapped, "Spill your secretive information."

"The Sunset Sliders are being released."

"Superb." A small spot on one temple started to throb.

"From what I heard, you had a hand in it."

She rubbed her temple. "No. I advocated for Ricky's release at his hearing six months ago. He didn't shoot anyone, and I think he's the only one salvageable from the group."

"Well, they're *all* out on parole tomorrow."

"*Sh... Sugar*," she swore. "You think I'm in danger?"

"I'm just the messenger. I don't think any of them are clever or ballsy enough to come after you, but you need to know they're out."

"Duly noted."

The line was quiet for several beats.

"I miss you."

"Eddy," she warned.

"Okay. Okay, sorry."

"Thanks for the heads up. I'm hanging up now." She disconnected the call.

Eddy's life was all about Eddy, which was one of the many reasons she'd stopped dating him. After her gunshot wound, he'd swept into the hospital room dramatically distraught, blubbering about how hard the event had been for him. *'I have been so worried about you. I haven't been able to work. My nerves are a wreck.'*

I, I, I. Me, me, me. Not once had he asked how *she'd* felt or how *she* was doing.

When she'd told Eddy about her frustrations with the FBI, he'd taken it personally, even though the botched heist had nothing to do with him. He couldn't stand the idea of someone being upset with his beloved agency.

Her phone rang. As Mica answered it, she pulled over to the curb and parked.

"Vivi, what news?"

"I should ask you the same thing." Her voice was smooth and husky, with a hint of playfulness.

"What do you mean?"

"Who was that hunk of yumminess you brought to my shop and when can I see him again?"

"David is a friend from high school. Well, we went to high school together."

"Now he's something more?"

"No, we just ran into each other the other night. Why are we having this conversation? Do you have an address for me?"

"He's not just a friend. Or, at least, he doesn't want to be. That man had eyes only for you."

"*Address*?"

Vivi made a disgusted sound. "Live a little, Mica. Life isn't just all about catching the bad guys."

"This week it is."

"I think your work obsession had spread long past one week."

Mica was silent. She couldn't argue with Vivi. Since taking the case to find Jeremiah Hughes' killer, work had been incessant.

She sighed. "Point taken."

"So, you'll enjoy Yumminess? If you don't, I might."

"His name is David."

"I'll take it, by your tone, he's off-limits."

"Yes."

"Good for you."

"Address?"

"Yes, yes. I'll text it to you."

Thirty seconds after Mica disconnected the call, the text message from Vivi came through. Mica stared at her phone: Buzz Lynch was in New Orleans.

Serrano first.

MICA SAW her target as soon as she entered the pool hall.

Kenneth Serrano was a short Brazilian with an athletic build, developed from playing semi-professional soccer once upon a time. After being convicted of rape five years ago, he'd hooked up with Kyle, the heroin dealer working for AJ.

The pool hall stunk of cigarette smoke and cheap liquor. The large room was poorly lit, but Mica could see faces clearly enough for identification. She caught suspicious glances and lascivious stares as she strolled to the back of the pool hall.

Serrano was perched on a stool against the wall, caressing his pool stick, chewing on a cigar, and flirting with a scantily-clad woman in high-heel boots. He wore faded jeans and a t-shirt that was three sizes too small, revealing his average, muscular physique. He was a mushy Brazilian papaya wrapped in a thin veil of machismo.

Noticing that everyone had stopped playing, he followed their gaze. The cigar fell to the floor. Mica saw beads of sweat form along his forehead. She felt a swell of satisfaction.

Damn right you're scared.

She had Serrano cornered. Only the pool table stood between him and the 'ghost,' which was what she must appear to be after the condition Serrano had left her in the other night. When he and Charlie had vacated the warehouse, she'd been barely conscious. She'd managed to use Kyle's phone to call for an ambulance just before slipping into unconsciousness.

How much of the fear in Serrano's eyes was concern about what she would do to him, and how much was fright at what AJ would do to him for failing to kill her?

The room remained silent except for the whine of an electric guitar humming through distant speakers. Mica knew the crowd could sense the tension, and they likely recognized the predatory glare in her eyes. The weak could always sense the strong.

Serrano stood and tossed his pool stick onto the table. With an attempt at a nonchalant smirk, he slowly shook his head. The initial shock of seeing her was wearing off, but fear still lurked in those *brigadeiro* eyes.

"Well, boys, guess I got a date with an officer of the law." He stared hard at Mica.

The room tensed as she went from being a mystery threat to someone associated with the law. She wasn't an officer or an agent. Not anymore.

Serrano darted to his right, but Mica anticipated the move. She grabbed the cue ball off of the table and slung it side-arm toward him. Her high school days of playing shortstop had come in handy more than once. The white ball struck the side of Serrano's head, knocking him to the ground.

Someone moved in to grab her from behind, but Mica had smelled the whiskey on his breath when he'd slid closer to her a moment earlier. She'd already calculated how he planned to join the fight. Grabbing her assailant's wrist, she pivoted left, using his momentum, in addition to the pressure points in the man's wrist and upper arm, to shove his full two-hundred-and-twenty pounds onto the pool table.

The stranger flopped, rolled, and crashed to the floor.

Mica sucked in a sharp breath from the way her motions had tugged at her stitches, but she worked to keep her face neutral. Never show weakness.

She glanced around the room. No one else appeared interested in joining the fight at the moment. She walked over to Serrano, who lay whimpering on the floor.

Come hither, my little rotten papaya.

Cinching a plastic zip tie around his wrists, Mica pulled him to his feet.

"Time to answer my questions," she hissed into Serrano's ear.

They'd almost reached the front door when, in her peripheral vision, she caught sight of a thin, young African-American reaching for a gun from inside his coat. Mica stopped as he pulled it out and pointed it at her head.

A Smith & Wesson.

At least he's got class.

"Can't let you leave with my boy Kenny," the young man shook his head. The whites of his knuckles demonstrated the tight grip he had on the gun.

Mica released Serrano and raised her hands shoulder high. She recognized this man as her photographic memory pulled up his rap sheet.

Tyrone Styles: Born in Georgia, twenty-five years old, previous arrest for distribution of cocaine and marijuana. Gun possession violated the terms of his parole.

She decided she'd have to come back for him later.

Mica moved swiftly—flawlessly—grasping and twisting Tyrone's wrist with her right hand and snatching the gun from him with her left. Tyrone hadn't even realized Mica had taken the gun until she'd twisted him around with his back to her by applying pressure to his wrist. Immobilized by pain and surprise, Tyrone let out a squeal.

Mica aimed the gun to her left as yet another man decided to involve himself, drawing a pocketknife from his back pocket. As soon as he snapped the blade open, he let it drop to the floor, staring down the barrel of the hijacked revolver.

"Drop," Mica told Tyrone.

He eased himself down to the floor.

Mica pushed Serrano out the door, slipped the gun into her coat, and left.

⁎

MAXINE SCRUBBED her hands across her face and pushed her chair away from her computer screen. She couldn't look at yet another employee application.

Maxine needed to hire more recruits for Rider Security and Investigation, but the difficulty was in finding new applicants with both the right level of experience *and* the right moral compass. They needed to know all the laws first, before learning the finesse of which ones they could break and under which circumstances. Private security could be compared to art—master all the rules first, before bending them to your will.

She struggled to discern on paper which applicants either possessed those required skills or had the aptitude to learn them. When she'd brought a select few applicants in to be interviewed, she'd found they either weren't comfortable with the workload, or they had inadvertently expressed hesitation about having a female boss.

David had no problem with a female boss. The ER chair was a woman.

David, she mused, had called his mother to mention a woman. That was a first.

Maxine sat up as an uncomfortable flutter hit her belly. Was the timing of this coincidental?

She stood and walked out of her office, down toward Claire's desk. Her blue-haired, computer-savvy millennial sat in her own office before three huge screens as she worked scrolling names, locations, and photos in multiple search engines. Maxine's young employee was still gathering information on Lucius Titan after he'd threatened to harm David.

"Claire."

The woman didn't move.

Damn earbuds.

Maxine pulled a business card out of her pocket and flipped it at Claire. The gold embroidery twinkled in the glow of the LED fairy lights strewn along the ceiling before the card embedded itself in Claire's hair like a throwing knife.

Claire brushed at the annoyance as she turned around. "Max?"

She pulled out her ear buds and laid them on the desk. "What's up?" She grinned.

"I need a background check on Mica McMillan."

"Business or pleasure?" Claire asked, her voice husky as she playfully wriggled her eyebrows.

Maxine blinked at her. Business. *Always* business. "David is interested in this woman, and I want to know why she's suddenly in his life."

Claire had already turned around to type on her computer. A picture of a woman—about thirty, with platinum curls and a sweet smile—suddenly filled one screen.

Maxine came beside Claire and leaned on her desk.

Claire swiveled to look up at Maxine. "Maybe because she's an attractive woman around his age?"

"Maybe."

Claire continued typing as she rattled off the facts. "Her dad's a former Marine. Oh, she went to the same high school as your son. She has a degree in criminal justice."

Claire turned back to Max. "What are you worried about?"

Maxine shrugged. "The timing. She appeared right after Lucius's threat."

"That was actually quite a few months ago." After looking up at Maxine, she added. "Okay. You want me to dig for a connection between Mica McMillan and Lucius Titan?"

"Yes."

"Does David know you're investigating his girlfriend?"

Maxine felt her eye twitch. Was Miss McMillan his girlfriend? "No."

"Oh-kay. Got it." Claire's mouth twisted with restraint.

Maxine narrowed her eyes. "*What*?"

Claire raised her eyebrows. "Well, we rented an apartment under an alias and staged a break-in just so David would have to buy a new door and electronic lock system for his apartment. During the installation of that alarm system, we proceeded to covertly install doorway and window cameras without his knowledge." Claire strummed her fingers on her desktop. "And *now* you're secretly investigating his love interest."

"Your point?"

"This is *not* the way to endear David to you. Or to heal the wounds of the past."

"As much as I'd like to reconnect with my son, I first have to ensure his safety."

Claire frowned.

Maxine sighed. "How do you think he'd react to me openly telling him I want him to invest in a better security system? Especially because it's *my* occupational blunders that have put *his* life in danger."

Claire's expression softened. "You're right. That wouldn't go over well. But don't call them blunders, Max. Everything you've done has been to help good people. It's not your fault there's a calculating, maniacal deviant who's after you."

Maxine looked at the ceiling and watched the twinkling lights for a moment. She'd never forgive herself if something happened to David at the hands of one of her enemies.

"I'll have the full background on Miss McMillan tomorrow." Claire gave a weak but reassuring smile.

Maxine straightened. "Thanks, Claire."

10

Mica returned to her house after dropping Serrano into police custody. He'd been another silent dead end.

She wandered into the backyard, aiming to center herself with Tai Chi. She needed to clear her mind. The sun had warmed the chilly air by mid-afternoon, but the temperature was growing cool again. A light breeze rustled through the bare trees around her small brick house. Cascading sunlight danced on a golden-brown floor of leaves.

Mica closed her eyes and swayed in rhythmic motions, letting the mist of exhaled air rise above her. The past flaked away like the foam on the crest of an ocean wave, rising against the wind. The future flickered as a distant white light. Only the present existed. Only nature, and only her breathing body.

The earth, the moon, the tides, and the seasons all flowed in cycles as she moved in rhythmic circles. As she melted into her surroundings, the world faded with each deep, flowing breath. She would realign with her soul and be whole again. Violence, greed, pessimism, and all the other impurities that clung from daily exposure floated away in the breeze.

Mica emerged from her peaceful meditation to the sound of her phone ringing.

She didn't recognize the number. "Hello?"

"McMillan."

"Ricky?" A flood of memories and emotions washed over her with the sound of that voice. Mica's chest tingled, eerily in the exact spot where the piercing bullet had left its mark.

"We need to talk."

"Talk," she commanded.

"In person."

Mica sighed. Ricky didn't know where she lived. No one did. The house was paid off, but she'd left the deed in the widow's name she'd bought it from, so she could remain anonymous. The utilities bills were still in the other woman's name, too, and Mica made sure to pay them monthly in cash. All of her mail went to a PO Box. Mica had explained to the seller that she'd made enemies because of the nature of her job and she needed discretion. She'd suspected that the woman had thought Mica was hiding from an abusive man, rather than the real reason Mica had told her, but regardless, she'd agreed to keep Mica's secret.

She thought about what Ricky had requested.

"Talk? In person?" Mica asked. "That sounds hazardous to my health."

"*Not* meeting with me is hazardous to your health."

"Is that a threat?"

"What? No. I need to pass along information."

Mica didn't fear Ricky, but she wouldn't take the chance of being ambushed.

She grabbed her keys and coat and headed for her truck.

"Sweetwater Creek State Park," she told Ricky, her mind planning the route like a GPS computer.

"Okay. And when I get there?"

"Start walking the Yellow Trail. I'll find you."

"It'll take me forty-five minutes to get there."

"I'll see you then."

THIRTY MINUTES LATER, Mica parked her truck at the state park and took the Yellow Trail. Autumn leaves decorated the floor in bright yellow, orange, and red, creating a trail of sunset colors. A cool breeze rustled the empty limbs of the looming trees. Just before Sweetwater Creek bridge, she stepped off the trail and hid in the woods.

When Ricky arrived, she trailed him for a short distance, ensuring he was alone. His choppy blond locks were longer, and he wore jeans and a brown leather jacket.

Moving quickly, Mica jumped from a boulder onto the trail. Ricky threw his hands up in surprise as she kicked at his side. He coughed in pain and buckled in two. Grabbing his wrist, she forced him against the rock. She frisked him with her free hand but found no weapon.

"Hello to you, too," Ricky gasped, wincing from the pain in his side and wrist. "I'm not into S&M, but I'm willing to make an exception for you."

Mica released him, and he turned around to look at her.

"You wanted to talk? So, talk." She wiped the sweat from her forehead with the back of her hand. Feeling less threatened, because Ricky wasn't armed, Mica stepped back, but she stayed ready for any sudden movements.

"I've had four lousy years to think about what happened." He had a brisk mid-Western accent, "and the way I figure it is: You took a damn bullet for me, and I went to fuckin' jail. So, I guess that makes us even. But I still lost a hundred grand."

Mica couldn't detect any anger in his voice. His foul language was part of Ricky's normal speech, used regardless of his emotional state.

"And you've come to collect?" Mica asked.

"No." He shook his head and licked his lips. "No," he repeated. "But I know that some of the others will."

Mica looked at him, puzzled. "You called a meeting to warn me?"

"Yes, I did," he replied. "I'm reformed and shit. I'll probably live out the rest of my miserable life flippin' soy burgers at a fast-food restaurant, makin' seven bucks an hour as I slap on a piece of processed cheese on top, sayin': 'You want fries with that?' All while I wade in six inches of fuckin' grease …"

Ricky often perused tangents of extended sentences, filled with vivid descriptions and intensified with sporadic cuss words. The style was entertaining, at least. Mica knew Ricky was smarter than minimum wage and had a college degree to prove it, but he'd forever be limited by his criminal background.

"Do they have the resources to pull off a hit?" Mica asked.

The other members of the gang—Tina, Troy, and Amos— would need money now that they were released. They wouldn't take her on without guns, transportation, and cash to hide. She doubted they'd hire someone to take her out. If the gang sought revenge, they wouldn't pay an assassin to do their dirty work for them.

"Yes, they do," he replied.

She narrowed her eyes at him. "You know this because?"

"Because someone approached me about a job the second I got clear of those prison walls. If I was asked to do the job, they were all asked to do the job too."

"And *I'm* the job?"

"Yeah." Ricky rubbed the back of his neck as he looked down at the beaten path. "You're the job. I turned him down."

"Who tried to hire you?"

"He didn't give a name, and I didn't ask."

A moment of silence passed before Mica said, "You should go, Ricky."

He nodded, but took a step forward. "And you should make yourself harder to find." His eyes looked her up and down.

She could smell his light cologne and see the intensity in his eyes. She stared back at him and didn't move. Knowing he couldn't defeat her in combat, Mica wasn't afraid or intimidated, but he wasn't *trying* to intimidate her. Instead, he searched for something.

Mica stiffened.

His face hovered close to hers as his eyes flickered down to her lips. "I knew there was chemistry there. *Here*," he corrected himself. "And I know it'll never work out between us. But I just wanted to see you. To warn you."

They hadn't had an intimate relationship. She'd consented to nothing. If he made a move, Mica felt she'd be forced to break his arm just to prove a point.

Mica wondered for a moment if this was the first time Ricky had ever done anything slowly in his life. He stopped only an inch from her lips. His eyes came back to hers and he must have seen the warning in them.

Ricky grinned and licked his lips. "It would have been sweet." He stepped back. "Good luck, McMillan."

"Stay out of trouble," she ordered.

Ricky opened his arms and raised three fingers in the air. "Scout's honor." He tucked his hands in his jacket and walked down the trail back toward the parking lot.

Mica turned and watched the water babble along the shoals of

Sweetwater Creek. A chill ran down her spine, followed by burning anger.

Someone had put a hit out on her.

A slow smile spread across her lips.

She was getting close.

———⁂———

CLAIRE AND MAXINE stared at the bouquet of flowers. Geraniums. When Maxine blinked, Claire noticed a drop of moisture vanish from her eyes.

Claire pried the card from Maxine's grasp to read it.

> *Happy Birthday, Mom*
> *From, David*

When she looked up at Maxine, the steely Marine swallowed.

Claire tried to dampen the swell of excitement she felt for her boss. "This is good, Max. This is progress."

"He's never sent me flowers." Her voice held sheer astonishment.

Claire leaned back in her chair. She needed to change the subject before Maxine lost her composure. She cleared her throat. "So Mica McMillan has a peculiar background. She started with a double major, criminal justice degree and psychology, followed by graduating the academy in Quantico. Several months out, she was pulled into undercover work to infiltrate bank thieves." Claire paused for effect and noted she had Maxine's unwavering attention. "During the heist, she was shot, but the bad guys were all apprehended. Then, McMillan quit the FBI."

"Quit?"

"Quit. After recovery and rehab from her trauma, she goes

somewhere remote in Colorado for six months—some type of martial arts training ground. Then she returns to Georgia and gets her PI license. Seems she has a knack for missing persons."

"Kidnappings?"

Claire shook her head. "No. Usually wanted adults, and she's reeled in some bounties."

"She's a *bounty hunter*?"

"At least in part."

"So, no connection to Lucius?"

Claire shifted in her chair. "That's where her story gets even more interesting. A while back, she was involved in a shooting where a former Titan employee was shot and died ... just after she'd located him."

"Did she kill him?"

"No. According to the police report, she'd brought him to the station on a false bounty claim. While she was discussing the case at the police station with the detective on duty, the perp wrestles a gun away from the officer in his holding room and shoots himself."

"Huh." It was a statement, not a question.

"Huh, what?"

"There's a connection," Maxine said. "We just have to dig for it."

"You think Lucius hired her to find the guy who shot himself? If so, then why bring him to a police station? Why a fake bounty BOLO?"

"I don't know. Keep digging. Check all the people McMillan's investigated or is associated with and cross reference them all with Titan Enterprises."

"What are you going to do?"

"I'm going to stare at my birthday flowers for the rest of the afternoon."

———

Mica's phone chirped with a reminder: 'Pick up Joey from park.'

Crap.

She checked the time and breathed a sigh of relief, knowing she could still arrive there on time.

She got back in her truck at the state park and drove toward another nearby park. As she drove, she contemplated Ricky's impromptu call and thought about the Sunset Sliders' bank robbery.

It was no coincidence that the Sliders would be hired when she was closing in on AJ. Killing her by using a group of people she'd previously jailed would keep AJ out of the spotlight. Law enforcement would assume the Sliders were acting on their own, motivated by revenge. Only she and Ricky knew they'd been hired by a third party.

"*Sh... Sugar,*" she swore.

Mica wanted to find AJ, but she didn't want to take on a hit squad. Was she in over her head with the Sunset Sliders?

...just like last time?

Aside from her father and David, Mica hadn't shared the details of those infuriating events—how everything she'd dreamed of had been destroyed in mere moments. Her future in law enforcement had ended with a sense of bitterness.

Following high school, she'd gone through college and earned a dual bachelor's degree in criminal justice and psychology. With exceptional grades, Mica had earned acceptance into FBI Academy Training where she'd excelled in both academic and physical training. Her hard work landed her in the Criminal, Cyber, Response, and Services (CCRSB) of the FBI.

Shortly into her career, the FBI needed a young woman to take an undercover field assignment and infiltrate a group of thieves believed to be scheming a bank robbery. At the age of twenty-three, Mica had felt up to the challenge and eagerly taken the career-propelling assignment.

I was so naive.

Before long, with her martial arts and weapons use, she'd proven herself to be a valuable asset to the robbers known as the Sunset Sliders. She'd literally fought her way into the group, proving her worth. The work was harrowing—being on edge all-day, every day. Working undercover, she could never relinquish her guard.

After successful infiltration, Mica was trusted enough to be included in an upcoming bank robbery. The Sunset Sliders kept the location from her as a precaution, because they didn't yet entirely trust the new woman on the team.

It was an insult. Mica had taken her licks. Still, they were right not to trust her. After all, she was waiting for them to commit the crime so she could make the arrest.

Mica had addressed several senior FBI formally in the small, local hotel conference room: "They won't tell me where the job is. They're dangerous and to let the heist proceed with no law enforcement puts innocent lives at risk. If we knew which bank, every person in the building could be an officer."

From the criminal lair, over a dozen banks operated within a ten-mile radius. Pinpointing the bank that the Sunset Sliders planned to target was impossible.

The conference room that day had been uncomfortably warm and tense. Surrounded by men in suits and ties, she felt the weight of their stares burrowing into her. Some fidgeted nervously with their pens and pads, others watched her with contempt. Mica knew she'd been given an opportunity for greatness early in her career.

She'd been the right person at the right time, but on that day in the conference room, the opportunity looked disastrous.

Do they want me to fail?

"When?" FBI agent Eddy Finch had asked.

"Two days."

Mica had been dating Eddy in secret for a few months at the time. His dark suit and trim ebony hair had made him an attractive authority figure. She'd been easily seduced, but found they'd had little time to spend with each other due to the nature of their jobs. Mica suspected they'd had nothing more substantial than mutual attraction and sex. She'd been right.

"You have two days, McMillan," her superior told her.

"And if they don't tell me?" she asked sharply.

Her bald-headed boss had slid a case across the table to her. Mica caught it and looked down. When she opened the rectangular box, she found herself looking at the pen within it—black with gold trim.

"Alert us with the pen." Her boss nodded her direction. "When you arrive at the bank, twist the pen to transmit a frequency. We'll track you to that location."

The Sunset Sliders had comprised a band of misfit robbers, mostly with backgrounds of petty theft and some juvenile time behind bars, who were recruited by their leader, Ricky Monroe.

Ricky had spiked brown hair and possessed a charming spunk. He talked fast, with an unmistakable mid-Western accent. He'd had no scores to settle with society, no chip on his shoulder. Ricky had just wanted money, lots of it, although he'd never killed anyone for it. He gave respect to those who'd earned it and always kept an even temper.

Mica's superiors had instructed her vaguely to "get close" to Ricky. By his lingering, sidelong glances and tendency to stand just a little too close, she knew he was attracted to her. But Mica hadn't known how to play the part. She'd been trained in weapons, combat, and deciphering the criminal mind. She hadn't taken any acting courses. Furthermore, Mica had no desire to nurture an attraction which could have dangerous consequences.

After the FBI conference, back in Ricky's planning room, Mica had experienced an ominous, bile-provoking feeling that something terrible would happen. Two days prior to the heist, when they'd finally permitted her to review the floor plan, Mica had learned that the targeted bank had two stories with the vault and customer service on the first floor. The other floor had consisted of offices, where investors toyed with other people's money. Ten cameras monitored the first floor. Four separate alarms under the service desk could be manually tripped by bank personnel. One guard stood at the bank entrance.

Tina, Troy, and Amos planned to position themselves at the locations of the bank tellers who stood within reach of the alarms. Mica's role entailed keeping the guard in check. Ricky would collect dues. The money would be collected at the bank in bags and then transferred to briefcases while driving their escape van. After changing clothes and disguises, the gang planned to switch from their getaway van to two sedans parked ten minutes away from the bank.

The twist? The Sunset Sliders didn't wait two days. A day before the planned strike, Ricky had suddenly declared they needed to act *now*. Mica had been the only person surprised. Having not been trusted quite enough, she'd been given a false date. Mica pretended to be copacetic with the change in plans.

"You okay?" Ricky had asked her at the time.

She nodded, forcing herself not to betray her discomfort and fear. "Yeah, no problem. Violence is something you have to mentally prepare for, and I thought I had one more day of mental preparation. But, now is good."

With a gentle hand on her shoulder, Ricky nodded.

The day of the surprise robbery, Mica had glanced at the group of thieves—all neatly groomed and wearing suits. They all appeared to be businessmen and businesswomen, aside from the concealed Berettas and bulletproof vests.

A hot sun had blazed above them that day.

Too hot for this Kevlar.

Wearing a light-blue silk skirt-suit, Mica shifted her shoulders to feel the weight of the pen in her blouse pocket. She'd worn a long, black-haired wig and had darkened her brown eyebrows to a matching black. She entered the bank at 1:59 in the afternoon and had twisted the pen in her pocket three minutes earlier.

Tina reached the front counter, feigning intentions to make a deposit. Troy and Amos waited in line. Four civilians also stood in line. Mica walked up to the guard, smiling casually, as Ricky and Milton entered the bank.

She raised her gun to the guard's head as the clock rolled over to 2 p.m. "Don't move," she said quietly.

The guard's rotund, sweating body was topped with a round face containing panicked eyes.

Please don't have a heart attack.

Tina, Troy, and Amos jumped the counter and leveled their guns at the tellers that had access to the alarms. With a wave of his gun, Ricky ordered everyone onto the floor.

Panicked screams were emitted as men and women dropped to the floor in fear.

Ricky and Milton collected money in bags.

Sweat trickled down the guard's prematurely balding head and streaked his face. Mica remembered noticing a wedding ring on his short, plump finger. She'd wondered if he had children, too.

Then, she noticed a twitch. A nervous twitch of contemplation.

Mica couldn't believe the guard was considering going for his gun in a room filled with five armed robbers.

Glancing over at Ricky, she saw his back was to her. One minute had passed. Mica reached and discretely pulled her suit jacket open. From the inside pocket, she pulled up her FBI badge. The guard looked at her with confusion.

Mica had taken a risk having the badge with her at all, but she'd thought having it might reduce the likelihood of getting shot by the authorities. Conversely, she'd known the badge might have increased her chances of getting shot by thugs.

"Time!" Ricky shouted.

The Sunset Sliders backed out the front door—Tina, Troy, and Amos, each with a bag of money. They went first, followed by Ricky.

Mica took two steps toward the door and swept the room with her eyes one last time. That's when the guard reached for his gun. She turned and leveled her gun back at the guard, and he raised his toward her.

She could not believe what was happening! What the hell was he thinking instigating a standoff? And why hadn't she disarmed him when she'd had the opportunity?

Ricky saw the situation and aimed his gun at the guard. The guard turned...

"No!" Mica remembered hearing her own voice echo across the lobby of the bank. She'd lunged at the guard just as he'd fired at Ricky. The bullet struck the right side of her chest. As Mica's weight plowed into the guard, he hit the floor hard, smacking his head against the tile floor and knocking himself unconscious.

Mica rolled onto her back on top of him, stunned.

White, hot pain radiated from her shoulder. Even the memory of it still hurt.

The bank tellers shrieked.

Approaching with haste, Ricky aimed his gun at the guard's head. By the wild look in his eyes, he had every intention of killing the guard. If he did, though, Ricky's prison sentence would be a lifetime.

Unable to speak through the searing pain, Mica raised her gun in warning at Ricky. He stopped just a few feet away and looked at her, perplexed.

As Ricky looked down at the blood soaking her blouse, he saw the inside of her jacket and the FBI badge on display.

Mica remembered how Ricky's look of confusion had quickly turned to anger and then to dismay. He lowered his gun, looking solemnly at her one last time, eyes destitute with betrayal, and then he left the building.

Before the Sunset Sliders could peel away from the bank in their van, the FBI and local police had surrounded them.

Mica's vest had prevented the bullet from doing much damage, but at such close range, and having struck the very edge of her vest, the bullet had puckered the vest and penetrated her skin, before burying itself into a rib.

Mica had been in and out of the hospital a few days following the shootout, but the emotional scar of that event would take much longer to heal.

11

David's phone rang. He looked at the caller ID. Maxine again. They were having an unprecedented number of conversations, but he genuinely felt like he wanted to talk to her.

"Hi, Mom."

"Hello, David. I got the flowers. They're amazing. Thank you."

"You're welcome."

"How's work?" Her voice held a twinge of excitement, but also the slight sense of angst, as though David might end the call at any moment.

"We had quite a bit of trauma this week, but I think we did some good."

"And Mica?"

"She's good. I really like Mica. I plan to see her again."

After she hopefully survives taking down a black belt.

"What do you like about Mica?"

"She's honest. She's tough. She wants more—wants better for herself and for the world."

She's not burned out like me.

He added, "She has this contagious energy. I saw her in action the other night. She's incredible."

"She brought you into a dangerous situation?"

David had already mentioned the street fight to his mom, but during that conversation he hadn't implied he'd seen it firsthand. "It wasn't her fault, Mom. Some thugs tried to steal my car. She defended us. She's an incredible fighter."

And I was only there because I pressured her to let me come.

"How many?"

"How many?"

"How many men did she take down?"

"Five."

Maxine fell silent again.

"I told you she used to be an FBI agent. Well, they tied her hands during an assignment. She got shot. After that, she didn't want any part of their stranglehold rules."

"So, basically, she got shot and quit," Maxine stated.

Ah. Mom has investigated.

David wondered what administrative report his mom had gotten her hands on—and how much of the story it actually revealed. Maxine had been shot, too; but she hadn't quit. Was she trying to pass judgment on Mica?

"She quit because they put her in a situation where she didn't have control over the outcome. She's certainly not a coward. Mica didn't hesitate, or cower, or give an inch to the men she fought."

Unlike me. I was ready to give them what they wanted and run.

"Bounty hunting."

"She prefers the term 'fugitive recovery agent.' I think she likes the autonomy of self-employment, but wants something more than picking up petty criminals."

"Dangers in her life can bleed into yours."

He already knew that firsthand. "It's just dating."

So far, just a date.

"Besides, my performance lacked bravado. She may already be conspiring to be rid of me." Even as David said the words, he recalled nothing of disapproval or reproach in Mica's tone or expression.

"Knowing what she does, you still like her?"

"I do. I don't think she'll stay a bounty hunter, but I imagine she'll always want to fight the good fight."

"Be careful."

VLADIMIR ACCEPTED kisses from his niece as his plane awaited him.

He patted Natasha's shoulder. "You're in charge, *tykva*."

She straightened the collar of his shirt. "I'm meeting with Yevgeny next week to discuss the trade routes within Kazakhstan. Mikhail is accepting the drug shipment from China on the twenty-first."

Vladimir started to open his mouth.

"I know, clubs over eighteen only and no school zones." Natasha took a step back, her lips downward in a pout. "When do you think you'll be back?"

Valdimir put a hand on her cheek. "I don't know specifically. I have an enemy to deal with, in addition to convincing Maxine Rider to let me help her team. You'll do fine here without me. You know the business better than anyone. If anyone hassles you, Mikhail will deal with them."

"You should take more people with you, not just Sonya and Boris."

Vladamir glanced at the Gulfstream parked on the tarmac. Sonya and Boris were already on board. "I'll send for more if needed."

"You know, the problem of Lucius Titan can be dealt with quickly and quietly. You have a dozen assassins at your disposal."

"*Da. Da, Odnako.* But Maxine wouldn't want it that way."

Natasha looked up at him with a wry grin. "And will you be spending any quality time with Ms. Rider?"

He smiled as he backed toward the plane. "*Babushka da nadvoye skazala—to li dozhdik, to li sneg, to li budet, to li net.*"

Natasha laughed.

We'll see what we'll see; maybe rain or maybe snow, maybe yes or maybe no.

MICA ARRIVED at the concrete skateboard park and spotted Joey. She approached and watched kids skateboard and defy gravity. Joey performed a kickflip, his thin limber body bending in the air.

As she watched his moves, she thought about when she'd first met Joey a year earlier.

She'd trailed Darren Wood—thief and petty criminal—to an abandoned warehouse in downtown Detroit. He'd been wanted for credit card fraud in California before fleeing to Detroit. He changed his hair and his name and started a used car business with mostly stolen vehicles. After all, a leopard doesn't change his spots.

Darren had come to the warehouse with accomplices to scope out a better place to hide and alter his stolen cars.

Cursed with Tourette Syndrome, a disorder of the nervous system, his neck and shoulders twitched irregularly and Darren was prone to occasional short, incomprehensible verbal outbursts. Unfortunately for him, this was a much more distinguishable trait than tattoos or scars. While he couldn't be found through database searches, putting her feet to pavement and questioning people quickly led Mica right to him.

Five men had arrived in two cars. After parking, they strolled about the warehouse, discussing the layout and renovation plans.

Mica had contrived a simple snatch-and-grab. She'd planned to hop in Darren's car while his gang inspected their potential new base of operations, then drive off with him the moment he got back into the vehicle.

Creeping up to his black Mercedes, Mica reached for the door handle when someone sneezed. The sound came from a stack of mildew-covered crates across the warehouse.

Four of the men hastily drew weapons and pointed their guns toward the crates—all except Darren, who didn't carry a gun. Mica wondered if that was because he wanted to avoid inadvertently shooting someone, or himself, during one of his twitches.

"Come out whitchya hands up," one of the men said, with a thick Boston accent. He had large hooked nose.

Mica remembered watching through the car windows as a small black boy marched out from behind the crates. He masked his fear with a look of defiance. They'd intruded on *his* playground.

Darren exclaimed, "*Damn*, it's a kid!"

"You live around here, kid?" Hook Nose asked.

The men holstered their guns.

"I don't have a home," Joey told them with mock pride, crossing his arms.

Mica had inched silently around the back of the car. If these men thought this kid's presence impacted the potential to use the warehouse, they would threaten the boy's life. Darren's threats usually involved a display of violence. She couldn't let them beat up a kid. Mica knew she'd have to take someone's gun, and the whole situation was going to get ugly.

With lightning speed, she went after the man closest to her whose back had been turned to her. Before he could turn around, she struck him with her elbow and the force of all her weight right between his shoulder blades. He crashed to his knees, grunting. With her left hand, Mica retrieved the gun from his holster, and with her right hand, she grabbed his wrist.

Everyone stopped their pursuit of the boy and turned in Mica's direction. They again reached for their guns. In response, Mica bent her prisoner's wrist forward by applying pressure, and he rose to his feet with a screech of pain.

Four guns had been pointed in Mica's direction that day. She stood safely behind her captive with two assailants at one o'clock, Hook Nose at noon, and Darren twitching at ten o'clock. The boy had hidden himself back behind the crates.

Smart kid.

"Easy boys," Mica had said. "Nobody has to get shot. I'm only here for Darren," she explained.

"Who the hell are you?" Darren asked.

Mica shook her head in disapproval. "You're in the middle of a standoff, and you want to ask irrelevant questions. You should be asking, 'How fast am I?' and 'How good is my aim?' The answers are fast enough and good enough. So everybody put your guns down." She calmly ordered.

"I don't think you're in any position to give orders, lady."

At that moment, the boy swung a two-by-four at Hook Nose, striking behind his knees. The distraction gave Mica much-needed seconds.

She shot one of the other men through his upper arm, debilitating him and crippling his ability to fire his weapon. The other two men shrieked, one after the other. Hook Nose fell to his knees while the other dropped his gun and reeled backward. The boy then kicked the gun toward Mica.

The man whose wrist she held sought to take advantage of the momentary disorder. He tried to bolt, but Mica twisted his wrist further. Her prisoner gritted his teeth and stopped wiggling.

Mica and the last gunman had faced each other. Her captive's writhing left one side exposed. She knew what the other man was asking himself. Was his aim good enough? Who was she? And what would be the consequences of killing her? A hardened killer didn't ask these questions, didn't hesitate. A man looking for an alternative to violence did.

Beads of sweat trickled down his face.

"You can climb in your car and drive away," Mica offered the man. "I don't know you, and I'm not here for you."

Darren had slowly slunk backward.

The final gunman contemplated for a moment, then holstered his gun and walked toward the driver's side of the other car—a black Lincoln Continental. Mica escorted her captive to the rear passenger door of the same car.

"Open it," she ordered.

Her prisoner opened the door, grimacing from the pain. Mica let him climb inside and shut the door. The men sped away from the warehouse.

Darren had taken off running.

After picking two Berettas up off the floor, Mica secured their safety catches and stuck them in the waistband of her pants. She then jogged after Darren, knowing his chubby physique didn't allow for a quick escape, and she caught up with him quickly.

"Ok, Darren, 'A' for effort," Mica told him as she secured Darren's hands behind his back with a plastic cable tie.

"Don't you have to read me my rights?" He asked.

"Fugitive recovery agent. Not cop."

Mica shoved him in the backseat of his own Mercedes and slammed the door shut.

So much for a simple snatch-and-grab.

She gruffly blew a blonde curl out of her eyes.

That was when the boy had stepped out from his hiding spot. "*Holy shit*, woman!"

"Watch your mouth."

The boy looked at her. "You ain't my mama."

"No," Mica agreed, "but I've got a gun."

"We cool." He took a step back and lifted his palm shoulder high before relaxing again.

"Good thing I was here to help you," the boy said with a large grin.

"You're lucky you're not dead." Mica stowed the guns in the glove compartment of the car.

The man with the gunshot wound sat bandaging his arm with his suit coat. The Yankee was also sitting, stretching to see if his knees still functioned.

"You want an ambulance?" She asked them. The men shook their heads.

"C'mon," the boy pleaded. "I went wham!" He motioned swinging the two-by-four. "And you went bam!" He used his hand as a gun. "That was teamwork. Like my uncle says, 'Ain't no *I* in teamwork.'"

"How old are you?" Mica had asked, reaching for her phone.

"I'm eight," Joey snapped.

"What's your name?"

"What's yours?" he sassed.

"Mica."

"Joey." He smiled.

AFTER THE WAREHOUSE INCIDENT, Mica had met Joey's uncle—who had a heart of gold but not the health to keep up with a rambunctious boy. She'd convinced his uncle to move to Atlanta, where he could stay with a brother so Joey would have two family members to look out for him.

Mica still checked in on Joey weekly and tried to help escort him to and from social activities when she was available. He was ten now and mostly kept out of trouble.

When Joey saw Mica standing at the edge of the skating bowl, he came to a halt and waved at her. He wore his helmet, but she noticed he wasn't wearing his elbow and kneepads.

Before she got close enough to scold him, he took off on another stunt. He flipped in the air off the ramp, but another boy skated too close to him and careened out of control. They struck each other and skateboards flew out from under them.

Mica held her breath as she calmly walked closer. Joey would lose face if a woman came rushing after him in concern. His playmates would tease him relentlessly. He rolled over, signifying he was still conscious, and gripped his elbow.

She resisted the urge to rush over, bend, and scoop him into her arms. Instead, she stood over him and crossed her arms. "That was quite the collision."

The other boy stood and ambled off.

She let Joey push himself up without offering assistance. Even amongst this group of young boys, weakness wasn't tolerated. If she offered to help and he took it, then he'd lose face. If he declined the offer to save face, then she'd be forcing him to be rude to her.

When Joey pushed himself to his feet, she observed the suppressed grimace. Instead of asking if he felt okay, she walked over, flipped the skateboard up and carried it. Some of the boys had resumed playing and others keenly watched Joey's reaction.

"Time to go home. Your uncle's waiting for you." Anybody

eavesdropping would think Joey had to leave as part of a parental obligation rather than his injury.

As they walked away from the park together, Mica glanced down at Joey, who still cradled his elbow.

With the skateboard in one hand, she pulled out her phone with the other.

"Who you texting?" Joey asked.

"A friend."

Need your medical expertise, she sent to David.

"I'm fine," Joey said.

"You're out of earshot of the other boys, and you don't have to lie to me."

His lower lip quivered.

"I wouldn't cry just yet. They may be able to see you still."

Joey sucked in a deep breath as he climbed into Mica's truck. She placed his skateboard in the back and sat in the driver's seat.

Her phone rang as she cranked the engine. "That was fast."

"Are you okay?" David asked.

She felt genuinely touched by the concern in David's voice. "I'm fine. A young friend of mine has a skateboard injury. I know you're not working today, but..."

"I'll take a look. How serious?"

"I think it's only his elbow." Mica glanced over at Joey, who nodded. "I can take him to an urgent care clinic if that would be more appropriate." If Mica hadn't formed a new relationship with David, she'd have just taken Joey to the nearest walk-in clinic.

"I'll take a look and decide. Do I need to meet you somewhere?"

Mica and David discussed each other's locations, and they decided she'd bring Joey to David's apartment. David gave her the address, and she entered it into her phone.

"Thanks. I appreciate it."

"No problem."

When Mica hung up the phone and pulled out of the parking lot, Joey gaped at her.

"What?"

"New boyfriend?"

"What? *No.* He's just a friend of mine."

"A friend you've never mentioned *and* who makes your voice all soft."

Mica shot Joey a scowl before bringing her attention back to the road.

12

fter parking her truck, Mica escorted Joey up the elevator to the tenth floor. She knocked on David's door.

He greeted them with a smile. "Come on in."

She glanced at the security pad in the entryway. "High tech."

"Is it?" He shrugged. "A neighbor had a break-in, so I got an upgrade."

David turned to Joey. "So, is this the patient?"

Joey looked around the apartment, still cradling his elbow. "Kinda sparse in here, for being such a fancy building." He walked into the living room, sounding disappointed. "And small."

"I'm one guy. I don't need much space. Especially because I'm in the ER most of the time."

Ad David leaned on the edge of his couch, Mica admired his rumpled hair, cotton t-shirt, and loose blue jeans.

"Well, young man, what happened to your arm?"

"Some fool plowed into me at the park."

"Have a seat. I'll take a look. You need anything to drink? I've got Coke, or orange juice, or water."

"No, I'm good."

As David palpated Joey's forearm, elbow, and upper arm, Joey eyed him suspiciously.

"Are you a real doctor?"

David grimaced with a slight grin. "Ouch. Sixty seconds in and you're already doubting my abilities."

Mica chuckled as she watched their interaction.

Joey continued, "Well, you look kinda scruffy and you don't have much of a living space."

"Aside from splurging on an overpriced car, I don't buy much stuff."

Joey grunted.

"Do you have a parent, or someone who can give me permission to treat you?"

"My uncle."

"He doesn't have transportation to come here," Mica said.

"That's okay. I can take verbal consent."

Mica withdrew her phone and called Joey's uncle. She explained the situation and handed the phone to David. He spoke with his uncle for a few seconds and then thanked him. He handed the phone back to Mica.

"So, a skateboarding mishap. Good thing you were wearing your helmet."

"How do you know that?"

Mica followed David's gaze to the indentation in his jaw from the chinstrap.

David leaned back. "Because you don't have a head injury."

Mica grinned but kept her face out of Joey's view.

"What you do have is a dislocated elbow. It can happen in kids —usually ones younger than you, though." As he spoke, David extended Joey's arm, turning it palm-down. He tugged and popped the elbow back into place.

Joey let out an "Ow" before jerking his arm back. Then, he marveled, flexing and extending his arm with ease. "Cool."

David went on to test Joey's sensation and finger movements, ensuring there was no nerve damage.

"Do you like to swim?" David asked.

Joey shrugged. "I guess."

"Well, I give kids free swim classes at the Y on Sundays. All you need is a ride there and you're in."

The boy grinned.

Mica marveled at the ease in which David interacted with Joey. He wasn't annoyed by them dropping in, he wasn't condescending to Joey, and he wasn't remotely bothered by a boy in dirty clothing sitting on his couch.

Mica closed her eyes momentarily and tuned out the discussion. Her side throbbed where David's stitches held her wound together. The injury would be a weak spot when she fought Buzz —and she knew she'd *have* to fight him.

Few of her marks ever came quietly. By the time Mica had hunted them, they'd already made up their minds to run from the law. Her petite size was certainly not enough to humble them.

Charlie had been a rare exception, and only because he'd already seen her fight. Mica chuckled to herself. The look on David's face that night had been priceless, especially because she imagined few events surprised an emergency room physician.

Yet, he'd surprised her as well. Mica had never seen a live birth before and the entire event had amazed her. Incredibly, in a single night, they'd each been able to take an intimate look into each other's lives, revealing more than they'd ever be able to over talks at dinner, or during leisurely walks.

Joey decided he wanted a soda after all. David retrieved it and handed it to him.

Joey jutted his chin toward Mica as he asked David, "So, what's your relationship with M n' M?"

David grinned at the nickname, but crossed his arms. "What's *yours*?" He asked the question in mock defensiveness, noticing Joey's smile.

"She's my big sister. It's part of this program, which basically means she checks in on me and takes me places."

"What kind of places?"

"Park, zoo, museums." Joey drank his soda.

"Well, my relationship is: I'd like to be her boyfriend."

Joey screwed up his face in disgust. "Eww! What for?"

"I kind of like her." David glanced at Mica.

She felt her cheeks flush.

Despite the danger she'd put him in, David was apparently still interested. Their lives were parallel in intensity and stress, enough that they could both understand each other. She and David could relate to each other—an essential component to any relationship.

But was Mica getting ahead of herself? Did they even have a *relationship*? The chemistry unquestionably sizzled when they were in proximity to each other, but Mica vowed to be patient and see where their attraction would lead them.

She rubbed a hand along Joey's short hair. "Come on, you. Let's get you back to your uncle."

Without further encouragement, Joey opened the door and stepped outside the apartment.

Mica stuck her hands in the back pockets of her jeans. "Thanks for taking care of him."

"No problem."

"You're back on shift tonight?"

David nodded as he stepped closer. "When are you back from your trip?"

"Hopefully in two or three days. Depends on how long I take to find my mark."

With another step closer, David placed his hands on Mica's hips. "Can I see you when you get back?"

Mica swallowed, feeling her heart flutter at his touch and his proximity. Yep. Chemistry.

"Yes."

"Can I see you *as soon as* you get back?"

David looked into Mica's eyes and down to her lips. She leaned closer and closed her eyes, ready to ignite the fire that had been building from the electricity dancing between them. As soon as she felt the barest brush of his lips, a loud throat-clearing came from the doorway.

Oh, right. *Joey*.

Instead of the heated kiss she'd desired, Mica gave David a brief peck before stepping back from him. "I'll text you as soon as I'm back in town."

She held the mental image of David standing in his apartment, with amusement on his lips and arousal in his eyes. Like a mental Polaroid, she took it with her as she left.

As Raymond finished washing the ambulance at the start of his shift, his usual partner, Cathy, arrived.

"The truck's checked off," he said as he sprayed the soap off the tires with the hose.

Cathy stood stationary and stared at him. "You've already checked all the supplies on the ambulance?" Cathy marveled. "*And* you're whistling."

Raymond rinsed off the back bumper. The sun had been

setting at the start of his shift, so he'd turned on the floodlights at the station to wash the ambulance.

Cathy put her hands on her hips. "Um. The stress-burdened, overworked, underpaid supervisor is in a good mood? Who are you? And what have you done with my partner?"

Raymond swung the water stream in her direction, as if he was going to spray Cathy with water, before he turned off the water faucet. A trickle of water landed at her feet before fading to a stop.

"Am I missing something?" Cathy inquired, putting her purse and bag in the ambulance.

"Yep. But you won't believe a word of it."

The radio sprang to life. They were being dispatched to a signal ten—a chest pain.

Raymond moved the water hose out of the station driveway, while Cathy cranked the ambulance. After mounting up, they turned onto the highway with the lights flashing and the sirens blaring.

Seven minutes later, Raymond and Cathy pulled onto the curb at an upscale restaurant. They rolled the stretcher, with an oxygen tank, bag of supplies and cardiac monitor on top, into the restaurant. The maître'd led them toward the sitting room of the lady's restroom.

As they made their way there, Raymond saw Cathy gawking at the crisp, white tablecloths and decorative, blown-glass lights hanging above each table. Dinner at a place like this would cost two days' wages.

The fire department had already arrived on scene. Two firefighters in navy uniforms reported to Raymond that the woman they were called to help was having palpitations. She had no history of heart problems, was taking no medications, and had an allergy to penicillin. One of the firefighters recited the woman's vital signs to Raymond and Cathy: blood pressure one-ten over seventy, pulse one eighty-six, and oxygen saturation at ninety-nine percent. They put an oxygen mask on her.

Sweating and anxious, the woman appeared to be in her mid-forties. Her blond updo was disheveled and her mascara was smeared, either from sweat or tears. The black splotches accentuated her pale skin.

Raymond asked her questions while Cathy connected the woman to the cardiac monitor through strategically placed electrodes on her torso. Still talking and assessing the patient, they moved her to the stretcher. As they strapped the patient into the stretcher, Cathy made eye contact with Raymond and directed his gaze toward the cardiac monitor. Following her cue, he looked at the screen. The woman had a rapid, regular rate known as paroxysmal supraventricular tachycardia.

After completing their initial assessment, they informed her husband that they would take his wife to Regional before pushing their way through the crowd to the ambulance. Raymond and Cathy loaded the patient, thanked the firefighters and first responders, and closed themselves inside the back of the ambulance. Cathy started an intravenous line as Raymond increased the woman's oxygen dosage and attached her tubing to the larger oxygen tank on the truck.

Ramon placed electrodes and ran a quick twelve-lead ECG, which he electronically sent to Regional with the push of a button.

Holding the radio in one hand, Raymond unlocked the drug box with the other.

Cathy chimed, "You're never going to get orders for it."

They both knew Dr. Rider was working in the ER tonight.

"Watch me," he fired back, his eyes sparkling.

Cathy secured the IV with tape then instructed the woman to cough. Coughing was a maneuver to stimulate the vagal nerve, to slow the heart rate down and hopefully convert the woman back into a normal heart rhythm. Unfortunately, the patient's heart only slowed for a few seconds with the coughing, then resumed at around one hundred eighty beats per minute. At one hundred fifty beats per minute or greater, the ventricles of the heart didn't have time to fill with enough blood before it emptied itself again. The physiologic effect was decreased circulation, which could damage tissue if it persisted.

"Unit twenty-two to Regional for a physician," Raymond said calmly. Confidently.

A few moments later, Maple answered, "Dr. Rider is listening. Go ahead twenty-two."

"Ten-four. We're on scene with a forty-six-year-old female complaining of palpitations. Patient is alert and oriented times three, but pale and diaphoretic. BP is one hundred ten palpated, pulse one eighty, respirations twenty-six, ECG showing PSVT at one-hundred eighty beats per minute. We sent the twelve-lead to you. Patient is on O2 at fifteen liters per minute via non-rebreather. We have an eighteen gauge, left A-C. Requesting orders for six milligrams adenosine."

The medication adenosine acted fast and had to be given through a large vein at the crook of the patient's elbow, upper arm, or neck, and preferably on her left side, where the drug could quickly reach the heart. Having only a six second half-life within the body, the drug had to be pushed into the vein quickly and immediately followed with a flush of normal saline. Upon reaching the heart, the adenosine would stop the electrical system of the heart briefly. For ten to thirty seconds, until the medication wore off, the patient would have no heartbeat yet remain conscious. Ideally, this would allow the heart to reset at a slower pace.

Dr. Rider's voice came over the radio, "Proceed with six

milligrams adenosine and twelve more as needed. Advise patient update before arrival. Regional out."

Raymond watched with enjoyment as Cathy's jaw came unhinged and her eyes bulged. She must have been wondering if she'd woken up today in an alternate world—a parallel universe.

Raymond prepared and administered the medication, and they both watched the cardiac monitor in anticipation. The heart rhythm on the monitor reduced itself to a squiggly line.

"Oh," the woman said faintly. "I feel light-headed all of the sudden."

That's because of the lack of blood flow, Raymond thought, his eyes glued to the cardiac monitor. "You'll be fine, ma'am. That's just the medication to slow your heart down."

After twenty seconds, which seemed like an eternity of flatline, the woman's heart resumed beating. It ticked along at a rate of one hundred twenty-six now—still high but not fast enough to warrant further treatment.

Cathy breathed a sigh of relief. She climbed into the driver's seat, calling to Raymond through the cab window, "I want to know everything."

As he pumped the blood pressure cuff, Raymond replied, "Well, Dr. Rider and I had a male bonding moment when we had a baby yesterday."

⁂

DAVID EXAMINED a scan of a patient's chest on the monitor, looking for evidence of a blood clot. The ER was bustling with patients, but everyone was working together smoothly to triage and treat.

He felt Maple staring at him, sensing that she wanted to ask him something. Maple never hesitated to ask anything patient-related, which meant something personal occupied her thoughts. He knew the emergency room rumor mill was churning about his relationship with Mica, but he had no interest in feeding the fire. Maple seemed frustrated that David wasn't volunteering information.

At last she spoke. "Bed two is hearing music. You want me to call a psychiatry consult?"

"Huh. How old?" David asked without looking up from his screen.

"He's an eighty-year-old man from a nursing home."

"Vital signs?"

Hallucinations could have multiple causes from neurologic to infectious. Something as seemingly simple as a urinary tract infection in an elderly patient could cause confusion.

"He's afebrile. Oxygen is ninety-six percent on room air, blood pressure one-ten over sixty, heart rate seventy and paced."

"Paced?" David turned to look at her.

Maple nodded.

"What type of music is he hearing?"

She arched a stenciled eyebrow. "I didn't ask."

"Can you page Dr. Jameson for me?"

"The electrophysiology specialist?"

"Yes, I think the patient's pacemaker battery is low."

Maple hesitated. "His pacemaker battery is low because he hears music?"

"Yes. Thanks." He knew sometimes patients could mistake the humming of a low battery as music.

Maple nodded and walked away, just as Raymond and Cathy rolled in a cardiac patient they'd called in a few minutes earlier.

Raymond wrote his narrative report on the lady with PSVT, while he pretended to ignore Maple who stood impatiently tapping her pen on the counter.

Cathy came in from the cold and to help Raymond fill out the electronic paperwork. Only a few minutes ago, he'd come out to the ambulance and explained yesterday's events with Dr. Rider to Cathy who had then told Maple.

Between Maple's tapping and Cathy's grinning, Raymond's annoyance mounted.

"Spit it out, Maple," Raymond demanded, without looking up from his tablet.

Maple shook her head. "I'm just absolutely astounded. He shows up on your call with his date, who's a bounty hunter! Last week, I'd have argued with anyone who claimed that Dr. Rider even knew what an emotion was. Now, I'm hearing he's infatuated with this woman."

Tom, who sat next to Maple, typed on the computer spoke as he spoke. "No way she's a *real* bounty hunter."

"Why do you say that?" Maple asked.

Tom shook his head. "She's five-foot-four and weighs a hundred and twenty."

Raymond interrupted: "I'm telling you, I saw her kicking some serious ass. Five of them, and these guys weren't little."

"She must have a pretty big gun then," Tom replied.

Maple looked at Tom slyly. "You saying a girl can't kick a little butt?"

"A *little* butt, yes," Tom agreed. "But not a big butt and definitely not more than one butt at a time. Little women just don't stand a chance against muscle."

"The bigger they are, the harder they fall," Robin squeaked, walking in mid-conversation.

Maple added, still speaking with Tom: "Uh-huh? So, a woman..."

"Don't start with the feminist crap. I'm talking about simple physics," Tom retorted.

Raymond shook his head. "You had to have seen it. A sight to behold."

"Now, *she's* a sight to behold," Tom said, turning around from the computer. "That, I'll agree with."

"Ugh. *Please*." Robin rolled her eyes as she leaned on the counter, her plump breasts squishing up to her chin.

Tom looked at Robin disbelievingly. "She's hot," he stated.

"She's *okay*," Robin scowled.

Tom snapped back, "Just because she's not a heaving mound of breasts doesn't mean she isn't hot."

Robin sent him a heated look of outrage.

"Raymond," Maple demanded, "You're the tie-breaker."

Robin interrupted: "You've seen her, Maple. She graced us with her presence the other night."

"She's a fox," Raymond replied.

Robin glared at Raymond, but he ignored her.

Maple looked at Robin. "She was in shock and doped on heroin. It doesn't count."

Robin rolled her eyes and walked away. "She's not even a natural blond," she mumbled as she left.

"Definitely a fox," Tom agreed.

"Who's a fox?" Dr. Rider suddenly asked, surprising them all as he walked toward the computer.

Tom jumped out of his way. "My, uh, brother's new girlfriend," he stumbled, shooting a warning look at Maple who concealed a smirk.

"Oh." Dr. Rider sat at the computer and logged onto the medical records system.

Raymond clasped him on the shoulder. "I'm off tomorrow night. You want to grab a beer?"

Dr. Rider pursed his lips, before nodding. "Sure. Dr. Cruz asked me to swap a shift later for him this month so I'm off tomorrow evening."

———

RAYMOND LISTENED to the rumble of his idling ambulance as he and Cathy sat in the parking lot of a fast food restaurant. The radio rambled on with traffic between dispatch and other units on calls. They rested in relaxed silence. He was attempting to quickly devour his food before the next emergency call, while Cathy picked at the bun of her grilled chicken sandwich.

"I can't believe the woman we picked up the other night—Mica is her name—was fighting in the streets last night. What's the connection?" Raymond narrowed his eyes. He wondered if drinks with Dr. Rider tomorrow night would solve the mystery.

Cathy glanced sidelong at her partner and shrugged.

He continued talking, "I don't understand how some people seem to just be a magnet for violence, or pain, or suffering. I mean, how bad is your karma that you're assaulted multiple days in a row? You'd think events like that might cause you to reevaluate your decision process!"

"You don't know her story. Maybe you're being too judgmental."

Cathy had accused Raymond of possessing a pedantic, pontificating persistence in expressing his opinion—no matter how callous that opinion might seem to others. Yet despite his intolerance for the shortcomings of others, Cathy seemed to enjoy Raymond's company. He could lapse into moments of wit and charm to make her laugh.

Cathy matched Raymond's proficiency at paramedicine, but their similarities ended there. She was short and stocky, with a heart big enough to swallow all of the ills in the world. She also possessed the patience needed to work with Raymond.

When Raymond's wedding band clinked against the can of soda he was drinking, he noticed Cathy stiffen. She glanced down at her own left hand as though noting the absence of her own ring.

Raymond had been widowed for a year, but still wore his wedding ring. He also always wore the pink ribbon on his collared work shirt. Breast cancer sucked.

Glancing at his partner, Cathy kept her focus intently on her uneaten sandwich.

He should take off the ring. He'd mourned. He'd worked relentless hours to keep his mind off his loss and keep his body away from their empty house. He should take the next step.

Raymond pondered during that moment of silence, wondering how to ask Cathy to share her thoughts.

The radio cackled, "Unit twenty-two, be en route to 1056 Martin Luther King Drive. Signal six."

Someone was having difficulty breathing.

"Shit," Raymond said, his mouth full of partially-chewed French fries.

Cathy shook her head at him in amusement.

He wadded the rest of his chicken sandwich up in its wrapper and tossed it in its paper bag. "That'll be too cold and soggy to eat by the time the call is finished," he grumbled.

He slammed the truck into drive and pulled into traffic with the lights flashing and siren blaring.

Cathy reached for her stethoscope and gloves. She pulled out two antacid pills, anticipating Raymond's needs.

"Thanks," he said with a sigh. He popped them into his mouth and chewed.

13

Mica walked down Bourbon Street in New Orleans. The smell of sweet liquor—mingled with vomit and urine—seeped upward from the pavement and hung in the humid air. Feeling the concoction stick to the soles of her boots, she thought about David for an instant, how his shoes would be sticking to the bodily fluids on the floor of the ER as he tended to his patients.

Similar smells would surround him: Liquor from the drunk driver who lay before him in a mess of bones and tissue, urine lost in a moment of fear before his car was halted by a tree, and the vomit he'd puked up earlier in the evening.

Jazz floating through the streets drowned out the clicking of Mica's boot heels against the street beneath her. Such a dirty city produced such beautiful music. Now, eleven o'clock on a weeknight, the bars were still filling. She wondered how intolerably crowded the street must become during Mardi Gras.

Mica came to a stretch of bars. The white of her shirt glowed in the black-light that surrounded the interior of the first bar.

Wearing black slacks and a black jacket, Mica blended seamlessly into the streets of New Orleans. She also wore a black wig. Dressing in disguise was effective because, if trouble occurred and police showed up, bystanders would then give descriptions inconsistent with her actual appearance. Mica wasn't there to cause trouble, and didn't care to be detained by police and forced to answer questions and show identification.

Finding herself encapsulated in the first bar by dancing men and women, Mica sought higher ground to look for Buzz Lynch. Half-naked bodies brushed against one another, dancing in rhythmic motion to the deafening music—a booming, heavy bass. In the shadows of corners, Mica couldn't make out people's faces clearly. She needed a closer look, but when she got it, she soon discovered that the shadows concealed the sexual encounters that were only hinted at on the dance floor.

At once, the discovery was both erotic and repulsive. The sweating bodies and clouds of cigarette smoke in the first bar were almost suffocating. The ones that followed were equally stifling.

Two bars and a half-dozen licentious invitations later, Mica spotted Buzz. He was flirting at the bar with a thin, pale-looking man.

Mica walked up and smiled. "Hey," she said cheerfully.

"Hello?" Buzz responded. He looked puzzled and somewhat irritated, as though wondering if this stranger had noticed she wasn't his sexual preference.

"Buzz Lynch?" Mica stated.

"Yeah?" he responded with bewilderment.

"I need to ask you some questions about a man named AJ."

"Are you police?"

The pale-looking man Buzz had been flirting with clutched his chest. "Oh, my God," he gasped.

"No," Mica admitted, "but I need answers. We can do this the friendly way or the hard way." She produced a pair of handcuffs.

Buzz set his drink on the counter. "You're joking, right?" When Mica didn't respond, Buzz continued, "I'm a black-belt in Karate. I think you should reconsider."

"Then perhaps we should take this outside," Mica countered, gesturing in the direction of the door.

"Right," Buzz smirked. "Where your partner is waiting with a gun."

"I work alone."

Buzz leaned forward, his teeth bared. "I'm not talking to anyone about anybody."

Mica turned, as if to walk away, and then lashed out her foot at the leg of Buzz's bar stool. The other man screamed as Buzz fell to the floor. The music stopped, and a crowd formed around them. Quickly back on his feet, Buzz took an offensive stance.

"I don't want to hurt you," he said sincerely.

Mica glanced around her as the crowd packed around them tightly. "I only want to talk, Buzz. But if you want to dance, we'll dance."

Buzz kicked at her ribs with some degree of limited mobility, owing to his skin-tight blue jeans. Mica pivoted right, then slapped one cuff on his wrist as she dodged a blow from his fist.

A man from the crowd attacked Buzz from the rear. Although a well-intentioned gesture, he was ill-trained. Buzz brought the man, plus a second vigilante, straight to the floor with a series of Karate kicks and punches. His show of force seemed to deter the rest of the crowd from any further participation except spectating.

They made a good crowd for her. Mica could always try to calculate how she'd be received in a particular crowd but rarely with certainty.

Buzz turned his attention back to Mica, who'd not taken

advantage of the distraction created by his other attackers. Fortunately for Buzz, Mica had enough honor not to fight a distracted opponent.

"I left that life behind," he sneered defensively.

Not so defensively, Buzz threw a punch out. Mica coolly blocked it.

"I just want to talk," she repeated. "I need information about AJ. I'm trying to find Jeremiah's killer."

She kicked, and Buzz barely bent in time to take the blow on his thigh instead of his knee. Wincing briefly, he managed to stay on his feet.

Mica understood the gravity of the situation, and the danger it posed to her own safety. She'd only ever encountered a few opponents skilled at martial arts, but all the scenarios had played out similarly. She possessed more speed and agility than her opponents, but also more fragility. One successful blow from a big man's powerful extremities could crack Mica's ribs or tear her tendons. Her defense had to be as good as her offense—better, even.

"He'd kill me if he ever finds me," Buzz growled, missing Mica with another swing.

Recovering from her duck, she kicked upward into his side. "I'm not leaving without information."

Buzz stepped forward, fire in his eyes as he fully engaged in hand-to-hand combat. Sweat now drenched his polo shirt. They swung, kicked, blocked and dodged, but Mica was consistently faster. About every third blow surpassed his defenses, until Buzz weakened in a moment of pain and breathlessness. That was when Mica took the opportunity and jabbed at his right kidney.

Buzz fell to the floor, but recovered in time to lash out a glancing strike before she could incapacitate him. His fist struck her side, near her stitches, and it knocked the breath out of her.

As Mica gasped and stepped backward, she threw up an off-balance kick that struck Buzz's jaw. He arched backward, then twisted to catch himself on his hands. Before he landed, Mica pounced on top of him, burying her knee into his back, right between Buzz's shoulders.

She caught his arms and secured the second cuff to his other wrist.

Claps and cheers burst forth from the entertained crowd.

For a moment, Mica remained seated astride Buzz's back, catching her breath.

After helping him to his feet, Mica paid the bartender for Buzz's tab and the broken stool. She walked out with her captive, and another round of applause spontaneously broke out.

It's not always a thankless job.

AFTER THE WAITER dropped off two beers, David stared at the foam and frosted glass. "Thanks for the invite."

Raymond shrugged before taking a long slow swig. He wore jeans and a t-shirt, rather than the paramedic uniform David was accustomed to seeing him in.

The two of them sat in The Bookhouse Pub in downtown Atlanta with two beers and a plate of fries between them.

"I half-expected you to turn me down, Doc. Wasn't sure you were a beer kind of guy."

"Is that so?" David drank his ale: Southbound Transilience—a tart and refreshing Savannah born beer on draft.

"Espresso. Wine. Not so much beer." Raymond leaned back in his chair, beer in hand.

"Because I'm a physician?"

"More because of the way you carry yourself. And that ostentatious car."

"The car *is* a bit much." David had bought the car thinking the luxury of having his lifelong dream car would make him happy. Other than a few carefree moments, the Aston Martin hadn't paid off.

Doctoring was what really brought him happiness, except when he was inundated with paperwork. Swimming brought happiness, releasing the day's tension with the feel of cool, smooth water parting around his skin. And Mica brought David happiness—her easy disposition, her propensity to right wrongs, and those big chocolate eyes.

She'd traveled to the jungle streets of New Orleans, putting herself in harm's way to find her mystery villain. David thought about her a lot.

"Don't look so worried, Doc. I get it: You have trust issues. Now you trust me and my medical skills. We're good."

David snorted. He hadn't been worried about his relationship with Raymond, but he didn't correct the medic. "Yeah, I suppose I do have trust issues." The situation with Raymond and the naloxone the other night could have been resolved or avoided entirely with better communication, and the blame lay on both sides. Regardless, the two of them were friendly now; so there was little point in belaboring how they could both have approached their working relationship better.

David leaned back and crossed his legs at the ankles. "Aren't we supposed to be discussing sports? Falcons, Braves, Hawks?"

Raymond shrugged and didn't lighten the conversation as David suggested. "We all have some type of issue. I've got dad issues, and he's been dead ten years."

David wondered at Raymond's meaning. Abuse? Alcohol? Drugs? David didn't ask.

"What about you, Doc? Who do you blame?"

He thought of Maxine, the source of his trust issues. She'd missed many major events in his life because she'd been gone serving their country.

"I think I'm done with blame and bitterness," David considered. "I have a good life—whether despite my resentment, or because of it."

"New chapter?" Raymond lifted his glass.

"New chapter. And don't call me Doc." David toasted his half-empty glass.

Raymond chuckled and then took a drink. "Does your new chapter have anything to do with that gorgeous blonde you've been spending time with?"

David felt an irritated flash of anger at Raymond's benign and accurate description.

Raymond grinned. "So, it *does*."

"Mica is unique. Always has been. I knew her in high school."

"High school sweetheart?"

"We barely knew each other then. But now..." His voice trailed off.

"Now?" Raymond prompted.

David beamed as he raised his glass to drink again. "Now I'm smitten."

After he drank, he turned a questioning gaze to Raymond. "What about you and Cathy?"

"What about us?" Raymond's brow furrowed.

"The ER rumor mill is that you two are either together or should be."

Raymond smacked his lips together. "You like the Falcons?"

David crossed his arms, not masking his annoyance that Raymond had no qualms about asking *him* personal questions;

but wasn't willing to answer any of his own. Still, he liked the man's laid back disposition. "I prefer college sports. UGA."

"Okay. Let's talk about them dawgs."

AFTER MICA REMOVED THE HANDCUFFS, Buzz rubbed his wrists. She watched him closely as they sat in a crowded coffee shop. His temper had subsided after she'd explained she was trying to find out what really happened to Jeremiah.

"You two served together, right?"

"Yeah. After that, he went into private security. I started a garage, tinkering with old cars."

"Oh yeah? My dad's a former Marine. Runs a shop now. His baby is a maroon 1964 Corvette. Sometimes I think he drags his feet fixing it up just so he doesn't have to sell it."

Buzz smiled. "I bet it's a beauty. I've got a 1966 Shelby. Purrs like a..." He stopped and glowered at her. "I know what you're doing."

"I told you what I'm doing: Jeremiah's sister thinks his death wasn't an accident. I know he was working in private security at the time he was killed. I think he got mixed up in something with a man named AJ, but I need more information."

Buzz's face turned pale. "Who told you that name?"

"Several people, but everyone clams up before I can get a last name from them."

Buzz pursed his lips.

Mica crossed her arms. "Case in point."

"Look, lady..."

"Mica."

"Look, Mica. You don't know what you're getting into. Sure, you've got some slick moves, but you're just one woman. Don't dig any further. Don't kick the hornets' nest, okay?"

"You know something."

Buzz gripped the edge of the table.

"His sister needs closure," Mica added. Not to mention that she needed to take down the man who'd manipulated her into finding Conrad Johnson for him. She'd delivered Co Jo to his death. He'd pulled his own trigger, but something had terrified him enough to take his own life.

"His sister's not gonna get the closure she wants," Buzz sighed, "but for what it's worth, his name is AJ Schlau. I only know that because Jeremiah told me his name at the same time he told me he was in trouble. I think it slipped out. Jeremiah said he wanted to uncover a human trafficking ring. Two weeks later, he was dead."

"Is that the only name Jeremiah gave you?"

"Yeah. Wait, no. He said if anything happened to him, give Ryan Walsh a message."

"Ryan Walsh?" Mica rifled through her Rolodex of a memory, but came up empty. "What did Ryan do when you told him the message?"

Buzz lifted his hands off the table. "I don't know this guy. I don't know where to find him, either, which I'm hoping also means he doesn't know where to find *me*. Because Jeremiah turned up dead after telling me what he did, I'm not risking my life to deliver a message to a stranger."

"Jeremiah obviously trusted him."

"But what if this Ryan guy is working for AJ? What if *he's* the one who killed Jeremiah? If I reach out to him, I'm just another loose end."

Mica leaned forward. "Tell *me* the message."

MAXINE ROLLED out of bed and pulled on her nightgown. She padded to the kitchen where she started a pot of coffee. Outside, orange light diffused the gray, early-morning hue. The pumpkins in her garden looked plump and picturesque. Their skin was still soft, but they'd be ripe soon.

As the coffee brewed, Maxine walked back to the bedroom and stood in the doorway. What the hell had she been thinking?

Vladimir Pronin propped his head up on a pillow and watched her. "We make a good team, Max." His deep voice sent heat through her body.

Gray hair covered his exposed chest. The memory of raking her hands along his chest only hours earlier made her mouth go dry.

Crossing her arms, Maxine steeled herself. "We are not a *we*. We are not team. You shouldn't have come to Atlanta."

Vladimir smiled as he rested his arms behind his head. "Your words say one thing, but your eyes say something different."

Her knees felt momentarily weak. She spun around and walked to the kitchen. After pouring a cup of coffee, she savored the aroma and the warm, sobering liquid as she sipped.

Maxine looked out of her window at her garden again. "*Tvoimi by ustami da myod pit'*," she whispered. The literal translation was 'I'd like to drink honey from your lips,' but the expression was used when something seemed too good to be true.

Strong, warm arms wrapped around her from behind. How could Vladimir be so large, yet so quiet and gentle?

He buried his face in her neck, and she felt a deep rumble of pleasure reverberate through his chest.

"Why can't we be a team? We're good together, *da*? I make you smile. You make me feel like a million rubles."

Maxine set down her coffee cup and turned in his arms. "We can't be a team—not with who you are, and who I am."

Vladimir tucked a strand of hair behind her ear. "You refer to our vocations. And our vocations are not who we are." He squeezed her closer. "This moment? *This* is who we are. If we need to change vocations to keep these moments, we can do that."

Was Vladimir saying what she suspected he was saying? That he'd leave the mob for her? One didn't simply walk away from the leadership role in the Russian mafia.

Maxine shook her head. "Impossible."

"We could find a way."

"Right now, we have to find a way to deal with Lucius Titan."

"Okay. Him first," Vladimir acquiesced. "Then we address *us*."

Maxine poured him a cup of coffee with two spoons of sugar. She should *not* know how the Russian mob boss preferred his coffee, but she did.

He accepted the cup and gave her a kiss on the cheek. "So, you mentioned you have a plan to trap Lucius?"

"I have ideas, but first you need to get dressed. I can't concentrate with a naked man in my kitchen."

He chuckled before walking unabashedly back into the bedroom.

Last night had been amazing, but it would have to remain nothing more than a one-night stand. Anything more would invite chaos and danger.

14

Mica stared out the small oval window into the night sky as she took a late plane from New Orleans back to Atlanta.

At last she had a name: AJ Schlau. Their history had begun with the fake bounty on Conrad Johnson and wounds its way into her investigation into Jeremiah's death. Their interaction would end with her sending AJ to jail. She would make sure of that.

It had been a hot August in Nevada when Mica had tracked Conrad Johnson, nicknamed Co Jo, to Reno and found him alone in a motel room outside city limits.

His thin, bony arms bore barbed wire tattoos. His bloodshot, green eyes and unshaven face betrayed his hangover. He'd missed his court date for credit card fraud, jumped bail two months earlier, and now had a $20,000 bounty on his head. In addition, Co Jo's gambling addiction had put him in deep to a nasty loan shark.

Mica had spent three days searching for him, knowing that he had to be in a gambler's paradise where he could nurse his addiction. Unfortunately, she'd soon discover she wasn't the only one after Co Jo.

That day, Mica had looked out of the window while Co Jo struggled to put on his alligator boots—difficult, with a plastic cable tie around his wrists.

"C'mon, baby," he'd pleaded with Mica. "You don't have to do this. I'll double your bounty pay." He spoke in a deep, Southern accent.

Mica stalked toward him. "With what? More loan-shark money?" She plucked his cowboy hat off the couch and set it on top of his thinning straw hair.

Co Jo looked down at Mica before lunging toward her neck with his bound hands outstretched. Mica easily dodged the clumsy move. She side-stepped then kicked her right leg out at the side of Co Jo's left knee. Conrad fell over backward with a grunt.

He rolled over and sat on his knees. "You're making a mistake. AJ will kill both of us."

"I don't know any AJ. I'm taking *you* in for jumping bail." Mica remembered standing over Co Jo as he told her:

"I didn't jump bail." He dropped his head.

"You can sort that out when I take you to the bail bondsman."

"I swear to God, I haven't been arrested."

Mica pulled Co Jo up by his ear.

"Ow!"

"Another stunt like that and I'll feed you to your loan shark," she warned.

Co Jo shook his head and adjusted his hat. "I'd rather go to him than your bail bondsman. Somethin' aint' right."

Mica had regarded him carefully when he'd said that. He seemed genuine. Was her information wrong? She could know for sure if she took Co Jo to a police station first.

"I don't think you want to cross me." Mica had taken him by

his bound hands and led him to the window. "See that rusty red van parked down there? That's Roy Burger's ride. He's another bounty hunter—ruthless, mean, and he stinks. Literally. Now, you could go with him, get ambushed by your loan shark, and Roy will hand you over to save his own skin. You could run from me and get caught by him. Or, you could cooperate with me, go safely to jail, and live to see your daughter graduate from high school."

Co Jo's shoulders slumped in resignation.

Heavy footsteps sounded, coming down the walkway outside the motel rooms.

Roy's tall, heavy-set body had looked oversized in his camouflage pants and snug, black t-shirt. He'd worn large, black, steel-toed military boots that practically shook the earth when he walked. Although big and slow, he was powerful and had accurate weapon aim. Often, he returned his prey to prison in a mangled heap, barely breathing by the time he'd finished with them.

Co Jo scurried into the bedroom as Mica unbolted the door. Roy would predictably try to kick in the door, but wouldn't be able to if it remained bolted; in which case he might resort to shooting the lock. That would draw far too much attention. Mica stepped into the bathroom that was adjacent to the door.

With a loud crash, the door flung open and the handle banged into the wall. Mica swung her leg in full force, delivering a precise blow to Roy's upper abdomen. Roy bent in half, falling forward. The sawed-off shotgun in his hands flew forward.

"Hello, Roy," Mica greeted him, picking up the shotgun.

"McMillan." Roy spat. He reached for his handgun.

"I don't think you want to do that, Roy." She raised the barrel of the shotgun toward him.

He pushed his arms forward in resignation.

Three minutes later, Mica had Roy disarmed and cuffed to a heater in the room.

"No hard feelings?" She asked him.

"Fuck you, McMillan," Roy growled.

"That's one fantasy of yours, Roy," she teased, as she and Co Jo left the room, "that will never come true."

Mica had escorted Co Jo to her rental car—a white Crown Victoria with a V8 engine. Knowing she wouldn't be the only fugitive recovery agent after Co Jo, she'd chosen a vehicle with speed and extra metal from interior to exterior. If anything predictably unpredictable happened—as often did--she imagined that most of her bounty would go toward damage repairs.

The damage factor had to be accounted for: broken doors, shot-up glass, destroyed hotel rooms, broken tables in restaurants. Most bounty hunters didn't worry about the damage factor, but Mica knew friends were needed at all levels and could easily be secured by reimbursing them for any damage to their property. If she gained the respect of a restaurant manager, or hotel manager, or shopkeeper, then she could call in a favor later.

Of course, there was a time for good public relations and a time for 'getting the hell out of Dodge.' That smoldering hot day, she'd known Roy wouldn't stay restrained for long. This time, she hadn't stopped at the front desk to pay for the damage that Roy had caused to the door.

Co Jo had been the first person to recite AJs name in fear, but at the time, Mica hadn't known the significance of it.

As they sped down the highway, Co Jo wrung his hands together nervously. "Holy shit," he gasped for the fifth time.

"Relax," Mica remembered telling him. "It's bad for your blood pressure."

Co Jo lowered his head.

"I do my homework," she explained.

"I must be outta my mind, trusting you. I'm gonna get my ass shot. Trusting a damn..." He stopped himself.

"Woman?"

"Yeah. A *female* bounty hunter." Co Jo shook his head. "This is how you get your kicks?"

"Well, it's not the thrill of gambling, but the work has its moments. Don't be so hard on yourself," she added. "Your options were limited."

Mica could have chosen to become defensive about the widely-held opinion that being both a fugitive recovery agent *and* a woman presented a contradiction of existence, or she could choose to challenge the misnomer by her actions rather than her words.

This job wasn't just about the money. People needed to accept the consequences of their actions. Co Jo was no exception. He would need rehabilitation for his gambling disease. He needed to confront the results of stealing and borrowing from loan sharks—short of serious bodily harm and death, that is.

Until Co Jo faced his weaknesses, he wouldn't be able to correct them. Until he corrected them, he couldn't reenter society at a productive level.

These were not Mica's own social reformist ideas, but simply the abbreviated facts according to criminal psychology.

Oh, how she'd thought she was doing the right thing that day. Right up until she'd taken Co Jo to the police station, found that no warrant for his arrest existed, and that he'd rather shoot himself than face whoever had tried to track him down.

THE WORST CALL?

Raymond thought about it, shifting in his plastic chair at the fast-food restaurant.

"The worst call I've ever responded to was a motor vehicle

crash. Pickup truck versus compact car on the highway. The driver of the truck was inebriated, plastered, stone-cold drunk. A mother and a child had been in the car he struck. The daughter was four and was wearing a seatbelt, but was too small for it. She should have been in a car seat."

Raymond didn't finish the description. He was fairly certain his grim expression conveyed the outcome of the crash.

The resident doctor swallowed hard and looked down at his soggy hamburger and limp fries. His expression was pale and devastated.

Raymond knew the youngster hadn't wanted a detailed description and a morbid story. He'd asked Raymond about his worst call just to make conversation while they ate. Yet, Raymond wanted this young man to understand what the streets were like— what life was like outside of the medical school classroom and hospital.

The physician would go back to working within the safety of his four walls, while the rest of the world lived the grim reality of life.

The image of that mother and child... Raymond forced them out of his mind. The belligerent drunk didn't have to live with these images.

That had been the worst call of his life.

He sipped his sweetened iced tea and ate his burger.

Resident doctors who were training in emergency medicine were required to ride the ambulance for some specified number of hours, and every once in a while, Raymond and Cathy were unlucky enough to have one of them ride with them.

On the surface, training day seemed like the perfect opportunity to educate these young doctors about the breadth and scope of a paramedic's knowledge and skill, but few of the trainees had the genuine opportunity to learn. The eager beavers hopped into the back of the ambulance in leather dress shoes and khaki slacks from a name-brand department store expecting to see a mass casualty disaster just like in the movies—a six car pile-up, a high-rise apartment fire, a hazardous material leak, a meteor shower—whatever they fancied.

But they only rode for a few hours at a time and were therefore unable to grasp what a whole day was like in the life of a paramedic; or what a day was like in the life of an impoverished patient. By the time patients arrived in the hospital, they were neatly packaged for the treating physician, not scooped off the street, which was a paramedic's job.

Raymond ignored Cathy's admonishing looks. He knew she'd say he was being judgmental.

The two of them might have only one or two calls in the short time frame the resident was with them for, or they might have none at all. The time on ambulance certainly wasn't enough for the crew and the resident to build any lasting rapport. That's why Raymond gave them all the grim descriptions and morbid details he could when they asked questions they had no business asking. Questions just like: "What was your worst call?"

After their meal, and after the resident had finished his four-hour stint, Cathy scolded Raymond, "You could have been a little easier on him."

"Why?" He turned down the volume on the ambulance radio. "He'll shuffle through the emergency room like the rest of them, denying us orders for nitroglycerine for a chest pain patient while sitting high on his damn soapbox, telling us the dangers of drug administration in the uncontrolled field setting. Meanwhile, our unused medication will sit in a drug box until it expires."

"You've got a good working relationship with Dr. Rider now," she offered.

"Uh—only due to a rare encounter of the third kind," he pointed out.

"Well, perhaps some of us para-gods are better off on a tight leash," Cathy observed. "There are some out there—and you know the ones I'm referring to—who don't know lidocaine from atropine and sure as heck couldn't tell you the contraindications. They're the ones who'd give procainamide rapid IV push and adenosine slow instead of vice versa."

Raymond grunted.

Cathy added, "I wouldn't mind more like Rider. You had to prove yourselves to each other, but you're good now."

"Yeah, we're good."

THE NEXT MORNING, David woke and went for a swim. When he arrived back home, he viciously cleaned his apartment to distract himself from worrying about Mica, at least until an appropriate hour to call arrived. At nine o'clock in the morning, there wasn't a corner of his apartment left un-scrubbed.

He finally sat down in his recliner and dialed her cell phone number. It rang three times, and he momentarily thought about hanging up the phone.

"Hello?" Her voice sounded low and raspy.

"Mica?" David asked, although he knew she had answered. "I'm sorry. I woke you up."

Damn, nine o'clock is too early.

"It's okay," she said.

He could hear the rustling of sheets in the background.

Mica continued, "I just got back a few hours ago. Took a late flight from New Orleans to Atlanta."

Her rich and sensual voice sent arousal coursing through him. What would waking up to that voice in the morning be like?

"Are you okay?" he asked.

"Actually," Mica sighed, "I was wondering if I could come in for a few x-rays."

His heart sank. Black belt. What trouble had she gotten herself into?

Then he heard her chuckle softly.

"Not funny," David growled.

"Had you, didn't I?"

He didn't answer.

"C'mon. I promise not to worry about you catching hepatitis, if you promise not to worry about me getting a little bruised." Her voice was still enticingly seductive.

"It's different," he insisted, though he thought it a good analogy. "Besides, I wouldn't worry about that happening to you if you hadn't shown up half-dead in my emergency room."

Defending herself, Mica responded, "That was a rare screw-up on my part. But just so we're clear, I did *not* lose that fight."

"Yes, you won the fight, but could have died anyway if you hadn't called for your own ambulance. Also, I seem to remember you mentioning the time you got shot."

"It was superficial."

David didn't respond.

"Fine," she eventually surrendered. "Waste your time worrying if you like."

"I'm sorry. I didn't call to harass you. I should let you go back to sleep."

"I'm awake, now."

Was she irritated? He couldn't tell.

"Brunch sounds good." That suggested she wasn't.

"What can I bring?"

———⚬———

WHEN MAXINE REACHED THE OFFICE, Claire had already arrived. She was tidying her office and rearranging the string of LED lights at her desk, whistling cheerfully.

"What are you so chipper about?" Maxine asked.

Claire jumped, squealed, and grabbed her chest. "Max! You can't sneak up on people like that!"

Maxine chuckled.

Claire straightened a stack of papers. "I had a date last night."

Maxine crossed her arms, intrigued. "Claire 'I-don't-do-people' went on a date?"

"I don't do crowds or groups of strangers—with the exception of Comic Con. But I *will* make exceptions for handsome actors."

"Actor? Wasn't Drake Somebody an actor?"

Claire huffed. "Drake Fitzgerald. And, yes, he's the guy I went to dinner with."

Maxine frowned. "I thought Bear didn't like Fitzy?"

Claire's dog was a good judge of character. The bullmastiff protected his owner, and all dates had to pass his inspection.

"Don't call him Fitzy."

"D-fitz?"

"No."

"Fitz on a Ritz?"

"Max, *no*. Anyway, the weirdest thing—I ran into *Drake* at the dog park. He was dog-sitting for a friend. Bear was friendly to him. Maybe Bear was having an off day the first time they met."

"I suppose we all do."

"Well..." Claire stopped arranging her yellow Post-It notes and scrutinized Maxine. "What's going on with *you*? You're practically glowing."

"I'm a Marine. We don't glow." Maxine turned and walked toward her office.

Claire scurried after her. "You... Were you *with* someone last night?"

Maxine started to close her door, but Claire pounced inside her office before she succeeded.

"We've got work to do."

Claire's eyes went wide as she threw her hand over her mouth. Unfortunately, that didn't keep her from speaking. "Vladimir!"

"What? How could you possibly come to that conclusion?" Maxine rubbed her cheeks. Was she glowing? Impossible.

"I'm *right*," the blue-haired pixy declared defiantly. "I have alerts in place for whenever he enters the US. He flew in yesterday and today you're..." Her voice trailed off.

Maxine sat heavily in her chair.

Damn.

Claire was too good at her job.

"How is he?"

"I'm not discussing my sex life with you."

"You had *sex*?" Claire shoved her hands in her jean pockets. "All *I* had was dinner."

Maxine pressed the power button to turn on her desktop computer.

Uninvited, Claire sat in the chair across from Maxine's desk. "You and Vladimir Pronin," she marveled.

Maxine pointed a finger at the other woman. "This stays between you and me."

Claire held up her hands. "Mum's the word. How are you going to make it work?"

Maxine sighed. "As I repeatedly explain to Vladimir, a relationship between us *cannot* work. It's impossible."

Claire smirked. "I'll bet at Ryan's wedding, when you danced with him, you told yourself you'd never sleep with him."

"Your point?"

Shrugging, she answered: "Love finds a way, Max."

"I can't be with a man who has committed the atrocities he has."

Claire's expression softened as she stood. "We're all products of our experiences—good and bad—and our decisions—good and bad. Sometimes, people want to put the past behind them. Start fresh." She walked toward the door. "Maybe you feel like you shouldn't love a man with his past, but maybe what he needs is a woman to love him for his future."

She left, closing the door gently behind her.

Maxine opened her email and set to work. She had projects to manage not relationships to ponder. She reviewed the status checks from her teams on their jobs and skimmed emails requesting Rider SI services. She accepted one invitation to discuss a proposal in person. Finally, she opened a memo Claire had sent updating her on her investigation into Lucius.

AJ Schlau handled Lucius's drug running and prostitution ring, but with Titan firewalls, Claire couldn't find anything incriminating on him or the organization. She'd been able to eavesdrop on a few casual mobile phone conversations between AJ's employees and learned that AJ's office was accessed via retinal scan and his computer via fingerprint identification.

If Maxine could facilitate AJ's arrest for his crimes, the antagonistic move would be the equivalent of firing a warning shot over Lucius' bow.

Let the battle begin.

15

avid stirred scrambled eggs in Mica's skillet while she buttered English muffins before drizzling honey on them.

"I remember in high school you were a swimmer. You told Joey you teach swim lessons."

"I'm not winning any trophies these days, but I still love to swim."

"And when you swim, what are you swimming toward?"

David smiled as he scraped the eggs onto two plates. "The cup is always half-full with you, isn't it? You didn't ask if I was swimming *away* from something."

Away from a broken home.

"Not *you*," Mica responded coyly, pouring the orange juice. "You have goals and future plans. How could you have gotten through college and medical school without ambition?"

David watched her as she set the table. Mica wore loose cotton pants and a fitted t-shirt. A thin rhinestone headband held her blond hair back from her face. If she was wearing make-up, he couldn't tell. Soft pink lips and sensual curves distracted him. Her skin was a light cream and her eyes a warm brown, with flecks of gold giving them a honey hue. He found that intriguing, because he hadn't noticed the color at the hospital. Honey flecks seem to appear whenever she was happy.

"I *do* have goals and future plans." As he stepped closer to her, a boyish nervousness swelled inside him.

Mica looked surprised, but didn't make the slightest motion to turn away from him. He reached out and rested his hands on her hips. He slid them up her sides, while gently pulling her closer. Mica obliged, and their bodies almost touched.

David leaned down, but stopped abruptly. Mica had flinched. The ever-so-slight, involuntary tightening of an abdominal muscle betrayed a response to pain.

"You know..." he began, with the tone of a lecture.

"The eggs are getting cold," Mica interrupted.

They ate in silence for several moments.

Way to ruin the moment, David.

Mica was right, though. He had to accept that she took certain risks; as a result, she might well become a regular patient of his. Mica seemed prepared both physically and mentally for her job, but would she know when she was in over her head?

Scolding himself for ruining a perfectly good moment together, David stared at his eggs, pushing them around his plate. He'd become so intrigued by everything about Mica—her young, soft exterior cloaked her tough, crime-fighting interior. Did she have any idea how arousing her personality was to him?

"Anything interesting at work?" Mica asked, breaking the silence.

David nodded, swallowing a morsel of English muffin. "A

couple of traumas from a DUI car accident the other night. And Raymond brought us a cardiac patient."

"Did the patient do alright?" She sipped her orange juice.

David shrugged. "Raymond had her heart problem abated by the time she got to us."

Mica raised her eyebrows, impressed. "When he delivered that baby, he remained so calm and collected. Such practiced motions." She added, "Like you with Joey."

"How's Joey doing?"

"His uncle texted to let me know he's back on his skateboard like nothing happened."

"How'd you meet Joey?"

She explained the warehouse and Joey's interference in her work. The kid had been living mostly on the street, and she'd reconnected him with his uncle.

When her story concluded, silence followed for several moments while David absorbed all the events. "Sounds to me like you saved him from the streets."

"Maybe," Mica said doubtfully.

"I'm not patronizing you. I've seen kids living on the street come through my ER—beat up in gangs, strung out on drugs, malnourished, or `with life-shortening chronic diseases."

"He's a good kid. He just needs positive role models."

"I meant what I said when I told him he should come to the Y." David finished his juice.

"I appreciate that. He can't come to swim lessons this Sunday, but I can drop him off next Sunday."

"Perfect." He laid his knife and fork on his plate. "Was the trip to New Orleans fruitful?"

They moved from the table to scrubbing dishes as Mica told him about AJ Schlau. After David and Mica had washed the dishes, they went back to the kitchen table and sat across from each other.

"I'd like to ask you on a date," David said, changing the subject. "There's a formal ball this Friday. It's a fundraiser a friend and colleague of mine is organizing for stem cell research. I was wondering if you'd be so gracious as to accompany me."

Mica sat back in her chair and crossed her arms. "Oh, a date, huh?" She said doubtfully. "Are you sure you want me there? On our last night out, I almost got your car stolen."

Dead. I was more worried about getting dead.

David shrugged, relieved that what had at first seemed to be heading in the direction of a decline might end up being a "yes."

"That was a small price to pay for quality entertainment."

Mica laughed. "Well, if you call *that* entertainment, I've got my work cut out to keep things interesting for you."

"On the contrary," David said flirtatiously, "I don't imagine I could ever be bored around you."

"With such charm, how could I refuse?" Mica batted her eyelashes.

"Excellent."

Mica leaned forward with a twinkle in her eye. "And shall you have me home before my carriage turns back into a pumpkin?"

"What do you mean?"

"I guess the offer just seems a little like a fairy tale—a ball and Prince Charming."

"Well," David cautioned, "don't get your hopes up too much. It'll be a bunch of stuffy doctors, socially awkward researchers, and gregarious pharmaceutical reps."

Mica nodded, smiling playfully. "If I'm with you, I'm sure I'll enjoy myself."

David could only smile. She was making no attempt to hide

her feelings or her desires. She was leaning forward with engaging eyes. Her body language exuded an invitation for intimacy. He wanted to kiss her—to kiss those full lips and feel their rose petal texture. But he'd ruined that moment last time, and the nerve seemed to escape him.

"Can I show you something?" Mica asked.

She wanted to kiss David, but because he seemed tentative, she decided to take the moment in a different direction. Perhaps his hesitation was a good thing. If they were going to be involved together, he needed to know more about her—her life and work.

"Of course." David straightened.

She led him into her office to show him the huge board laden with clues. She pointed to the name at the top of her list. "The lead is AJ Schlau—drug runner and human trafficker with no rap sheet and no photo, so AJ is probably a pseudonym. But this is the first time I even *have* a name."

David inspected the board carefully. "So Jeremiah Hughes—who died under sudden and mysterious circumstances—was working for AJ?"

"Technically, he was employed by a security company called Titan Enterprises. He either worked for AJ as well, or was working undercover to try and expose him. By what Jeremiah's sister has to say, and his military record, he was an upstanding soldier and model community citizen. So I believe he's the hero of this story."

"You think AJ's the villain who killed Jeremiah?"

"Him and his family. He had a wife and children." Mica wrapped her arms around her torso as goose bumps gave her a shiver. "I tried reaching out to his former employer, but the company gave me a standard line about being unable to breach confidentiality. They wouldn't share any information about Jeremiah's clients or anyone he may have worked with."

"Think you can catch AJ?"

"I sure as hell hope so."

Mica stared at her board for several long seconds, before finally speaking softly, "I joined the FBI to make a difference, but I learned I couldn't thrive in an environment with outdated technology and mind-boggling red tape." She swallowed. "Leaving the agency was the first time in my life I'd quit anything. Now, on my own, I've apprehended some fairly awful criminals, but I've also been manipulated by AJ. I have to find him and stop him. For me, for Jeremiah, and for the women AJ enslaved."

David hugged her from behind. "You'll get him." His voice sounded firm with conviction.

His validation with those simple words made Mica feel positively invincible.

She turned into him and embraced him. "Thank you."

As David held her, she felt the quick beat of his heart. She looked into his eyes and felt her defensive walls melt. When she arched up toward him, he met her for a deep, exhilarating kiss. The world around Mica seemed to burst with warmth and light as his lips moved over hers and their tongues explored.

In that single kiss, she felt all of David—his strength, his vulnerability, and his sensuality.

When he pulled away, they were both breathless.

David gave her a crooked smile. "There's more of that to come on Friday night."

She bit her lip and nodded. Although she didn't want to wait until Friday night for more of him, she reminded herself that he had to work tonight and needed sleep before his upcoming shift. She was also exhausted from her late flight home.

David hesitated before bending down to give her another kiss, deeper and even more intoxicating than the first. Her entire body tingled with anticipation. He pulled away, smiling.

Mica felt her cheeks flush. Could he tell she'd lost all self-control in the moment? One more kiss and she'd be begging him to stay. She needed to get control of the chemistry she felt whenever he touched her.

"I look forward to seeing you Friday."

"I'll go buy a dress," Mica said.

AFTER DAVID LEFT, Mica lay on her bed with the intention of grabbing a few more hours of sleep. Instead, her thoughts focused on David.

Although she'd never dated a physician, she felt certain David was unique. He had wit and charm, but also a semblance of uncertainty with her, as though he was cautious not to move too fast or push her away.

He seemed genuinely interested in helping people. Stopping to help the paramedics was certainly not in his job description, and David had nothing to gain financially by doing so. He didn't do it for self-edification—evident in the way he hadn't tried to control the scene. He'd worked in tandem with the paramedics to help them with the delivery and save the baby's life.

She'd had so few and such short relationships that Mica had never learned the rules of the game. A few rogue men were turned on by her occupation and her skill, but she found them uneducated and unmotivated. They quickly receded from her regimen of exercise and healthy living. The more professional men that weren't already married were usually self-absorbed or seeking someone more polished than her to complement their ambitions.

Eddy had been her only serious relationship, but in retrospect, lust drove them together, not love. Their time together had been about stealing moments without the hint of a promise of anything more. It was sensual, sexual, and short-lived. Eddy fixated his interests on Eddy—*his* life, *his* career, *his* ambitions. He had aggressive career plans and imagined that if he gave one-hundred percent to a relationship, then he wouldn't be able to give one-hundred percent to his career. He seemed frightened by his cravings for her and too emotionally stunted to explore his feelings.

David was different. He was eager to see her and be seen with her. He didn't hide his emotions, and although he'd been the most exposed to Mica's lifestyle, he didn't shrink away from it. Furthermore, his interests weren't purely sexual—evidenced by his control that morning when she'd had none. Mica sensed a growing intimacy; the promise of something more.

Relationship or not, there was nothing normal about Mica's life—a fact that she attributed to an eccentric childhood. After her mother had left, Mica's father had to raise a six-year-old girl on his own. He was an ex-Marine who'd had an only child after the age of forty. In his youth, he'd been part of countless special operations, including Iraq, Somalia, Afghanistan, and other places that weren't even declassified yet.

As a civilian, Mica's father had enjoyed repairing vintage cars, but every weekend had been an adventure with him. Her father had missed the adrenaline rush of combat, so he'd recreate the feeling of excitement through different sports and games. Together, they partook of paintball with a group of ex-military misfits, hang-gliding and parachuting with adrenaline junkies, and skiing every winter on frightful inclines laden with perilous moguls. On calmer trips, they did roller coasters at the state fair, hiked the Appalachian Trail, and rode horseback across the Big Sky state of Montana.

Her father had lived by a 'work hard, play hard' motto. Her

father's approach had given Mica a unique childhood and taught her the axiom that 'the only thing to fear is fear itself'. She'd always been treated as an equal by her father's friends, never as a child, and never any differently because she was a girl.

She'd learned the value of truth and friendship. But what rooted the symbiotic relationship between two people who loved each other? Her father had never remarried, and he'd never put much effort into the plethora of short-term relationships that followed. He'd explained to Mica once that there was no point, because he still loved Mica's mother.

Mica felt a sudden urge to visit her father. She pulled on a pair of blue jeans and a gray, long-sleeve shirt. She sent a quick text message to him to let him know she was coming.

After pulling her short hair away from her face with barrettes, Mica grabbed her keys, opened the garage, and climbed into her old, green pickup truck. She drove north to her father's body shop.

When she arrived, her father was already waiting, waving at her from behind the glass partition that separated the garage and the office. He sat behind a desk cluttered with invoices, receipts, and unfiled tax forms, while he talked hurriedly on the phone.

"Hey, Dad," Mica said when he finally hung up the phone.

Her father stood and greeted her with a hug.

"No action today?" He smiled, the lines around his eyes crinkling.

They took seats in his office. Her father swiveled restlessly from behind his desk, his hair protruding in short spikes of black and white. His large forearms bulged from the sleeves of his shirt. The big man looked out of place behind a desk.

"Today is a 'think' day."

"Oh? What's his name?"

"AJ Schlau. He's behind..." She cocked her head to one side. "Wait. How did you know I found my bad guy?"

Her father chuckled. "I didn't. I threw the question out jokingly, as if you were coming to talk to me about a man. A *relationship*. Which you never do."

Mica's brow furrowed. "Did you hear something about me?"

He leaned forward. "No. Should I have?"

"No."

He narrowed his eyes at her. "Are you *dating* someone?"

"Do you want to go for a walk?" Mica offered.

He accepted her stall tactic, and they left his office. They walked through the garage. The familiar scent of grease, gasoline, and antifreeze filled the expansive room.

"I tracked a Black Belt to New Orleans yesterday. He was physically resistant to answering my questions ... at first."

"Karate." He grunted.

If Mica's father had ever worried about her, he'd never let it show. As far as he was concerned, no criminal could defeat her physically or mentally. He'd always been her coach in the corner of the ring—always believing, always faithful, and always unwavering.

"Yes."

Her father scratched his chin. "But that's not the relationship we were going to discuss."

Always insightful.

"No." Mica smiled. "Another relationship. I've seen someone a few times now, and I like him."

"*Someone*," he repeated, frowning. "'A few times'? Are you going to make me drag it out of you, or did you come here to talk about him?"

Always to the point.

Mica looked around the garage as she tried to sort out how to tell her father about David. She saw the red 1964 Corvette parked in the corner, waiting patiently for an engine. Her father restored the cars with original parts and sold the vehicles for obscene amounts of money at car shows. Her eyes wandered to an old Jeep Wagoneer with restored plush leather seats and its original side wood paneling. Despite all of the adventures she and her father had shared, she'd always envision him leaned over the hood of a car, smelling of oil and lubricant and wearing his faded blue coveralls.

"Does this man who has your tongue tied have a name?"

"David."

"And David knows what you do?" He prodded.

"Yes."

"And he's still interested?"

"Apparently."

"Well?"

"He's an emergency room doctor."

"Uh huh?"

"And... He's charming, caring and..."

"*And*?"

"And," Mica paused, then added with heightened excitement, "And he's *still* interested."

"And the problem is?" Her father hooked his thumbs through his belt loops.

Mica picked up a ratchet from a utility cart and spun it between her fingers. "The problem is that he's wonderful, he likes me, and I don't want to screw it up."

Her father arched an eyebrow.

"Dad, he invited me to a *ball*. Not a ball*game*. A formal ball."

He nodded. "And he doesn't want to change you?"

"I don't sense that," she answered.

"Then, I don't see a problem." Her father stopped walking and turned to face Mica. "You like him, he likes you. Relationships with you don't usually move beyond the discovery of the danger in your life, so you're nervous when it does. Be nervous. Have butter-flies. It's normal. Just don't be afraid because you're nervous. Don't hold back, don't play games, and don't stop showing affection. I lost your mother because I stopped showing affection," he added.

Mica looked at her father curiously. He rarely spoke about his relationship with her mother. When he did, the corners of his mouth would droop down and his eyes would momentarily shift to some distant focus in the past.

"But a *ball*?"

"Let the man pamper you with a fun night. Your carriage won't turn into a pumpkin at midnight, I promise."

"I'm just excited, Dad."

"Yeah, I see that." He smiled wryly and threw an arm over her shoulder.

"So, still into that Ying-Yang, healthy lifestyle crap?" He joked.

"Something like that," Mica replied.

"Look at me," he stepped back, then continued walking. "I don't worry about my health by doing Yoga, microwaving soy burgers, or eating tree bark. I'm a healthy sixty-five-year-old."

She didn't do any of those things, but she knew her father just wanted to tease her.

"No, Dad. The Grim Reaper took one look at you and decided you were too mean and tough to take on."

"*Hey*," he protested. "Be nice to your old man."

AN HOUR LATER, Mica parked her truck in the lot and walked into Vanessa Vogel's store. A mixture of lavender and vanilla diffused through the air. Incense burned in a bowl next to the cash register.

Mica picked up a pink feather decorating a stand of aromatherapy lotions. She ran the soft barbules along her fingers.

Vivi emerged from the back room. "Back so soon? Your

tenacity is commendable. Who are you after this time?" Copper bangles on her wrist jingled musically as she tucked strands of long hair behind one ear.

Mica chuckled. Who was she after, indeed. "I'm here for advice."

Vivi arched one perfectly sculpted eyebrow.

"I have a date," Mica explained. "A formal ball and fundraiser. I want to dress appropriately."

Vivi's eyes widened. "You want fashion advice?"

"Yes."

"And would this date involve that delicious-looking hunk you brought here the other day?"

"Yes, it does."

"Well done," Vivi purred. Her plump, purple lips curved in a slow smile. "You've come to the right place."

TWO HOURS LATER, Mica arrived at the skate park to pick up Joey.

He tossed his skateboard into the bed of her truck and climbed into the cab. As he buckled his seatbelt, he brushed the evening gown she had laid across the seat back. It was safely inside a protective plastic garment bag.

Joey eyed her suspiciously. "That a body bag?"

She grunted. "It's a ballroom gown."

She pulled out of the parking lot and started the drive to take Joey home.

"What do you need *that* for?"

Mica chuckled. "I have a date. I'm going to a party with David Rider."

"You're going to a party?"

"Is that so surprising?"

Joey shrugged. "I guess not. I'm just used to thinking of you fighting, not dancing."

"You and me both." Mica felt tired after having tried on over a dozen dresses under Vivi's watchful eye.

Joey laughed. "David seems like a nice guy."

"I think so. Do you want to take swim lessons with him?"

"Yeah. Sounds cool."

16

That Friday, Mica met David on her porch dressed in a long, champagne gown. Loose, blonde hair circled her oval face.

"You look fantastic," David said, taking the few steps up to her porch and unabashedly drinking in her appearance. "Although the duffle bag doesn't go with your dress."

"I know." She stuck out her bottom lip in a pout. "I couldn't find shoes to match both."

David's expression became momentarily heavy-lidded as he looked at her lips.

When he picked up her bag, he shot her a skeptical glance and put it in the trunk. "I'm not going to ask what's in this bag, but I hope there's at least a gun."

"Could be," Mica shrugged, admiring David's tuxedo and clean-shaven face as he opened the passenger car door for her. "I put it together after the warning about the Sunset Sliders. It's just a little extra protection I've been carrying around in my truck, but because we're taking your car..."

Mica had spent the days leading up to the ball researching AJ Schlau. She mostly did tedious online searching and feet-to-pavement investigation. Hookers and drug dealers admitted to knowing about him, but no one knew his whereabouts, or they knew enough not to share that information.

Tonight, though, Mica was determined to take the night off and enjoy some leisure time with David. She'd just make sure she was *also* equipped to deal with any eventualities.

Before she entered the car, David gently took Mica's wrist and turned her toward him. "You look amazing."

She touched her necklace. "They're not real, but I thought the dress needed some bling." She'd had to solicit Vivi's help in selecting the dress, and the jewelry was on loan from the eclectic woman.

"I wasn't referring to your jewelry, though it is a nice compliment to your beauty."

She felt her cheeks flush.

David continued, "And because I never know when the next adventure with you will strike, I'd like to kiss you now."

A tingling excitement swept through her as he leaned closer. Arching up, Mica met David's lips for a slow, sensuous kiss.

This is heaven, complete with clouds and existential floating.

Mica felt his reluctance as he broke the kiss, though the electricity between them still crackled. Raw, hungry sensuality filled David's eyes. With a long breath, he seemed to rein in his desire. He stepped back, allowing her room to slide into the passenger seat.

Still dazed by the kiss, she sat down, watching him stroll around to the other side of the car. Fortunately, he had pulled away from their kiss, because Mica had been on the brink of losing herself in it. If he'd asked her to stay at her house for the night and skip the ball entirely, she might have willingly obliged.

With the sun setting behind them, they drove east toward Atlanta. David gently placed his hand in hers and winked at her.

THE FUNDRAISER TOOK place in a large, elegant room inside a conference center just beyond the I-285 loop. Extravagant chandeliers cast brilliant light on the vast room, filled with round tables covered in white linen. At the front of the room, a few couples occupied a hardwood dance floor as they swayed to jazz music played by a band dressed in red, sequined vests.

As Mica walked with David past a buffet table of hors d'oeuvres and people milling about, making conversation, drinks in hand, she felt oddly out of place. She reminded herself that she'd worked multiple undercover roles over the years—whether for the FBI, PI, or fugitive recovery work. She could blend into any scene.

As David escorted her around the room to meet his colleagues, she realized what being arm candy felt like. He kept her close, made her the topic of conversation only when she seemed comfortable with it, and handed her a crystal glass of champagne.

Mica eagerly drank the cool, bubbling beverage. She'd been so busy preparing for the evening that she hadn't eaten dinner. On an empty stomach, the champagne sparkled its way through her senses.

"Pinch me," David whispered into her ear.

She shot him a quizzical glance.

"I still can't believe I'm here with the most beautiful woman in the room."

Mica giggled. "I'm not pinching you."

"Then dance with me." He took her champagne glass, set it aside, and led her to the floor.

Mica felt lighter than air dancing on the ballroom floor. She was enchanted as she swayed through a sea of champagne and swirling attraction. She definitely had plans for them tonight. Intimate plans.

As David turned and spun her across the dance floor, Mica caught a glimpse of someone walking at the periphery of the room like a predator stalking prey. Troy!

A shockwave of pins and needles catapulted her into sobriety. Across the room, she could see Amos flanking the east entrance. They wore waitstaff uniforms. Mica scanned for Tina, who would undoubtedly be working with her partners.

David must have felt her stiffen, because he slowed his pace and looked down at her.

With roaming eyes, Mica explained, "The Sunset Sliders are surrounding the exits."

He started to reach inside his coat pocket for his mobile phone. "I'll call the police."

Mica shook her head. "If they think they've been spotted, they'll act sooner, and we'll have just created a hostage situation."

"You have an alternative plan?"

Mica sensed the anxiety in his voice, but also the absolute conviction and deference to her expertise in this situation.

"Their primary target is me. They want revenge. We have to draw them away so no one gets hurt. They've always been trigger-happy."

As they danced their way to the exit, Mica explained the plan.

Naturally, when all hell breaking loose was eminent, Mica's equipment bag lounged out of reach in the trunk of a car. Best laid plans and all.

At least the Sunset Sliders hadn't spotted her yet. Perhaps the dress, heels, make-up, and flashy jewelry were working in her favor. Oh, and the hair. They hadn't known her as a blonde.

She unlocked the large window leading to a balcony and glanced down at the lawn below. Not a small drop, but doable. She could simply escape now. The Sliders would be none the wiser. But then she'd be leaving violent criminals in a room full of wealthy civilians. Not a good combination.

But if Mica tried to confront them here, one by one, they could pull their weapons and bystanders could become casualties. She had no doubt these criminals were armed.

Mica picked up a glass of champagne and pretended to drink as she walked to one side of the ballroom.

When she reached her destination, she gave a quick, hard tug on the fire alarm. Noise wailed as the sprinklers sprouted.

Mica walked to the center of the room and waited to be spotted. As people gasped, cried, and ran toward the exits, they flowed around her. Troy and Amos watched the crowd, obviously suspecting the fire alarm was a ruse. When their eyes met hers, they reached inside their white jackets.

Mica spun and dashed for her planned exit. When she reached the balcony windows, she shoved them open. In two quick strides, she'd reached the bannister, straddled the railing, and then dropped over the edge.

Shattered glass exploded around her from the window above. *Of course,* the delinquents would open fire in a crowded room. Hopefully, the firing line between them and the window had been clear of patrons.

Outside, as planned, David waited dutifully in his Aston Martin with the powerful engine running, passenger door open, and her bag on the front seat. Mica dragged her heels out of the soft grass where they'd embedded themselves and sprinted to the car.

Another shot rang out, the bullet splintering a nearby tree. As Mica slammed shut the door to David's car, she glanced in the direction of the shooter. It had been Tina.

Of course. Tina was their getaway driver.

The woman stood near a car, taking aim in the direction of David's vehicle. Her brown hair was pulled back in a pony tail, accentuating her strong cheekbones and large overbite.

The Sunset Sliders were more organized than she'd anticipated. If AJ had put them up to this, perhaps he had coached them.

"*Go!*" Mica yelled.

DAVID SPED AWAY in the Aston Martin. As he zipped between cars and ran red lights, he hoped a nearby police car would come to their rescue.

Beside him, Mica reached into her bag and withdrew two thick vests—bulletproof vests, he realized. Twisting around, she slid the vest over his torso and secured the Velcro straps around him. She did the same with her own vest, before putting on her seat belt.

Hoping to outrun the Sunset Sliders, David took a hard right onto the on-ramp of West-bound I-20. He accelerated, weaving between vehicles. The rear window suddenly burst, shattering to the sound of gunfire behind them.

David swore.

He glanced at Mica long enough to see the gun in her hand. She must have pulled it out of her bag. She peered out the back window at their pursuers. He felt a mix of reassurance and awkwardness, recalling that only a few minutes earlier he'd been dancing with the woman who now wielded a gun.

"You planning on using that thing anytime soon?" he asked.

"You're traveling over eighty miles per hour," Mica responded.

"I've got no accuracy with a handgun in a high-speed chase. I'm more likely to hit a bystander's car."

A loud metal *thunk* sounded as a bullet struck the trunk.

"*They* don't seem to have difficulty hitting us," he retorted, not liking the higher pitch his voice had taken. He shrank behind his seat, wishing the bulletproof vest was larger.

"They've got automatic weapons firing thirty rounds every fifteen seconds. So, yeah, they're bound to land a few close hits." Her voice sounded strained for the first time, and David regretted snapping at her.

As the traffic thinned out, David put more distance between them and their pursuers. He weaved through cars as he pushed his Aston Martin beyond one-hundred miles per hour.

He turned to look at Mica, who grinned slightly through flushed cheeks. She turned back around and re-attached her seatbelt.

We escaped.

David was jetting around a pickup truck when he saw tire debris in his path. He didn't have enough room between the other car and the railing to safely swerve around it. Letting his foot off of the gas, he braced for impact.

The force of the shredded tire against the undercarriage of his car jerked his axle. He felt the tug at the steering wheel. He gripped it with all his might, desperately trying to hold the car steady.

Despite his efforts, the hit was enough to drag the right front tire onto the coarse shoulder of the interstate. Hardly able to control the car in that split second, the wheels quickly pulled further right until they slid off into the grass. At that instant, David knew he'd lost all control of the vehicle.

The speed of the car transformed into spinning momentum. With the decline of the embankment, the car violently tumbled.

Mica scream as his world plunged into a devastating spin. His body jerk in every direction like a rag doll in a dryer. He waited for the moment when the car would simply implode in upon itself, reducing them both to squashed grapes.

SEVERAL MOMENTS PASSED after the car stopped tumbling before David's world stopped spinning.

Mica.

With a dull ache on the side of his head, he stumbled out of the car. Steam billowed from the wrecked hood. The dirt and shrubs along the hillside were marred by the rolling car as it had gouged its way to a shuddering stop. The scarred ground looked as though a beast had raked giant claws across the dirt and grass.

Their pursuers would certainly see the destruction and follow the trail straight to them. They had to run away from the scene.

Mica.

He ambled on wobbly legs to the passenger side of the car. The door was caved in toward her. He looked inside and could see her uselessly trying to push open the door.

"Exit on my side," he instructed.

She crawled, and he noticed blood streaks on her champagne gown. Whatever her injury, she was conscious and moving, which worked in her favor.

He came around and helped her out of the car.

"We have to go," David snapped. He didn't know where, but they couldn't wait here for the Sliders to appear with their automatic weapons.

"My bag." Her voice sounded weak and shaken.

Not Mica. Not my beacon of strength.

"Can you walk?"

She nodded.

He reached in and snagged the bag. With one arm under her bicep, they moved together toward the looming black woods bordering the interstate.

They set a relentless pace until fifteen minutes into their brisk hike, when David finally forced Mica to rest. They both panted from the exertion. He needed to inspect the source of her bleeding. The quiet stillness around them suggested they hadn't been followed, so now was as good a time as any.

They sat together in a bare spot of dirt, deep in the woods. Mica dug inside her bag and pulled out a flashlight. David snagged it and inspected her, looking for a source of bleeding as she pulled off her Kevlar vest.

A small cut on her forehead had already coagulated. At some point, she'd lost the heels of her shoes. Mica was shivering, whether from the post-adrenaline rush or the cool ambient temperature, David couldn't tell. Maybe both.

She hadn't complained about pain or cold, though. She was tough.

"My turn," Mica said.

She took the flashlight and shone it over his head and body. She stopped on his thigh.

"You're bleeding."

"It's small and already dried," he said.

He pulled out his cell phone and called Maxine. "Max, we're in trouble. You have anyone who can pick us up outside Atlanta?" He ignored Mica's stares.

"You're with Mica?"

"Yes."

"I'll pick you up."

"Thanks."

"Not so fast. I need to know what I'm walking into."

Mica and his mom were going to meet. He felt sick that he

hadn't talked to Mica about his mom yet. His mother's work and mannerisms would be a shock he couldn't prevent. It might drive a wedge between them.

David put the phone on speaker. "Mica, can you tell my mother what we're up against?"

Mica looked at him skeptically. "Three assailants. We're on foot. I've got two handguns, four clips."

"Professional hit?" Maxine asked.

"No. Amateurs. But you don't have to be good when you've got automatic weapons."

"True."

"We can figure out our coordinates to text to you," Mica said.

"Don't bother. I'm already tracking you. There's a gas station one mile southeast of you. I'll pick you up there."

David cringed slightly at Mica's incredulous glare, as she heard Maxine inform them she was already tracking him. David knew his mom had some fancy equipment and computer genius at her disposal. Hell, as careful and thorough as Maxine was, she'd probably had his phone tagged, or bugged, or traced, or whatever it was called.

"David, are you injured?" Maxine asked.

"Just scratches."

"Okay, stay safe."

"Thanks, Mom."

He disconnected the phone and met Mica's eyes.

"*That* was your mother!" She gaped at him.

AJ PACED in his living room as he called Lucius. His plan had been flawless. He had used Titan's technology to clone McMillan's phone and discovered—through her text messages—that she and

Dr. Rider were going to a fancy fundraiser. He'd given the time and day to the Sunset Sliders. All the amateurs had needed to do was kill her. Even *those* delinquents should have been capable of killing one woman.

"Titan," Lucius answered the phone.

"They failed, boss." McMillan had outlived her usefulness and was fast becoming a liability. "It's okay," AJ continued, hating how his speech sounded pressured and nervous. "I'd planned to take care of them anyway, but the high-speed chase did the job for me. An eighteen-wheeler demolished their car. There's nothing to tie me to them. If *I* can't be tied to them, you can't be tied to any of it either."

AJ had followed the chase, but had lapsed some distance behind on the interstate. He'd thought they'd left him behind until he saw the wreck—both wrecks, in fact,—the crash that wiped out the Sunset Sliders, and the crash that had left the doctor's car a mangled heap of metal. If AJ hadn't glimpsed Mica's bright evening dress in the distance, heading into the woods, he'd have thought them both dead, too.

Police had pulled onto the scene almost immediately, so AJ couldn't give chase to the couple on foot.

AJ practically felt Lucius's irritation brimming through the phone like froth from a boiling cauldron. Lucius was schmoozing at some fancy tuxedo-only function with a Georgia congressman, and AJ had interrupted the dinner. But Lucius needed to know that the bounty hunter and the physician were still alive.

"What's your proposal to fix this situation?"

AJ hesitated as he squeezed his stress ball. He needed a cigarette. Why had he ever bothered to stop smoking?

"I'll take care of it personally."

"Damn right you will." Lucius disconnected the call.

EVERY MUSCLE in Mica's body ached, but she pushed through the pain as they walked through the woods. One mile through the dark woods took longer than it should have. Or so she thought.

Through her fatigue and pain, Mica considered David's destroyed vehicle. Looking at the stars through the trees, she suppressed a hysterical laugh.

My carriage did turn into a pumpkin, Dad.

A squashed pumpkin.

The front and side airbags had protected both of them. She took a sobering breath and focused on the present. Now, David's mom was picking them up. Max, David had called her. And he was Dr. Rider.

Max Rider's son?

Maxine Rider of Rider Securities and Investigation?

The CEO of a reputable protective agency.

Mica had to dig deep in her photographic memory for that nugget. She remembered her father thinking of taking a security job there. She'd teased him about being a night watchman, which prompted her dad to explain that the woman he'd be working for was a decorated and highly esteemed ex-Marine who now orchestrated an elite security team.

Her dad hadn't taken the job, but he had piqued Mica's interest. She'd still worked for the FBI at the time, so she used her contacts to find out more about Rider SI. Apparently, the organization had a reputation for quality protection and covert investigation.

And beside me is Maxine Rider's son.

Mica had stumbled across the son of Maxine Rider, working late nights in the bowels of an emergency room.

"Maxine Rider is your *mom*."

"You keep saying that in surprise, but you haven't actually asked me a question yet."

"I'm shocked. I honestly hadn't put that together."

"We're estranged."

Instead of that statement answering any questions, it raised new ones.

"Why?"

David shrugged. "She wasn't around much during my childhood."

"I know nothing of her personality, or what type of mother she is, but I hope you know she's a war hero, and she uses her company to help people. Good people."

Mica tried to keep judgment out of her voice.

David didn't respond to her comment as they limped together toward the gas station.

"I'm sorry. It's not my business." The hardships a woman like Maxine suffered may have made her difficult to love. Mica only wanted to make the suggestion that David should reconsider his relationship with her.

"Mom was gone for long stretches at a time, fighting someone else's fight. When she did come home, she always stayed restless and distracted. I think I was a typical teenager, wondering why her world didn't revolve around me. When I left home, I assumed that because she'd mostly lived without me for the last decade, she could probably continue to do so."

Mica reached out and took David's hand. Her father had been done with his covert escapades by the time she was born. He'd devoted an abundance of time to giving her a rich childhood.

"What about your dad?" Mica asked.

They stepped over a fallen log without slowing down.

"He complained about her absence and having to raise a son without her."

So, his father acted like a dejected teenager, too.

Mica frowned. "I wonder if he'd painted a heroic picture for you and emphasized her self-sacrifice, you might have seen your mom differently."

David fell silent.

"I'm overstepping again. Sorry."

"You're right though. You've never met her, and yet her reputation is enough to have you defending her. Perhaps my dad should've held her in higher esteem."

David pulled Mica's hand to his lips and kissed the back of it. "I like your honesty."

"My big mouth."

"You don't say it condescendingly. You say it like you care. Like you want my Mom and I to mend our relationship."

"I do care."

And my life isn't usually this violent all the time. And I hate how the Sunset Sliders screwed up my chances with you.

Mica cared, and because she cared, she needed to stop seeing David. She couldn't risk putting his life in danger again.

17

*D*avid slowed as Mica squeezed his hand.

Gas station rendezvous.

She shivered once they were no longer moving. Taking off his bulletproof vest and tuxedo coat, he placed the vest in the bag and draped the coat over Mica's shoulders.

Maxine's car wasn't there yet, so they decided waiting at the edge of the woods would be safest than in the opening.

He thought about Mica's comments about his parents. They'd all been things he had actually considered as he got older. His dad shouldn't have pitted the two of them against his mom. Dad should have given him both perspectives and let him decide how he felt about Maxine's absence. Ironically, Mica was making an argument to reconnect with his mom, and yet he'd already started the process—all because of her.

Once Max arrived to pick them up, his time with Mica would end. There'd be questions, and police, and the need for a rental car. Days would pass before things settled down enough to get back to their relationship.

Mica dug in the bag, pulled out a phone, and dialed a number. "Dad. Sorry it's late. The Sunset Sliders attacked... Yes, I'm fine. David is with me. "

David?

She spoke as if her father would know to whom she was referring.

She's already told her dad about me?

David grinned at her.

Mica's lips curled in a suppressed smile as she shook her head. "We're getting a ride, Dad, but can you secure my house? Why? I'm unlisted... Okay, okay, the cabin... Thanks."

Mica glanced back up at David as she continued talking to her father. "Guess who is picking us up? Maxine Rider. David's mother."

She mentioned the name to her dad as if Max was some type of celebrity. David felt a twinge of guilt as he discovered this side to his mother—a side of her that people revered, and he'd never taken the time to get to know.

"Okay. I'll see you there." Mica shoved the phone back in her bag and turned to David.

"My dad has a cabin in Allatoona. It's not under his name. AJ won't know about it. We'll be safe there."

Mica starting dismantling her phone.

"What are you doing?"

"Dad's rules, mobile phone batteries out en route and during stays at the cabin. Your too. We'll wait until your mom arrives."

***

MAXINE FLASHED her headlights three times when she arrived at the gas station. Two figures emerged from the woods.

"I've got eyes on them. Thanks, Claire. Stay on the line."

She watched David and his girlfriend walk toward her. In the headlights, she could see his lean figure in a tuxedo. Too much time had passed since she'd seen him, and her heart squeezed the way only a mother's could. His thick, brown hair was a mess and his clothes were torn, but he still looked good. How she and her sorry, despicable ex-husband had managed to produce such a handsome, smart man was a mystery.

Fury burned through her at the miscreants who'd attempted to kill her son.

She watched Mica McMillan holding David's hand. Her evening gown hung in shreds and looked like something Frankenstein's bride might wear. Spots of blood dotted the dress, but she carried herself with dignity. Tough girl.

You wouldn't know it by those fluffy platinum curls.

Mica was both the one who brought danger to her son's doorstep and saved him. Former FBI. Squandering her talents as a bail enforcement officer.

They climbed into her backseat.

"Thanks, Mom."

"Anytime."

"Thank you, Mrs. Rider."

"Maxine will do." She looked at Mica through the rearview mirror.

When they were buckled in, Maxine pulled out of the gas station.

"Any injuries needing a hospital?" She doubted it, because they were both ambulatory.

"No," they both confirmed.

Maxine glanced back and saw their hands entwined. Good. Because they'd be spending more time together in the immediate future, they might as well still like each other, despite these dangerous events.

"My dad has a cabin in the north Georgia woods. We can use it as a safe house," Mica said.

Maxine nodded. "Claire, my informatics specialist, has been eavesdropping on Atlanta PD. After your crash, an eighteen-wheeler collided with your pursuers. Three dead on the scene."

"So Mica is safe? No more pursuers?" David asked.

"No more Sunset Sliders," Maxine agreed. "But there's a bigger issue." Through the rearview mirror, Maxine noticed Mica's face blanch slightly. She wondered if Mica had something to hide or had just assumed the next issue would also be her fault. "Let's get to Mica's cabin, and we'll discuss the situation further."

Claire's voice came through the car's speakers. "Max, I let Atlanta PD know David's in your custody so they don't start a search."

"Who's that?" David asked.

Maxine shook her phone in the air and then set it back on the dash. "David and Mica, meet Claire. Claire, meet my son and his date."

"Hello."

"Hi, Claire," they both said in unison.

"She's my computer genius," Maxine explained.

"*Extraordinaire*," Claire added. "You forgot extraordinaire."

Maxine rolled her eyes. "And she fits in well with the rest of my humble employees."

MICA GAVE Maxine directions to her dad's cabin. She had explained the mobile phone rule, but Maxine assured her that her phone was checked daily for unauthorized access.

David stayed mostly quiet during the trip. Mica wondered if he sensed their relationship coming to a close as much as she did.

As they pulled into the winding drive, relief washed over Mica to see the familiar, dark wood structure surrounded by its curtain of dense pine trees. Her dad's jeep was parked outside, and she could see smoke billowing out of the chimney, signaling her dad had already started the fireplace.

Maxine and David followed her inside. Mica's father was waiting by the fire.

She hugged her dad. "Thanks."

He looked over her dress and scrapes blandly. "Now you know why I never spent money on pretty dresses for you. You make a mess of nice stuff."

Mica chuckled. "I'm going to make everyone some tea."

He kissed her cheek. "You know how I like mine."

David, Maxine, and her dad sat in the living room exchanging introductions while Mica washed her face and hands. As she boiled water and steeped the tea bags, she heard the leather of her recliner squeak as Maxine sat in it. The legendary Marine and entrepreneur, dressed in combat pants and a flannel shirt, sat in the recliner.

Mica had counted at least two guns and a knife in the woman's armament. She wondered if Maxine was upset about Mica putting her son in danger. For now, Maxine was preoccupied with a new threat, but she may still feel she had a score to settle with Mica later on.

Pissing off a deadly war hero. Add that to my list of blunders.

Mica would either have to guard her flank around Maxine or owe her a debt. Perhaps both.

As she brought both David and Maxine a cup of steaming, herbal tea, Mica heard Maxine explaining the orchestrated car chase to her dad.

David's face and hands looked scrubbed cleaned, and he'd attempted to tame his disheveled hair.

Maxine sniffed her tea. "You got anything stronger?"

David looked appalled by his mother's manners, but Mica took no offense.

"Yes, ma'am." She produced a bottle of whisky her dad kept in the cupboard.

Mica went back to the kitchen and brought out tea for her and her dad. Maxine handed him the whisky, and he added a shot to his tea.

When Mica brought the cup to her lips, the robust scent of the black tea filled her nostrils. The hour was late to have so much caffeine, but the night wasn't finished. She needed something to keep her functioning after the adrenaline crash earlier.

She leaned back on the couch and kept the warm cup close. Because she was still filthy from the walk through the woods, Mica knew she'd have to wash the blanket later. The heat from the fireplace warmed one side of her and the crackling flames threatened to lull her to sleep.

David had taken one sip of his tea and set it down on the coffee table. He looked tense as he leaned forward on the couch. He ran his hands along his face. "I don't want to offend anyone, but does anyone else find the criminal hit out on Mica outrageous?"

Maxine gulped her spiked tea.

"Your mom is the person people go to for help with outrageous conspiracy theories," Mica's dad explained.

Mica watched the rugged woman pull out her phone, speed dial someone, and then set the phone on speaker on the table before them. She sat back and rested her teacup on her belly. "We—as in Rider SI—have been watching a man named Lucius Titan closely for a few years." She looked at David. "When you told me about Mica, Claire dug for a connection to Lucius. AJ Schlau is the link."

"AJ works for Lucius?" Mica asked. Jeremiah had worked for Lucius's company, so she saw the connection.

David scowled. "I knew it. I knew the minute I told you her name you'd violate her privacy."

Maxine didn't recoil from his bitter words.

"She had to," Claire said through the speakerphone. "Lucius threatened to go after you, David, to get to Max. She had to investigate everyone in contact with you."

"Why is he upset with you?" David asked his mom.

"I've been antagonistic to his enterprise."

"She fights for the forces of good. He fights for the forces of evil. They were bound to clash," Claire explained.

Maxine shot an irritated look at her phone.

Mica leaned over to her dad, whispering, "That's Claire on the phone. She's Maxine's investigator."

David rubbed a hand through his hair. "You should have told *me*. You should have come to *me*."

Mica could tell he was testy. He'd had a long night of being shot at, driving in a high-speed chase, surviving a crash, running through the woods, and now being told he was the target of his mother's sworn rival.

"You still weren't speaking to me at the time." The loose skin on Maxine's face sank down as she frowned.

As David and his mom exchanged heated words about how she should have talked to him, Mica fought her own raging sense of inadequacy. AJ and Lucius had used her so thoroughly—their personal hound dog, which they'd then conspired to put her out of their misery.

Mica's dad took a swig of his enhanced tea, but kept quiet during the bickering. He seemed thoroughly entertained.

David looked back and forth between Mica and his mom. His expression transformed from frustration to surrender. When he leaned back on the couch, he slipped his hand into Mica's. She suspected the motion was intended to steady himself, but it served to ease Mica's worries about his jeopardized safety.

"So, Mica's investigation led her to AJ Schlau who hired the Sunset Sliders to kill Mica. Now, although they're dead, AJ is still alive. Meanwhile, he works for Lucius, who's threatened to target me as retribution for what you did to him." David pursed his lips. "Everyone in this room is a target except for Mica's father. What's the solution?"

"We need to assemble the Rider team," Maxine said. "Brainstorm. Come up with a plan."

Mica spoke, still feeling the tension between mother and son, "I want to be part of the solution." Despite feeling like she'd been cycled through an industrial clothes dryer, she *needed* to be part of the solution.

Mica's dad interjected. "It's late. Why doesn't everyone rest here tonight? Max, I have a guest room, and the hall bathroom should have everything you need. I'm going to head home. I'll come back in the morning with coffee and breakfast. Everyone will think more clearly then."

"This location is secure?" Maxine asked.

Mica's dad nodded. "No one knows about it except Mica and I."

Maxine nodded. "Then I'll head out, too. I'm going to be more effective from my home and the office. I'll be in touch with everyone about a meet."

Maxine cast a glance at Mica, who straightened as soon as she saw it. She sensed a silent communication—a message that she was now charged with keeping David safe. The nonverbal message made Mica feel she'd somehow earned Maxine's trust.

DAVID WATCHED Mica and her dad hug before he left. So, *that* was what a functional parent-offspring relationship looked like.

Mica then excused herself for a shower and walked toward the back of the house.

David stood and looked down at the couch. It wasn't long enough for his long legs, but his exhausted body told him he could sleep on the floor if needed.

"It's good to see you, Mom."

Maxine attempted something like a smile, but it was almost as though her face didn't know how to shape itself appropriately for that emotion. "It's been too long."

He tried another sip of the pungent tea. The stuff tasted like watery coffee, but with a strange hint of licorice. Despite the flavor, it served the purpose of warming him and clearing his mind.

"I've been busy." He wasn't in the right frame of mind to talk about regret.

"I'm proud of you."

Well, damn.

It would be easier to stay bitter toward Maxine if she manipulated him through guilt. Wasn't that the motherly thing to do?

"Thanks, Mom." He shouldn't have lashed out at her earlier, and he regretted it now.

"We'll get through this."

Maxine's statement was so matter-of-fact that he believed her.

"We?"

"You, me, Mica, and the Rider team."

He scratched at his chin. "You like her?"

"Does it matter?"

No. Yes. Maybe.

Maxine added, "Despite having made up my mind *not* to like her, I like her."

David felt his mouth quirk. He looked into his mom's face. She'd never been vibrant and youthful, but she looked especially aged tonight. Had he contributed to that aging process? Decades without her son. Worry. He felt an unexpected pang of guilt and remorse.

"The important question is: Do *you* like her?"

"Yeah, I like her."

She patted his shoulder. "Goodnight, David."

"Bye, Mom."

They didn't manage a hug, but nevertheless, he felt like all the hard feelings about their bickering tonight had been resolved.

After Maxine left, David heard the shower water running in Mica's bathroom. He used the guest bathroom to shower. Afterward, he borrowed Mica's first aid kit from the duffle bag she'd assembled and bandaged the cut on his thigh. He didn't have a change of clothes, so he put his slacks back on and kept the towel around his neck.

MICA STOOD inside the cabin by the fire feeling battered—emotionally and physically. She'd been manipulated by AJ Schlau and then targeted for elimination. In addition, whatever had been stirring between her and David was now as irrevocably damaged as David's Aston Martin.

After her shower, she'd changed into a hoodie and cotton shorts, leaving her tattered evening dress on the floor. The simple act of cleaning and dressing had given her time alone to think.

David entered the main room in his tuxedo pants, a towel...

...and nothing else.

Why did he have to be shirtless? The mouthwatering view only made this more difficult.

She glanced at David as she tried to remember what she'd rehearsed in the shower to say to him, now that they were finally alone. He probably blamed her for putting him in danger. And he'd be right.

Mica noticed a bruise forming on his left shoulder. The sight of it squelched the swell of desire she'd begun to form and served as a reminder of why she needed to have this conversation.

She straightened up and took a steadying breath. "I know what you're thinking."

"You do?"

"The danger in my life put you in danger. My life isn't fancy parties and country clubs."

"Neither is mine."

Mica continued quickly, "My life is chaos, turmoil, and grit." She ran her fingers through her damp hair. "*Sh... Sugar*! I destroyed your car!"

"It's just a car."

"You could've been killed!" Mica paced the floor, unable to make eye contact. She needed to get this over with–like ripping off a Band-Aid. "Let's not drag this out. I know the lines."

"Lines?"

"My life is too messy, David. Too complicated. Men need women to provide stability and complement their lifestyle. They certainly don't want a woman who can physically best them. We don't have to see each other anymore."

David crossed his arms, the towel still over his shoulder from his shower.

Mica waited for his resigned agreement.

He scratched at the stubble on his jaw. "Just so I'm understanding you correctly, you're releasing me to walk away? Because you think I couldn't possibly still be interested in dating you after everything we've been through?"

Mica tugged at the string on her hoodie. "It's okay. I'm not mad at you."

"I'm a little mad at *you*."

She startled at the harshness in his voice.

"You're dismissing me."

"Guys I've dated..."

David stepped forward and gently turned her chin up toward him. "I'm not any of *them*. I'm David."

The warmth from his hand spread through Mica like wildfire, but she resisted the urge to step into him. If she got any closer, emotionally or physically, she would only hurt more when it ended.

"I know, but..."

"No, you don't. You don't know where we're going, and you're not ending this relationship when we're just getting started." His firm expression softened as David raised her scraped knuckles to his lips and kissed them tenderly.

Mica felt her heart kick into overdrive when his lips touched her skin. She closed her eyes and swallowed.

"I know you, Mica. I know you need to right wrongs and defend people." He curled his finger around her hand. "Maybe adult life is more complicated than your Justice League from high school, but I still don't see you as anything less than Wonder Woman."

Mica opened her eyes to meet David's intense green stare.

"Your abilities are amazing. I don't feel in competition with them." With a wink, he added, "I heal people, so I have my own superpowers." He moved his hands to embrace Mica's shoulders and stepped closer.

The air between them felt electric.

"The only time I've even seen you weak was just now, when you wanted to cut me loose for my own protection. That's the last time I ever want you to feel weak because of me. We can be strong together."

Mica closed the gap between them and stepped into his arms. He squeezed her to him. His embrace gave her solidarity. She felt simultaneously grounded and light as a feather.

DAVID RELISHED the feel of Mica in his arms. He pulled back just enough to lean his head down and claim her mouth. As the kiss grew deeper, it became hot, and hungry, and full of need. A need for *her*. A need to be stronger together.

Their tongues explored and connected, sending waves of arousal through Mica. His warm hands and long fingers trailed down her waist and around to her buttocks. When he squeezed her up against his body, she groaned with pleasure.

David felt the yearning in Mica's kiss, embrace, and purrs. As he scooped her up and carried her to the bedroom, he considered how wonderfully unplanned everything with her had been—a chance meeting, a late-night delivery, and a date turned into a harrowing escape. Falling in love with Mica hadn't been planned either, yet it had happened somewhere along the way. Considering she was waving him out of her life two minutes ago, he didn't need to share those feelings with her yet.

After setting Mica down on the bed, David hovered above her, taking in her beauty and wide, hungry eyes. "We can stop. Slow down." He didn't want to stop, but he also didn't want to overwhelm her.

Mica tugged the towel off his shoulder. "Don't you *dare* stop."

Her breathless voice sent heat dancing along his spine. He grinned as he undressed before her.

Mica gaped at David before pulling him down for another kiss. Between kisses, she pulled off her hoodie, revealing her round, pale breasts. When he cupped the soft, tender skin, she gasped his name.

Mica tugged off her remaining clothes before he buried himself—body and soul—into her soft strength.

18

*D*avid was rolling emotions of elation, dread, and exhaustion. His entire body still floated since spending the night with Mica, yet the aches and pains from the car wreck had settled into his muscles overnight.

What's more, they still had the issue of Lucius and AJ.

After only a few hours' sleep, David spent the day talking to the police about the motor vehicle crash. Fortunately, he'd taken his mom's advice and taken the company lawyer with him, because the police were on the verge of arresting him for leaving the scene of an accident. They firmly informed David that there'd be a formal investigation, but didn't arrest him. David took this to mean they'd found the automatic weapons in the car that had been chasing him, which gave validity to David's claim that his life was at risk if he'd remained at the scene of the accident.

Mica had given her statement separately, but David suspected her connection to Detective Bose and the high esteem the cop held her in eased the trouble they faced.

After the police interrogation, David and Mica went to his

insurance company's office to complete paperwork. The stale coffee in the small office wasn't palatable enough to drink.

"Are you okay?" Mica squeezed David's shoulder as they waited for his rental car.

"Yeah, I'm good. You don't have to wait on the car." He kissed her cheek, knowing Mica must be as tired as he was. She didn't seem nearly as rattled by a half-day at the police station as he did. He supposed that was one of the perks of being in her line of work.

She leaned into him. "Let's rent you a car, then we'll get some rest. You need to stay with me. I don't want to answer to your mom if anything happens to you. My dad's already confirmed my house is untouched. It's not under my name, so no one can trace me there."

David gave a nod. "I'll need my clothes. And I need to work tomorrow night. I have a shift to cover."

"We'll buy you new clothes. I don't want to risk going back to your apartment and being ambushed, or picking up a tail. After I meet with your mom and her company tomorrow to work on our criminal problem, we'll discuss what protection to put in place for you."

David felt simultaneously out of his depth yet grateful to have Mica by his side.

"My Mom's already made arrangements to have one of her team meet up with me and provide protection until you catch AJ."

David tugged the belt loop of her jeans to pull Mica's body against his. "That being said—I'm not turning down the opportunity to stay with you until this is all resolved."

Mica put a hand on his cheek and turned his head toward hers. "Together."

He leaned closer and kissed her. "Together."

MICA EXITED the elevators and gazed at the offices of Maxine Rider's private security business. The reception area was clean and simple, with a single elegant sign that read RIDER SECURITY AND INVESTIGATION. No extravagant paintings or statues decorated the room. Nothing elaborate. No secretary staffed the desk. Instead, a small dome, obviously a camera, sat on the countertop where one might expect a bell to be.

Footsteps approached from down the hallway, followed by a girl with a squeal.

Mica looked over to see a pretty woman in her mid to late twenties, with a bright blue bob of hair, bounce into the room. With her buoyancy and enthusiasm, Mica half-expected the woman to introduce herself as Tigger: "T-i-double-uhg-rrr."

The new arrival extended a hand toward Mica. "I'm Claire Maltisse." She gave Mica a beaming and contagious smile.

"Mica McMillan."

"I know. It's great to meet you. Maxine told me David had seen you take down an entire street gang by yourself."

"That's an exaggeration."

"And this online buddy of mine told me you'd disarmed a man with his own belt in Cuernavaca."

"That's *not* an exaggeration." Mica followed Claire down the hallway, passing several offices along the way.

"I really hope you take the job."

"The job?"

Claire blinked at her. "Working for Rider SI." She stopped in front of a closed conference room door.

"Maxine wants to hire me?" Mica glanced down at her fitted gray yoga pants and loose cotton top. Was this an interview? She wasn't dressed for an interview. Did she *want* to be dressed for an interview?

Claire rested her hand on the door handle. "Who wouldn't want you? Your résumé is awesome."

"I never gave Maxine my résumé."

Claire laughed. "It wouldn't matter what document you gave Max, even if you had one. What matters is what I pull about you from the Internet. That's your *real* résumé."

"I see."

Claire pushed open the door to the conference room. "Come meet the team—well, most of the team. Barry and Billy are on assignment, but Mason, Ryan, Reece, and Dorian are here."

When Mica followed Claire inside, she was surprised to see a room full of muscled men. She hadn't arrived late, so there must have been a meeting right before this one. She wondered if it had been to discuss her.

Mica walked over to Maxine and shook her hand. "Thanks for the show of support."

Maxine's grip felt firm. "Each and every one of us wants any leverage we can find on Lucius Titan. This is about taking him down and keeping my son safe."

Mica nodded. She appreciated Maxine's honesty. She wasn't trying to coerce Mica into helping them by implying they were all there to help her. The Rider team was here to help Maxine— nobody else.

Claire began introductions. "This is Mason Stone, former SEAL."

Mica shook the hand of the tall blond, who looked like he'd be better suited wielding Mjölnir—the hammer of Norse mythology —than wearing a suit. He gave her a welcoming smile.

Claire continued, "This is Reece Owen, former Ranger. Fastest draw in the south."

The man looked like a gunslinger with his handlebar mustache and crooked smile.

"Next is Ryan Walsh. He was in the Rangers with Reece. He also worked with Titan for a spell. He got out when he realized how ass-backward they are. His wife's a physician, different specialty than David, though."

Ryan's warm handshake and easy expression almost masked the intensity behind his brown eyes. "In addition to keeping Maxine's son safe, I have a list of personal reasons why I'd like to bury Titan Enterprises."

Ryan Walsh. Mica recalled the name from when Buzz had mentioned it.

"I bet you do. I've got a message for you from Jeremiah Hughes."

Walsh raised his eyebrows. "I'm interested to hear your message. And how you became its courier." His square jaw tensed slightly. "Let's have you meet the rest of the team first."

Claire led Mica to a tall, brown-skinned man who appeared closer in age to Maxine. Little gray patches of hair above his ears were mixed with his dark brown hair. "This is Dorian Chapman," her voice dropped to a whisper, still audible to the entire room. "Spy extraordinaire. Nobody except Maxine knows his background."

"I'm delighted to know someone of your talents, Ms. McMillan." Dorian's voice was a silken British accent. The tone matched his immaculate appearance and manicured nails.

"Thank you. I'm humbled to meet everyone. You seem like a formidable group to bring down Titan." Mica felt the swell of ... *something.*

"We're still David against Goliath," Dorian admitted.

"That makes him big, clumsy, and slow."

Ryan grinned, revealing an attractive set of dimples. "So, you'll join us?"

Belonging. Mica realized she felt a swell of belonging.

"I'm in." Mica was unsure if she'd agreed to join them for this single mission, or if she'd just accepted a permanent position at Rider SI.

Maxine stepped forward. "We work as a team. We look out for each other."

"And we take orders from Max," Mason added.

"I can do all of that," Mica promised. She'd thought she'd never take orders from anyone again—not after that botched bank robbery. But standing before Maxine and this room full of her employees, all of whom trusted her explicitly, Mica knew she could do the same.

Maxine nodded and moved to take a seat at the head of the conference table.

Claire seemingly skipped to her chair in front of her laptop.

Mica and the men followed Maxine's lead, taking seats around the table.

"Now," said Max. "We need a plan. Several, in fact."

MICA MET with Eddy Finch at a Starbucks off I-20.

He stood as she entered and then hugged her. "When I heard the Sliders came after you, I was mortified. I'm glad I warned you." He rubbed his neck as he took a seat. "It took hours to handle all the fallout—what with the director wanting all the details."

Mica walked to the coffee bar, bought a tall, black coffee, and came back to Eddy's table. "That must have been difficult for you."

"You're right about that. You're safe now, so that's good."

"Yes and no."

Eddy leaned back in his chair. "I'm guessing the 'no' part is the reason for this meeting?"

"That's correct. The Sliders' attempted hit on me was funded by a man name AJ Schlau."

"You got this information from Ricky?"

"The 'where' isn't important. Stopping AJ is."

"Don't know him."

"Perhaps you don't, but perhaps the enormous FBI database does."

"I'm not putting my career on the line to investigate someone for you."

"I'm not asking you to." Mica now had access to Claire, who could do all the online investigation she needed. Mica needed Eddy on the clean-up crew, except he would detest it being called such.

Mica produced a flash drive and slid it across the table to him. "I'm giving you this."

He arched an eyebrow, but didn't accept her offering.

"That's an electronic arsenal against AJ Shclau. It belonged to my client's deceased brother. Everything's there—photo, video, and shipping details of all AJ's illicit business activities."

Jeremiah, through that last cryptic message left for Ryan Walsh, had directed Rider SI to a safe deposit box. The contents would end AJ's reign, though they did nothing to incriminate Lucius Titan.

After Ryan had seen the contents of the flash drive, he'd suspected Jeremiah had been trying to gather enough information to bring down Titan as well as AJ. He had died before he'd had the chance.

Eddy eased a hand to take the flash drive. "You're giving me this so I can apprehend AJ?"

"Yes."

"Why don't you bring him in yourself and get all the glory?"

Mica suppressed the urge to tell him she didn't need criminal busts to stroke her ego the way he did. "I know you'll do it right. If *you* do it, it'll be a clean arrest. You'll give justice to my client's family."

Eddy's eyes sparkled at the compliment. He pocketed the flash drive. "Assuming I look into this and agree that the evidence supports the FBI's involvement, where do I find AJ?"

"I'm working on that as we speak. Look at the flash drive, let me know if you're in. If you're in, as soon as I have his whereabouts, you'll be one of the first to know."

AJ FELT the mounting stress and annoyance at having to deal with Mica McMillan. His men hadn't taken care of her at the warehouse. The Sunset Sliders had similarly failed to eliminate her. Now, she was *his* problem.

He didn't have time for this. He had drugs and women to move.

However, a little ingenuity would go a long way. He was beginning to visualize his plan. To AJ's good fortune, Dr. Rider and Ms. McMillan were apparently involved in a relationship, though where they were currently hiding out was a mystery. AJ still had the clone link to McMillan's phone, and the capability to send Dr. Rider a text message that would *appear* to originate from McMillan.

He'd just have to wait to send it until they weren't hiding out together.

AJ's plan was to summon Dr. Rider, fooling him into thinking McMillan was the one sending the message. He'd then arrive at the location AJ had selected, thinking he was coming to see his woman. Instead, Dr. Rider would find AJ and his team.

AJ could *then* send an SOS to McMillan on behalf of Dr. Rider. He'd dispose of David Rider while waiting for the nuisance of the woman before eliminating her as well.

If AJ set the scene especially well, he was even hoping he could make events appear as if *she'd* shot Dr. Rider.

Once he eliminated both of them, AJ hoped Lucius' faith in him would be restored.

He studied the text-messaging transcript on his computer. The messages Rider and McMillan exchanged were simple and without punctuation. No emojis. No terms of endearment. He could mimic the style so his text wouldn't raise suspicion.

Now, he needed only to determine where to lure his lambs for their slaughter. And where to dispose of the bodies afterward.

THE PARAMEDICS WHEELED a cardiac arrest patient into one of David's treatment rooms. David recognized the young paramedic as the rookie from the apartment delivery who'd been partnered with Raymond. He didn't know the other paramedic, though. Raymond, David knew, was off-duty tonight.

"Sixty-two-year-old male, status post cardiac arrest at a restaurant. He got five minutes of CPR from an off-duty nurse before first responders arrived. Upon EMS arrival, he was in V-fib. He got one shock and converted. He has amio hanging."

"Great work."

Maple and Robin worked to remove the patient's clothing and place additional intravenous lines and a Foley catheter, while a respiratory therapist connected the patient's breathing tube to a ventilator.

Although few patients survived an out-of-hospital cardiac arrest, immediate CPR and shock of the heart rhythm were good prognostic indicators for this patient.

David ordered a stat ECG, continuous infusion amiodarone, and the usual slew of post-arrest labs. He pulled the ultrasound machine to the bedside to see what heart function the patient still had.

An hour later, David had stabilized his patient and sent him on his way to the heart catheterization lab. Next, he stared at an x-ray of a ten-year-old girl's arm. She'd fractured her ulnar bone when she fell off a trampoline.

David suddenly remembered an antibiotic order he'd forgotten to place. "Maple?"

She swiveled in her chair to look at him.

"Bed one. Pneumonia. We talked about antibiotics, but then the cardiac arrest patient arrived." David and all the other emergency room physicians were under hospital scrutiny to start antibiotics on septic patients and those with suspected pneumonia within one hour of the patient's arrival.

"No worries." Maple winked. "I hung them on a verbal order."

He gave her a grateful smile. "Thank you."

David's phone buzzed.

A text message from Mica. *Need help. Can you give me a lift?*

The message was followed by an address and then: *I'm in the basement level parking deck.*

David replied: *No problem. Let me get the rest of my shift covered, and I'll be there.*

David began to sort through his contact list for somebody who could help on short notice. After a few phone calls, he found shift coverage.

When his coverage, Dr. Cruz, arrived, David briefed him about the patients in the emergency room and then headed out into the night.

Mica needed his help.

19

AJ waited triumphantly in the parking deck for Dr. Rider to appear.

He'd posted five Titan security men in or near the garage— one at each of the three exit/entry points for vehicles, one on the basement level with AJ, watching the stairwell, and one street-side to report activity. He'd also had the parking lot cameras disabled and put the elevator out-of-order.

Once the physician was in his grasp, Mica would have no undetectable means of entry into the parking deck, and no way of escape.

"Location check," AJ hissed into his earpiece.

"Beta-one check. Clear."

"Beta-two check. Clear."

"Beta-three check. Clear."

Outstanding. The garage was secure.

"Beta-four check. No incoming traffic."

"Beta-five check. Stairwell quiet."

Planning and patience would yield the payoff. AJ felt practically giddy with the simple ingenuity of his plan, as he waited by the out-of-order elevator at the basement level. Only a few parked cars occupied spaces. Otherwise, the garage remained quiet. His vehicle was one floor up and parked on the street, providing a simple getaway.

"Beta-four. Incoming blue Nissan Xterra. Confirm. This is the target's rental car."

The good doctor had to downgrade while the insurance company prepared to fork over payment for his totaled luxury sports car. With a smirk, AJ wondered how the doctor had explained the bullet holes to his claims adjuster.

"Alpha copy." AJ said.

He heard the engine and then saw the headlights as Dr. Rider drove down the ramp to the basement level.

The doctor parked the car and turned off the engine. When he exited the vehicle and stepped into the light, AJ's mouth went dry.

His mind raced. He'd texted Dr. Rider, but one of Maxine Rider's men had showed up instead. The tall, blond man had a chiseled jaw and a hard expression. Mason Stone. AJ knew him from the file Titan kept on all of Maxine's employees.

AJ could take the former SEAL, but if there was one Rider team member present, others would be closing in on him.

"Betas, we've been compromised. Status check." He backed toward the stairwell.

No one replied.

Shit.

He pulled his Glock and fired.

MICA STOPPED and watched as her prey paced in and out of the shadows near the garage exit. He outweighed her by over fifty pounds and outgunned her with his semi-automatic Glock. Because he was one of the Titan crew, he'd be ex-military and no easy takedown. This wasn't a cocky street fighter. Unlike some of the average criminals she targeted in the past, this man wouldn't hesitate for a second to kill her.

Mica wore all black—even her quiet sneakers were black. As she crept through the shadows, she slipped on her brass knuckles.

When the man stopped pacing, Mica held her breath.

"Beta–three check. Clear." He continued his silent walk with his short, spiked hair unmoving and his dark eyes attentively roaming his surroundings.

When Mica sprang from behind the pillar, her mark's lightning-fast reflexes made her wonder if she'd been as stealthy as she'd thought she had. Instead of the debilitating blow to his solar plexus as planned, the most Mica managed was a crack to the man's wrist as he brought his gun toward her. With her force, in addition to the brass knuckles, the big man's tendons would be stunned just long enough to keep him from pulling the trigger.

Her target let out a grunt as the gun fell from his grip. He never slowed, though, as he pulled out a twelve-inch blade with his other hand and took a swipe at her.

But Mica was already making her next move—a kick to his knee. As she dodged the man's knife, she couldn't plant her foot precisely enough to tear the tendon, but the strike was still solid.

The man with the call-sign 'Beta–three' gritted his teeth and dropped to one knee, still swinging.

As Mica blocked the knife with her brass knuckles, she brought a knee up into the man's jaw. The sound of metal scraping metal—steel knife to brass knuckles—drowned out the crunch of bone.

She felt Beta-three's upper and lower teeth jar together through the reverberation in her knee.

Yet, even as blood gushed from his mouth, Beta-three pushed up and swiped at Mica once again with his knife. She caught the glint of silver and the sound of whooshing as the blade cut through the air.

Mica dodged but not entirely. The sting of skin parting on her calf caused her to grimace. The man's hammer-sized fist came at her in a right hook and caught Mica's left shoulder as she twisted away from him. Pain flared through her shoulder, arm, and neck. She jabbed her brass knuckles into his larynx.

The man fell back, gasping for air.

Mica blinked through eyes watering with pain. As she glanced at her cut, she noted blood oozing, but the wound could wait for a patch up. She collected the man's fallen knife and gun.

Beta–three lay on his back, gasping for air before passing out. She rolled him onto his side so blood from his bitten tongue wouldn't suffocate him. Then she felt for a pulse, confirming it was strong and steady.

Beta-three would survive. Between the blood in the back of his mouth and his throat swelling up, she suspected his vocal cords had spasmed shut, rendering him unconscious. She could still feel him breathing, though, and his exhaled air condensed in the cool night air. Mica secured his hands and ankles with zip ties.

Claire's voice sounded crisply in Mica's earpiece as she addressed the Rider team. "Confirmed hostiles down. Thor?"

"West side, confirm."

"Hulk?"

A sigh followed by, "East side, confirm." Ryan sounded slightly winded, which made Mica feel better about her own struggle.

"Hawk Eye?"

"Watch tower, confirm," said Reece.

Claire had let the team know the nicknames she'd planned to use. Apparently, Ryan's wife Jenna had initiated the Avengers analogy, and Claire had opted to incorporate it during missions because they used code names anyway. Maxine had accused Claire of being juvenile, but the head of Rider SI had used more of a bemused tone than an authoritative one.

"Stark?"

"Stairwell confirm," Dorian replied.

"Black Widow."

"North side, confirm." Mica had always been partial to Wonder Woman growing up—what with Diana being a badass warrior princess with a cool lasso—but Natasha Romanov was a respectable alternative so as not to disrupt Claire's Marvel superhero theme.

Mica added, "Clean up on aisle nine." They had strict instructions from Maxine to maim and not kill, but they also had a paramedic on standby for incidentals.

"Copy, will send in medic," Claire replied.

Because everyone had seamlessly incapacitated his or her target, only one prize remained.

AJ Schlau.

And Mica was coming for him.

David paid the driver and hopped out of the taxi. His shift had taken a while to find coverage for, and he raced directly into the parking garage from the ER.

After he had received a text from 'Mica', he got a call from Claire letting him know the text had been the anticipated 'trap' from either Lucius or AJ. Rider SI hadn't known if an attack would be straightforward or conniving, and they didn't know who Titan's team would try to lure away from the group: David, Mica, or Maxine.

All three of them had been on alert.

Precious minutes ticked by from ER to taxi to now the parking garage.

Why the rush? He asked himself.

What could he do to help? Perhaps nothing. Mica had incredible skills and the full support of Rider SI. Perhaps he could provide moral support. David just hoped he wouldn't be needed as a physician tonight.

When he reached the entrance to the parking garage, a man dressed in black approached him, materializing out of the shadows.

"I'll escort you to the basement level, Dr. Rider."

David recognized the tall, broad-shouldered man as Ryan Walsh, one of his mom's crew. He was married to Dr. Jenna Masters, who, as David understood it, was interviewing at ICUs in Atlanta to move near her husband's home base.

"Please, call me David." He was slightly winded from the block he'd jogged. Maxine had initially told him not to come, but amended it to say—because she'd known David would come anyway—that he should at least ensure his movements were untraceable.

"David," Ryan motioned to the mounted cameras in the parking deck, "the cameras have been disabled, so none of us will be seen coming or going."

"Is it over?" David wondered if they had custody of AJ and Lucius, or the information needed to prosecute either of them.

"Let's go find out."

When they reached the basement level, David saw his mother dressed in black cargo pants and a long sleeve black shirt. She wore a gun on her belt. David wondered if it was the same Marineissued Beretta she'd had when he was growing up. Her wispy, frayed brown and gray hair waved loosely.

Mica, dressed in black leggings and a black turtleneck, stood a few feet from AJ Schlau. Mica's mystery man and nemesis towered over her, an intimidating hulk, twice her size and twice her age. David glanced around the concrete walls as he approached, wondering where AJ's team was. Surely he hadn't come alone.

As Mica spoke, she made AJ an offer, "You're a small fish, AJ. We want dirt on Titan. Enough to bury him in a maximum-security prison."

David noticed gashes on her leg and arm. His gut clinched. He'd gotten here late, and Mica had already been in at least one fight.

AJ scoffed. "The Rider team plays within the law. Lucius doesn't. The only reason you pissants are still alive is because he hasn't bothered to take you out yet."

David frowned. Lucius *had* bothered. They'd gone after Mica twice now. The reason the Rider team still lived, David knew, was because they were clever and underestimated.

Mica unobtrusively eased her way toward AJ. Why? She didn't have a gun, and he did. It was holstered, but his fingers danced along the handle. David dampened his worry, reminding himself that she'd defended herself proficiently in the street fight. Mica did this for a living. She wouldn't interfere with him performing CPR on a cardiac arrest patient anymore than he should interfere with what she was doing right now.

"I'm not going with you," AJ said.

David suspected that whatever plans Rider SI had for AJ were nothing in comparison to what a man like Lucius would do to him if he failed his objective.

With Ryan on one side and Maxine on the other, David watched the stand-off between Mica and AJ.

In a blur of speed, AJ drew his gun. His gaze focused, hard and determined, on Maxine. Fear coursed through David as he made a protective step toward his mother.

Mica was faster. Before AJ had his gun fully raised, Mica kicked. Her boot connected with AJ's elbow with a loud crack. The gun flew out of his hand and skittered across the concrete floor.

He made a quick one-two punch, hitting Mica in the ribs and then her jaw. She stumbled backward before dropping to one knee.

David clenched his fist and took a furious step forward.

Ryan placed a hand on his chest.

David glared at him.

"Sorry, David. This is Mica's fight."

"What the hell kind of crap is *that*?"

Ryan kept calm but kept his hand in place. "She's been after this man for months. He used her, and then he went after the man she loves. Mica deserves this."

David sunk back onto his heels.

Mica spit a mouth full of blood onto the concrete, before standing to face AJ.

"This is barbaric," David complained.

Ryan lowered his hand. "In your sheltered world above ground, it might seem that way. In the underworld, though, this is how the other half establish their hierarchy."

The fight commenced. Blows and blocks blurred too fast to keep track of the swift movements. Two things were certain, though: Mica was tiring, and her small frame couldn't take much more of a beating.

David's heart raced. Any minute, Ryan or Maxine would end this madness. Right? As time seemed to slow, David's mouth went dry. Mica was back down on one knee, this time with AJ's massive fist barreling toward her head. With his power and downward momentum, he could inflict serious damage—intracranial hemorrhage, or a fractured orbit, or a broken jaw.

At the last instant, and with the glint of light reflecting off metal, Mica's right fist came up and impacted with AJ's fist. When her brass knuckles collided with his balled fingers, the crunch of breaking bones was audible. AJ's face twisted in pain. He stumbled back, clutching his shattered hand.

Mica reached toward his waist. In one quick motion she unbuckled AJ's belt, yanked it off him, and then whipped it around his ankles. When she yanked, AJ smacked down hard onto his back.

Mica cinched the belt and tied it off—the same way a ranchhand would half hog-tie an animal.

In a relaxed, barely audible tone, Ryan murmured, "Cleanup, basement level." He stepped toward AJ and secured the prisoner's hands with cuffs.

David rushed to Mica.

She sank into him.

MAXINE SURVEYED THE SCENE. Zero casualties. David was inspecting Mica's injuries while she drank from a bottle of water. Ryan and Reece guarded the entrances and exits.

Raymond approached with his medic bag and Dorian in tow. The Rider SI employee wore a nondescript, navy-blue medic outfit with an embroidered caduceus. They walked toward AJ.

David addressed Raymond, "Thanks for being available."

"I'm glad the good guys won."

"Are they calling you The Cleaner now?"

Raymond set his bag next to AJ, who now wore handcuffs

following his loss to Mica. "That title has a negative connotation. I'm just here to patch people up."

As Raymond knelt to attend to AJ's injuries with ice packs and bandages, Dorian busied himself as well, except Maxine knew he wasn't performing a physical exam. Dorian was just posing as a medic. As he "tested" the function of AJ's broken hand, he discretely took fingerprints onto a silicone imprint. As he wrapped the bleeding knuckles, he swabbed DNA samples and dropped them into a plastic tube. As he pretended to check AJ's eyes for pupillary reflexes, Dorian performed a retinal scan with a hand-held digital device.

Raymond, the paramedic David had suggested for this job, was proving helpful and good at playing along with Dorian, even as he administered actual medical care.

"Max, that was *awesome*." Claire spoke into her earpiece. She'd been watching through the video feed they'd set up earlier in David's rental car.

"Everything's under control. You can call in Eddy Finch now."

Mica had explained that her FBI contact would be happy to swoop in, claim AJ while taking full credit, and lock him up, because Eddy'd seen the incriminating evidence on Jeremiah's flash drive. With whatever Claire would be able to uncover from AJ's computer—now that they had his fingerprints and retinal scan—Maxine hoped to bring Lucius down right after AJ. But that would be a much longer endeavor.

"Did you see Mica's moves?" Claire asked, excited. "That's what she did in Cuernavaca."

"She's smooth," Maxine admitted.

"I hope she stays on. How is everyone else?"

Maxine looked over at Mica, resting in David's arms. She held an ice pack to her side as David whispered something in her ear that made her smile.

"We're all good."

"And my samples?"

Maxine glanced at Dorian as he zipped a small doctor's bag closed. "We've got everything we need." Everything to break through Lucius's security and bring him to his knees.

20

Raymond sipped his cabernet as he looked across the table at Cathy. She'd curled her strawberry-blonde hair and wore a pink dress with a purple design.

"Thank you for having dinner with me."

Cathy took a drink of her wine. "I thought you'd never ask."

He smiled.

She set her glass down with more force than necessary. The red liquid sloshed inside the rim. "Seriously. I thought you'd *never* ask."

Raymond fidgeted with his fork, turning it over and over on the table. "I'm sorry. Thanks for being patient."

"You've been different lately," she remarked.

"Have I?"

"Ever since you had that shift without me, you've been different. Since the delivery with Dr. Rider."

Raymond shrugged, even as he gave deeper contemplation to Cathy's words. "I made a new friend. I hadn't put forth any social effort since Miriam's death."

He paused, but Cathy remained silent, letting him work through his thoughts. "Then, the other night, when I helped Rider SI, I felt this fulfilling rush." He shook his head. "I wasn't doing anything earth shattering. Just the same trauma care I do every shift... But it *felt* different. I was suddenly working for the good guys, with more purpose than my day-to-day job."

Raymond took a gulp of water. "This woman—Maxine Rider. She's gruff, like a female Clint Eastwood, and she commands respect like him too. You can sense she's a good person, looking out for other people's well-being."

"Are you planning to continue working with her team?"

"I hope so. She asked if she could call me again sometime, and I said yes. There's some larger conflict between her team and another security firm."

"I'm glad you found a new outlet. New friends."

Raymond extended his left hand across the table and curled his fingers around hers. "Thank you for waiting until I was ready."

Her fingers ran over the absence of a ring. "You're worth waiting for."

In some of his darkest hours, after his wife's death, Raymond hadn't thought he was worth much. He'd been powerless against the sinister spread of metastatic breast cancer, unable to do little more than hold the hand of the woman he loved as she slowly faded away.

Slowly, painfully, day by day as the sun rose in the east and the coffee brewed on his kitchen counter and the ambulance's wheels turned, his damaged heart had healed. Now, a fresh start awaited him.

MICA EASED CLOSER to David's warm body. As she slid her hands over his broad shoulders, she relished his swimmer's physique.

He wrapped an arm around her. "You're okay?"

She smiled and kissed his cheek. How had she been so fortunate to find this man who would start his morning by asking how *she* was? "Better than okay. I'm sublimely happy."

"Oh? Am I to infer that my performance last night was passible?"

"You were amazing."

"I could get used to being called amazing." David pulled her hand to his lips and kissed her knuckles.

Since the fight against AJ, Mica had mostly healed. David has sutured one of her cuts with the precision of a plastic surgeon. The other needed only butterfly strips to keep it closed until it healed. Despite the worry on his face, not once had David implored her to consider a career change.

"I've no doubt that any morning I wake, naked in your arms, will be deemed amazing," she added.

He brushed a thumb along her jaw. "I love you, Mica."

She saw his eyes widen slightly, as though he'd surprised himself by saying those words. His expression turned to apprehension. Did he think his declaration of love would scare her away?

Mica needed to wipe the worry off his face. "I love you, too."

He pulled her to him for a hug. When he eased away, he said, "You got your closure yesterday."

"Yes." She'd met with Jeremiah's sister and explained Jeremiah's heroic attempt to unveil Lucius Titan's human trafficking, which had led to one of his criminal leaders being apprehended: AJ Schlau.

With the drug dealer in custody, in addition to all the evidence Jeremiah had amassed against him, AJ would be in prison for life, however long or short Lucius deemed that to be. Unfortunately, tying AJ's work to Lucius's payroll would be difficult and time consuming.

Mica was up for the challenge, especially now that she was part of a team working against Titan Enterprises. "One door closed and another one opened."

"What's on today's agenda?" David asked.

"Just another day at the office." She wriggled closer. "But neither of our shifts start for another hour."

David rolled to straddle her and pressed his lips to Mica's neck.

She gasped in delight.

"Let's see if I can top *amazing*."

Mica walked into the garage with her dad by her side.

"AJ is wrapped up nice and tight in a bow?" Her dad asked.

Mica looped an arm through his elbow and sighed contentedly. "And it's not even Christmas yet."

"How do you like the new job?"

"Love it. My next assignment will be working with this high-profile weapon's manufacturer—Bill Sharp."

"Oh, I've heard of him." Her dad's tone was filled with pride.

"Because I'm the only Rider team member with the experience, I get to go undercover. Bill Sharp is investigating corporate espionage, and he's concerned someone's trying to steal his design ideas."

"Congratulations."

Mica beamed.

"And, simultaneously, Maxine has her hands full with Lucius Titan?"

"She's a multi-tasking woman."

"Think she'd say yes if I asked her on a date?"

Mica frowned. "I'm not in the gossip circle, but Claire seemed to suggest Max is in a relationship with someone. The way Claire implied it, I'm not sure everyone knows."

They came to a stop in front of a mound of bent and twisted metal.

Mica looked dispiritedly at the corpse of the car. "Anything salvageable?"

"Maybe just the engine." Her dad crossed his arms. "This was your carriage to the ball?"

"It was. Now, it's squashed."

"Damn shame. I bet it was a fine-looking car."

Mica turned to her father. "Can you come to Thanksgiving? We're spending the holiday with David's mom and some other Rider SI employees."

"I would, but I already promised Hicks I'd head to Florida and scoop some rock lobster over the holidays. I'm sorry. You're usually working holidays, so I've never made a point to have them off."

"It's no problem. We'll plan something with more notice next time."

"Sounds great." He gave her a kiss on the cheek.

⁂

MAXINE GLANCED over at Vladimir as he pressed the pie crust into the pan and shaped the edges. He seemed at ease in his cotton shirt and slacks. Tattoos decorated his thick biceps.

She stirred the pumpkin filling. "With AJ taken care of, we have to make a move soon against Lucius. He'll be planning retaliation."

"Patience, *prekrasnyy*. We will plan, but it will take time. Enjoy the holidays first."

"We need to tie everything to him so the weight of it sinks him —the drugs, the human trafficking, murders."

The oven beeped, signaling the temperature was right.

"I could suggest a *literal* sinking, but I know you'll decline."

"I don't kill people. I stopped doing that a long time ago." Maxine poured the pie mix into the crusted pan.

"I know. We do things your way, Max. Time, investigation, proof of crime." Vladimir took the pie and slid it into the oven.

Maxine turned to look out the window at the gray November sky.

When Vladimir turned back around from the oven, he put a finger on her chin and turned her face toward him. Leaning down, he kissed her softly. "Can I come to Thanksgiving dinner?"

Maxine blinked and stepped back from him. "No. Rider people only, but whatever we discuss pertaining to Lucius, I promise to share with you. I'm not ready for the team to know about us, yet."

When Vladimir grinned, she knew he was congratulating himself on getting her to agree that the two of them were an 'us.' They shared a relationship, even if she couldn't define it yet.

Maxine pursed her lips, drew back the dish towel, and whipped one corner at him. As it cracked loudly, but harmlessly against his pant leg, he chuckled.

The doorbell rang.

Vladimir arched an eyebrow. Maxine threw a devious smile at him as she went to answer the door.

David stood in slacks and a button-down shirt. He greeted his mother with a hug.

"Mica's in the car. I have the butter you asked me to drop off."

"Great. You got the ham?"

"It's cooked and ready to eat."

Vladimir came to the entryway.

David straightened. "Hello."

"David, this is my friend, Vladimir Pronin."

Vladimir extended a hand. "*Rad vstreche s vami.*"

David took the hand with a smile. "Oh. Is that Russian? Sorry, I don't know any Russian."

Maxine glanced at Vladimir. "And his English is perfectly fine."

"Pleased to meet you, David. Maxine has told me so much about you."

Maxine was certain she'd told him *something* about her son, but the rest he'd learned through his own channels of investigation.

David handed Maxine the butter in a grocery bag. He looked back at Vladimir. "Pleasure is mine. Will you be joining us for Thanksgiving?"

"Not this time," he replied.

David glanced back at his mom, seeming to wonder how he was to interpret a man at her house baking with her but not joining in with the holiday festivities.

"Vladimir is going to help us with our Titan problem."

"Oh. Then I assume you have a special skill set; like my mom's other employees."

"He's *not* my employee," Max quickly clarified.

"Maxine has only just begun to learn my skill set."

David's lips quirked as he backed away from the two of them. "Then I suppose I'll be seeing more of you, Vladimir."

"*Da.*"

<hr>

MAXINE LOOKED around the table and the abundance of food—turkey, ham, gravy, green beans, sweet potatoes, rolls, cranberries, and more.

David and Mica sat next to each other, drinking red wine and conversing easily with Ryan and his wife, Jenna. Jenna would hopefully be moving from Chicago to Atlanta soon, perhaps even work at the same hospital as David. Ryan would take his new family—Jenna and her son Cal—to Moscow the following summer for a vacation. During that time, Cal would have some visitation with his biological father, Brad.

Due to poor life decisions, Brad was Vladimir's indentured servant. Vladimir had been the one to suggest the visit. Although the Russian mobster had a ruthless reputation, he understood family.

Billy had made the trip to the company Thanksgiving dinner and was listening to Reece complain about his on-again, off-again relationship with a feisty physician friend of Jenna's—Jess. Billy flicked a strand of dark hair from her bob cut out of her face, drinking her wine and rolling her eyes so only Maxine could see her exasperated expression.

Claire was sulking even while talking to Cal, Jenna's son. Maxine hadn't let Claire bring her boyfriend, Drake. Although he and Claire were dating, Maxine didn't know Drake well enough to trust him at an intimate dinner where the topic of conversation would be Rider SI and Titan Enterprises.

Maxine had invited Raymond, though, because he'd been helpful on-scene and off-duty during the AJ takedown. He declined, having already made plans with someone named Cathy.

Maxine had gotten Raymond offsite before the police arrived, so he'd remained unassociated with events. He'd enjoyed administering his clandestine medical care enough that he'd agreed to help out on occasion—from a distance, at least until after the fighting and bullets flying were done.

Maxine now had two physicians and a paramedic agreeable to

pro-bono work for Rider SI. God willing, they'd never need any of them.

Dorian and Barry weren't present, because they had their own families to spend time with on Thanksgiving.

As she stood, Maxine raised her glass and cleared her throat. Everyone gave her their attention.

"I want to thank everyone for coming. This is our first company holiday celebration together, and I hope this will be the first of many. We have a great deal to celebrate—our newest addition, Mica McMillan, our successful mission, and our business growth. Sharp Industries has hired us again. There's a Russian saying: '*If the family is together, the soul is in the right place.*' Today, my soul is in the right place. I'm grateful for family, and all of you are family."

"Here, here," Ryan's deep voice boomed.

Everyone raised their glass and toasted.

Claire shot her a knowing glance, causing Maxine to wonder if citing Russian philosophy was a dead giveaway that she was dating a Russian.

After they drank, Maxine took her seat.

David unexpectedly stood. "I've a lot to be grateful for. I'm humbled to be a part of a great gathering for Thanksgiving. I'm grateful to all of you for being part of my mother's family, and I'm almost speechless every time I see Mica." He smiled down at her.

"And," David added, "I have gifts for everyone. I know it's not Christmas, but I'm whisking Mica away to Jenna's family resort in Antigua for Christmas, so I have to distribute them now."

David pulled a bag from against the wall and handed out rectangular boxes wrapped in red paper. He gave one to Maxine, Mica, Ryan, Reece, and Billy.

Maxine tugged at the paper with a puzzled expression. When she opened the box, she smiled.

David explained, "As phenomenally trained as all of you are, your weapons of choice are your fists or your guns. I give you option C. Those are top-of-the-line, electroshock stun guns."

Everyone chuckled.

Maxine took a drink of her wine and enjoyed this moment of bliss. David was mostly right, but technically, the Rider SI top weapon of choice was their intelligence. They'd be using every ounce of it in the inevitable battle against Lucius Titan, and if savvy failed, stun guns wouldn't be enough to defeat him.

****QUICK NOTE FROM THE AUTHOR****

ARE you ready for the showdown between about Maxine and Lucius? Wondering what's in store for Claire? Find out more in *Maltisse File*, The Rider Files Book 4.

DEAR READER

Want to keep in touch?

If you enjoyed this book and want to know about future releases by CB Samet you can visit www.cbsamet.com to sign up for my mailing list! I promise I won't spam you. I only send an email when I have a new book released, giveaways, or special discounts. You can also unsubscribe at any time.

If you loved McMillan File, kindly let others know by posing a brief comment on social media or leave a review where you purchased it so readers can find their next favorite romantic suspense series.

Even more ways to follow me below!

Thank you for reading,
CB Samet

THE RIDER FILES SERIES

Meridian File / Masters File / Box Set 1

McMillan File / Maltisse File /Box Set 2

Storm File / Sullivan File / Box Set 3

Sharp File / Sizani File / Box Set 4

Rivera File / Rucker File / Box Set 5

Richmond File / Redwood File / Box Set 6

FREE EBOOK WITH NEWSLETTER SIGNUP

Rick Swanson loves his job as a firefighter, but his world is sent on a tailspin when an arsonist has an agenda of revenge. He needs to deal with this threat if he's going to get his life back on track.

Mackenzie Rivera is falling fast for fireman Rick, until he inexplicably distances himself. When she learns he's trying to protect her from a crazed arsonist, she won't be idle. And she won't back down from danger. But will her determination and his strength be enough to save them both from the fire?

*~~~***<<<SIGN UP HERE>>>***~~~*